praise for *If He Had Been with Me*

"[Autumn and Finn's] romance is Shakespeare-worthy in its tragic dimension. Autumn's reflections on love's possibilities and near misses will surely resonate with the unsettled teen soul, and readers will get exactly what they came for, and then some."

—*Bulletin of the Center for Children's Books*

"Tender prose that makes it hard not to care about the main characters... When Nowlin reveals why Finny should have been with Autumn all along, readers are sure to feel the ache of life's capriciousness."

—*School Library Journal*

"Hypnotic writing style."

—*VOYA*

"Friendship, love, secrets, hope, and regret... *If He Had Been With Me* by Laura Nowlin is a page-turner that you won't be able to put down."

—*Girls' Life*

"Sweet, authentic love story. Nowlin keeps the story real and fast paced, avoiding the melodramatic."

—*Booklist*

if only i had told her

also by laura nowlin

If He Had Been with Me
This Song Is (Not) for You

if
only
i
had
told
her

laura nowlin

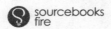
sourcebooks
fire

Copyright © 2024 by Laura Nowlin
Cover and internal design © 2024 by Sourcebooks
Cover design by Elsie Lyons
Cover image © Juan Moyano/Getty Images
Internal design by Tara Jaggers/Sourcebooks

Published by Sourcebooks Fire, an imprint of Sourcebooks
P.O. Box 4410, Naperville, Illinois 60567–4410
(630) 961-3900
sourcebooks.com

Cataloging-in-Publication Data is on file with the Library of Congress.

Printed and bound in the United States of America.
PAH 10 9 8 7 6 5 4 3 2 1

This book is dedicated to the memory of

Aliksir Dragoman Jaan

And in honor of all parents
whose children live on in their hearts.

author's note

In the winter of 2009, my husband found me crying over my second-hand IBM ThinkPad. He kneeled in front of me in my "office" (a deep window ledge in our tiny studio apartment that I'd claimed as a desk), and I sobbed to him,

"I have to let Finny die inside my brain now!"

As I first drafted Autumn's narrative in *If He Had Been with Me*, I crafted Finn's side of the story within me, and I could feel all his thoughts and passion. I had even written a page and a half of Finn's story. When my husband found me crying, it was because I had realized that I needed to delete those pages. I had no agent, no literary prospects; I couldn't write a whole new novel from his perspective when my energy would be better spent revising the novel that I'd already written from Autumn's point of view. So I dried my tears and focused on making sure Autumn's story was the best it could be. I let Finny's voice fade. I let him die again within me.

Over the years, so many readers have asked for a Finny POV, and I've always said, "I'm sorry, he's dead; I can't bring him back."

And it was true. I didn't have that power. But Gina Rogers had that power.

I hadn't planned to listen to the audiobook. The idea of my words in someone else's mouth terrified me. But then Gina sent me a message asking that if I ever listened, I provide feedback—even if it was negative—because she too was an artist striving for an ideal. I was so touched by her sentiment and dedication to her craft that I decided to give it a listen.

The moment I heard Gina as Finny say "Hey" to Autumn at the bus stop, I felt him stir within me. Before I was done listening, he was alive and, dear reader, Finny was mad at me. Not for killing him—he understood I had to make *If He Had Been with Me* the best story that I could—but he had a few things that he wanted to say, some things he needed to clarify. Given his miraculous resurrection, his request seemed reasonable, and I was compelled to let him finally have his say.

So forgive me if I ever swore to you that this book would never exist. At the time, I believed it with my whole artist's heart.

But life is like that sometimes, and that's a good thing.

content warning

This novel includes depictions of death, depression, suicide, and pregnancy.

If you or someone you know is experiencing mental-health distress or crisis, please reach out for help.

Suicide and Crisis Lifeline:

Call or text 988 or chat at 988lifeline.org.

finn

one

——

AUTUMN IS A TERROR TO sleep beside. She talks, kicks, steals the covers, uses you as a pillow. The stories I could tell if I had anyone to tell them to. Autumn is uncharacteristically embarrassed about her nocturnal chaos though, and it's one of her eccentricities for which she will not tolerate a bit of teasing. Our mothers—"The Mothers" as Autumn started calling them when we were young— have their own tales of Autumn's nighttime calamities, and the look that she gives them has been enough to stop me from sharing my childhood memories of her violent, restless sleepovers.

This summer, I discovered just how much she hasn't changed. The other day, she fell asleep watching me play video games. I had finally, finally, made a specific timed jump when she flung her arm onto my lap, causing my guy to fall to his death. I gently lifted her hand off me and scooted over a few inches, but not too far. I didn't tell her about it when she woke up; she would say something about going back home when she starts to feel tired, and I'd rather give away all my games than lose a minute of whatever has been happening between us since Jamie broke up with her.

I made sure to insert myself between Autumn and Jack last night for this very reason. It was clear that we were crashing at my house, and I felt it was my duty to be the one to take the blows.

I have to admit: I'd hoped for something like this.

It was her fingers twitching against my ribs that first woke me.

Aunt Claire is right. Autumn snores now. She didn't when we were children. I'd believed Autumn when, again and again, she insisted that her mother was only joking.

But here we are, in this blanket tent I made for her, her head under the crook of my arm. She's on her side, curled in a tight ball, snoring, though not loudly. Her breath comes in hot, short puffs.

After Jack fell asleep last night, she and I stayed up talking for a while. Autumn was drifting, but I hadn't wanted to give her up yet, so I kept her talking until she said, "Hush, Finny. I need to focus on sweeping."

I turned my face and, in the darkness, saw her closed eyes, her gentle breathing.

"You're sleeping?"

She frowned.

"No. Can't you see me with the broom? It's so messy in here."

"Where are you?" I asked.

"Oh, you know…in the room…in between…"

"Between what?"

"Huh?"

2

"The room in between what, Autumn?"

"Pretend and reality. Help me. It's so messy."

"Why is it messy?" I asked, but she didn't answer me.

I went to sleep much like I am now, on my back, staring at the quilt above us. I remember stretching my arm above my head, vaguely aware of the way she was twitching and mumbling a few inches away from me, presumably cleaning the space between this world and the next. We weren't touching, but it felt like the atoms between us were warm with my love for her.

Later on in the night, I woke up when she smacked my face. I pushed her hand away and turned my head toward her. She was close but not touching me, the covers bunched in her other fist, the hand that clocked me resting between us. I made myself look away and close my eyes, go back to sleep.

But now...

This is heaven: her forehead pressed into me, her head under my arm, and my hand on her shoulder. We found each other by instinct. Even if I was half-asleep, I would never have done this knowingly. I wouldn't know if she was okay with it. I don't know it now either, but I am unable to move.

My penis, based on very minimal evidence, has decided that today is going to be the greatest day of both our lives. I understand its enthusiasm, but it's (sadly) vastly overestimating the situation.

If I move, Autumn will wake up.

If Autumn wakes up, she'll see my body's assumption.

This is what I get for putting myself in this position. Again.

Not that I've been in this *exact* position with Autumn. But like I said, the tales I could tell.

The toilet flushes. I hadn't wondered where my other best friend had gone off to.

I am not going to be able to keep up the brave face with Jack. I don't think he'll let me this time. He's always known that I was still in love with Autumn after all these years, in spite of my being mostly happy with Sylvie. He let it slide all through high school, but he's not going to let me pretend anymore.

A couple of weeks ago, after we went to see that silly horror movie that made Autumn scream three times, both of them—Jack and Autumn—said they had fun. They said they could understand why I liked my other friend so much, and sure, maybe we could do it again.

Autumn had meant it. I could tell.

It wasn't that Jack didn't mean it. There was just a lot he wasn't saying.

I don't know if last night helped. I want Jack to see that Autumn isn't a poseur who thinks she's a princess like Alexis or Taylor make her sound.

It's more like Autumn is a real princess but from an alien planet. She is the most confident and insecure person I've ever known.

Except for Sylvie, of course.

Remembering Sylvie robs my penis of the delusion that a miracle is about to occur and adds to my already bloated guilt.

Jack retches and spits. The toilet flushes again, then the sink runs. I hear Jack get a glass of water in the kitchen.

I try to remember what Sylvie said about her flight itinerary. She must be in the air now. Over the English Channel? I can't say. I picture her in her seat, on the aisle, like she told me she prefers. Her Discman rests on her tray table, and her golden hair falls back as she tilts her head to listen.

I hope this trip was everything she needed, helped the way her therapist thought it would.

At first, I was doubtful. Sylvie in Europe on her own with no one to rein her in? Sure, she'd been to Europe before, is fluent in French, and has a cell phone. But I still couldn't believe that her therapist insisted she get away by herself without a single friend or parent on the postgraduation trip he'd prescribed.

I see now that Dr. Giles had been onto something. Sylvie knows how to take care of herself when she's not trying to impress other people. Sylvie gets drunk to impress people. If no one had dared her first, Sylvie would have never pulled her legendary inebriated stunts.

On her own, with her backpack and her maps, hostel listings and train schedules, Sylvie trekked across that continent. She got herself in a situation in Amsterdam when she didn't realize some guys were trying to get with her, but she got herself safe, and it was all over by the time she called me.

I hope Sylvie sees how capable she is, how smart and resilient. I hope she can feel good about herself for her own reasons, not for how other people think of her. Sylvie could be anything she wants if she just stops caring what the wrong people think about her.

I'm one of those people, and I hope I'm not going to ruin whatever progress this summer gave her.

Jack enters the room. I close my eyes. Though my penis remains somewhat optimistic, the blankets provide cover. I should move, wake Autumn, pretend my arm was never around her, but I can't bear to yet.

I hear the flap of the blanket tent flutter. Jack sighs. He says the same thing he told me the night I trusted Sylvie to sober drive for us and I had to drunkenly call him for a ride.

"We both should have expected this, you know," Jack mumbles.

He drops the blanket and it sounds like he goes to the couch, but I'm paying less attention to him now.

Autumn won't be asleep for much longer. She twitches occasionally, moving her face in reaction to things I cannot see. She makes a soft noise, the sort of noise I wish I could be responsible for while she is awake and consenting. And with that thought, I lift my arm and shift away from her. She frowns at the loss of heat, and I pause, waiting for her to stir. She whimpers and curls into a tighter ball.

I allow myself the brief luxury of gazing at her face.

It is cosmically unfair how beautiful Autumn is. It puts me at such a disadvantage. Her brilliant, goofy brain was already enough. Why must she have a perfect face too?

I never stood a chance.

Even before she grew breasts.

I need to stop this train of thought.

Might as well get this over with then.

———————————

Jack is typing on his phone at the end of the couch. He doesn't speak until I sit down.

"Finn, man—"

"I know," I say.

He flips his phone closed.

"No. You're in way over your head. You have no idea."

"I have an idea."

He stares at me.

"I know what I'm doing," I try.

"What *are* you doing? And what about *her*?" Jack nods toward the tent. Even though we're talking low, he starts to whisper. "She would have to be the stupidest person on earth to not know you're bonkers in love with her."

"She's not stupid. She just doesn't know how much I"—I can't bear to say the word—"care about her. She thinks it's an old crush."

I get that stare from him again, but I don't know what he wants me to say. Autumn doesn't flirt with me. She doesn't make suggestive jokes or give me any false reason to hope. Not when she's awake.

I'm the problem. My heart gets confused when she looks at me with affection that's only natural given our history.

7

"Finn," Jack says, "look at it this way. I'm not like you. I wasn't raised in a house where people talked about feelings and stuff. This is hard for me, and I'm doing it anyway. Again."

Again.

It's true.

"You're a good friend," I say. "And thanks. But she needs me. She's in a weird place with her other friends."

"She was laughing with you all night," Jack says, like he's trying to nail each word into my head.

"She was drunk, and besides, she's—" I realize what I'm about to say, but it's out of my mouth before I can hold it back. "—like Sylvie. She's disturbingly good at hiding how much pain she's in."

Jack groans and rubs his face. He says something I don't quite hear, but it ends with the word "type." Autumn makes a noise in the tent, and we both hold our breaths and listen.

Silence.

"Since you brought up Sylvie," he whispers. "Yeah, I complain about her, but she's my friend too, and I—"

"I know. I'm going to—"

Autumn makes a noise.

"She's about to wake up," I tell him.

Jack sighs. He's right about me when it comes to Autumn, and he knows that I know that he's right.

Jack and I can both see what happens next. Autumn and I will go off to Springfield. We'll make friends, probably mutual this time, but eventually, Autumn is going to meet someone she likes, someone

8

who has whatever made her want to be with Jamie. And I am going to be more than devastated. I will be obliterated. Jack and I are close enough that it kinda makes this his problem too. But I can't give up what I have with Autumn, and when she does meet that guy, I'm going to make sure he's supporting her, not treating her like a troublesome but valuable acquisition. Or a sidekick. Or a punch line.

"Fin-nah," Jack sings. He snaps his fingers in front of my face. "Hello!"

"Sorry, I—"

"Zoned out the way she does? You have been so, so... Like last week!" Jack asks, "How could you have missed that game?"

"Autumn and I were at the mall."

"You never miss it when the Strikers are on TV," Jack says.

And it's true; I was annoyed with myself when I remembered that the game was on. St. Louis barely has a league, and I'm on a mission to support it. But Autumn was talking about how the mall was like a neglected garden with some patches dying more quickly than others. According to Autumn, the area around the movie theater is a sunny spot with good rainfall. We walked around and decided that kiosks were weeds, and the department stores were neglected topiaries.

My shrug has not satisfied Jack. He waits for me to explain myself.

"I'm going to break up with Sylvie when she gets home tomorrow."

"I figured," Jack says. Simple words, but his tone has the recrimination I deserve. "Then what?"

9

"Oh God!" Autumn moans as she dashes out of her cave.

"Autumn," I say involuntarily as she heads to the half bath near the kitchen, the one recently vacated by Jack. I warned her she would be miserable if she had that fourth drink. It was her choice, but I still feel responsible. Plus, Jack made it, so unlike the previous three that I'd made her, it probably contained more alcohol. I am about to comment on Jack's bartending skills when I see the look on his face and remember that I do not have the high ground. "I'm going to check on her," I say.

"I figured," Jack says again. "Then what?"

"Then we'll hang out?" I try to make it sound flippant, as if I think he's only asking about today, but I don't fool either of us. We both know I'm avoiding the real question: How am I going to live the rest of my life in love with Autumn Davis with no hope of reciprocation?

two

―――

"Go away," Autumn says when I knock. She sounds like she's dying.

"You okay?" I know what she's going to say.

"Yes. Go away."

Autumn hates being vulnerable. She inherited that from her mother, despite all her complaining about Aunt Claire's veneer of suburban perfection.

"Okay." I have the urge to wait outside the door, even though I know she wants privacy. I turn and ignore the sounds on the other side of the door. When I was lusting after her a few minutes ago, what I should have been doing was worrying about her hangover.

Sometimes it feels like Autumn brings out the worst in me. She makes me feel like the kind of guys I hate, the jocks who say things in the locker room that stun me. I tried, especially after I was an upperclassman, to intervene in those conversations, but often I was so floored by what I'd heard that I missed my chance to interrupt.

A few times over the years though, when something was said specifically, vulgarly, about Autumn, my mouth spoke before the rest of me knew what was happening.

I was able to speak up those times, berate them for their disgusting observations, because I agreed with them. I wanted what they wanted or had seen the sight they recalled. Their words were a grotesque reflection of my own feelings.

Then, after the very last track meet of senior year, a freshman came up to me and said, "You've let Rick say worse stuff about other girls," laying bare my hypocrisy.

I sneered at that poor kid. "Then I should have had higher standards before today. I'll be gone soon. You can take over as chivalrous knight next year." I slung my bag over my shoulder and stomped off. I can't remember the guy's name, but he's probably going to remember Finn the asshole for a while.

In high school, Autumn only had eyes for Jamie. She didn't want those jock jerks thinking about her, and she doesn't want me thinking about her like that, then or now. She made that clear years ago. I get why she needed to make it clear. It's for the best that she did. But someday if we talk about it, I will tell her that she could have at least told me that she didn't feel the same way. She didn't have to leave me the way that she did.

That's probably what my mother meant yesterday. Aunt Claire is celebrating her divorce from Autumn's dad, Tom, with a wine-themed weekend. She and Mom left Autumn and I cash and surprisingly few instructions for while they were away. When Mom hugged me goodbye yesterday, she whispered, "For fuck's sake, kiddo. Talk to her."

It's been hanging between Autumn and I, this mutually incomplete knowledge. She knows I wish she felt differently about me. She needs to know it's much worse than she thinks. My love for her is the closest thing I have to religion. But it's okay that she doesn't feel the same. I'm fine. I can handle it. We can be friends, like when we were kids. I was in love with her back then, except this time I'm not going to wig out and try to prove anything to her. I learned my lesson when I tried to kiss her and she didn't kiss me back.

But my mother is wrong about the timing. This is not the weekend for that conversation. I need to get through today and breaking up with Sylvie tomorrow. After that, maybe I'll talk to Autumn. Or maybe it should wait until Christmas. I don't know.

———————

Once again, I have forgotten about my other best friend. I came to the kitchen to make toast out of habit, though Autumn has never been hungover at my house before.

Jack appears in the doorway. He watches me.

"Are you going to put cinnamon and sugar on it too?"

"That's not how Autumn likes her toast, loser." There I go again, lashing out instead of dealing with my fucking feelings like a man. I try to sound more like myself. "Do you want some too?"

"Sure." He sits and yawns. Jack has decided to let me off the hook for today. "Did she like *Goodfellas*?"

I laugh.

"We'd barely started it when you fell asleep. And you talked about it enough last night that she basically didn't need to see it."

"There is no way that can be true," Jack says. "That film is like a carefully constructed house of cards…"

He continues, but I'm not listening. The bathroom door has opened. She's back.

Behind me, I can hear her cross the kitchen and sit at the table.

"Feeling better?" Jack asks.

"More or less," Autumn says. Her eyes are closed when I turn around, and she's curled up in the chair, chin on her knee.

I pass Jack the first plate of toast and turn back to make more.

"So if you go back to the original source material, *Wiseguy*," Jack begins. He talks about this movie all the time. I don't have to listen to know what he's saying. I can agree or say the right thing while focusing on her.

I butter Autumn's toast the way she likes it, and she gives me a weak, grateful smile that melts me. I'm not sure what's keeping me upright.

Jack is only trying to save me from myself with this Scorsese monologue, and I'm being a terrible friend.

Her breathing is focused and slow. She chews, swallows, and takes a deep breath. Chew. Swallow. Breath. It's working. She's relaxing. Her eyes are still closed; she still leans her cheek on her bent knee.

Jack says, "I think you'd dig the narrative style, like, as a writer."

Autumn opens her eyes and blinks at him. I'm certain she has not been listening to the film history lesson either.

"Why don't we restart the movie? We can all watch it." Jack gives me a look to remind me that our other conversation isn't over.

Autumn shrugs and finishes her toast.

———————

I don't pay attention to the movie. We all sit on the couch in a row, the tent abandoned. They're watching the movie. I'm just here, near her. It seems like the toast did the trick for the nausea she had when she woke.

When had she woken? What had Jack and I been saying?

When I warned Jack that she was about to wake up, we'd been talking about—

Sylvie or soccer. That's what she could have overheard.

I already told Autumn that I'm breaking up with Sylvie. I don't think I said anything that could have revealed the real reason. It's one thing to be in a relationship with Sylvie while in love with the girl next door; it's a step too far if she's going back to being my best friend too.

"She's just not who I want to be with," I finally said when Autumn asked me why. It was the truth, even if it omitted so much. She nodded like she understood, and it felt like we both said more than we were, but I'm a fool like that.

———————

My best friends sit on either side of me for two and a half hours. Last night, we joked and teased. Today, we are quiet. Either way,

15

hanging out with both of them at the same time feels so right. I hope in the fall, when we're all in Springfield, they can be friends too. Just friends though.

It's a silly thought to have, but the point remains: I need to convince both myself and Jack that when Autumn does meet someone again, I'll be ready to let her go this time.

"Hey, Finn," Jack says. "Come get your cleats out of my car." He's getting ready to leave, and my cleats are not in his car. His car is a dumpster, and I'd never leave something of mine there, even cleats.

"Sure." I glance at Autumn before I get up. She's nestled in a blanket, finishing the glass of water I got her and having another slice of toast. I take note again of how unfair it is that she can be so beautiful while hungover.

I walk Jack to his car, and when he turns to me with that look on his face, I know what he's going to say. I open my mouth.

He beats me to speaking. "Your story doesn't make sense."

That's not what I expected.

"My story?"

"That she knows but also simultaneously doesn't know that you're in love with her."

"That's not what I said."

"It basically is. Maybe you are the two stupidest people on earth who somehow don't realize you're in love with each other, but I'm

16

leaning toward she knows you love her and she's fucking with you to make herself feel better."

"That is not—"

He gives me a look, and I stop talking.

"Break up with Sylvie tomorrow. Call me after. Think about what I said."

"Fine." I shrug one shoulder and look away.

"We're cool?"

I meet his eyes again. "Yeah."

He nods and leaves. I head back inside.

I wonder if I should have pretended to go upstairs and put away my imaginary cleats before sitting next to her on the couch, but she doesn't seem to notice.

"Did you have fun?" I ask her.

She smiles faintly. "You were right about that fourth drink and maybe about Jack's bartending skills."

"I was definitely right about both things. You're looking better though."

She looks amazing; that's how she looks by default.

"The toast helped. Thanks." She flashes me another smile, which fills me with warmth.

"Just a trick I learned." *From taking care of Sylvie*, I don't say.

"I think I'm going to go home and take a shower," she says.

I'm surprised and disappointed. I feel myself blink.

"Okay." Perhaps it's for the best. I need to collect my thoughts. Figure out what I'm going to say to Sylvie tomorrow.

Autumn stretches her arms above her head and groans before getting up, and I wish I could have that moment, like so many others, on instant replay.

She calls, "Bye, Finny!" over her shoulder as she heads to her house next door.

I pause, then rush to my room to catch another glimpse of her before she goes inside, perhaps see her again when she goes to her room, since our windows are across from each other.

Not that I'm trying to see her in any state of undress. Believe me, I've had my chances, and there've been close calls, but I've always made myself close my curtains when she forgets to close hers. Today though, she comes into her room and closes the curtains with efficiency. I leave my curtains open and stretch out on my bed. I should be thinking about what my mother and Jack have said to me about my relationship—my friendship—with Autumn. They both agree that I need to tell her.

But all I can think about *is* Autumn. The way her brown eyes shone as we built the tent yesterday. The way I could smell her soft hair as she was curled up against me this morning. The way she had arched her back and made that noise before getting off the couch. That she is now undressing to take a shower.

I am thinking about Autumn intensely, but not in a way that is going to make me feel better, now or in the long run.

three

I CANNOT LOOK BACK AND say when I fell in love with Autumn Rose. Something I felt for her before I even learned to read had grown and sharpened as we grew up together. If I tried to pin it down, I would guess the first time I had thought of myself as "in love with Autumn" would have been before fifth grade. I don't know if a psychologist would believe someone that young can be in love. All I know is what happened to me.

I was in love with her, but we were only eleven, so being just friends felt natural, even if in my mind it was assuredly temporary. We always talked like we were living our whole lives together like The Mothers; surely she would realize we should get married. But I never got the sense she was preoccupied with me in the same way. She did not understand why The Mothers said we could not have sleepovers in the same bed anymore. And I did. She did not, when our hands happened to touch, try to make the moment linger. And I did.

Those early years of being in love with her were hard, but I had no idea how much harder it was going to get.

———————————

I met Jack on the first day of middle school. Autumn and I did not have a single class together—I would be less distracted, for one thing—but not having lunch together seemed like a joke. Surely the school administrators knew we had always been together, were meant to be together. Surely, if I looked around the cafeteria, she would be there?

But she wasn't. Autumn ate during the first lunch, where she'd meet her new friends and my future friends, though I knew none of that right then.

When I finally sat down next to Jack at a mostly empty table, he reacted as if he had been waiting for me. We had been in the morning gym class together and kicked a ball around with a few other guys after the teacher had given us free time. I didn't sit down because I recognized Jack though; I simply sat at the first empty seat, defeated. But Jack remembered me. He asked me if I ever watched pro soccer. I said yeah, not really interested in conversation, not really listening, wondering what Autumn was doing.

And then Jack sealed our fates.

"Paolo Maldini is the reason I play defense."

My head shot up and I looked at him for the first time, noticing his freckles, the reddish tint to his hair.

"Me too," I said. "He's my—" and we said "favorite" together. I don't remember the rest of the conversation, but we were friends.

At dinner with The Mothers that night, Autumn talked about the girls she had eaten with, especially a girl named Alexis, and I was glad we had both worked out our lunches. For those first two weeks, I thought maybe everyone had been right: it would be good for us to have other friends. I could have Jack for lunch and soccer and Autumn for everything else. Autumn would have those girls for going to the mall. All those girly things were starting to be important to her, and she would still have me, like always, for everything else.

When my mom sat me down and explained that this year, after we had Autumn's birthday dinner as a family with Uncle Tom, Autumn's father, Autumn would be having girlfriends over for a slumber party and I couldn't participate, I understood. I didn't mind. The only thing that confused me was why my mom was telling me instead of Autumn.

I decided it was a timing thing. I was in all honors classes and Autumn wasn't, not even in honors English. She'd gotten a B-minus in English the year before. She'd read all the assigned books back in fourth grade, so she used her in-class reading time to secretly read Stephen King. Then she wrote her book reports based on what she could remember from two years earlier. I thought it was impressive that she'd gotten a B-minus under those circumstances.

Because we weren't in the same classes, our homework was different. There wasn't much purpose in doing our work together unless she needed my help with math. So we were spending less time together in the evenings. I told myself Autumn meant to tell me herself but didn't have time.

I had been talking to Jack all month about Autumn. How fun she was, how cool, how funny, how she always remembered to say "Paolo" and not "Pablo." (Not that she talked about soccer. It was more that she cared enough to remember when *I* talked about Paolo Maldini.)

For my birthday, one week before Autumn's, Jack came out to dinner with Mom, Aunt Claire, and Autumn. (Tom didn't appear for my events, and I wouldn't have wanted him. My own father sent a notice that he'd taken out another savings bond in my name.) I was excited for Jack and Autumn to meet.

Autumn smiled at him, and his eyes popped. He shook himself like he was getting out of a pool. I had talked about my friend Autumn, but I had not told Jack about her face or the new shape of her body. He said, "Hi," and the evening had seemed fine and normal, like every other birthday celebration with The Mothers and Autumn, except Jack was there too. It was only later that I realized how much time Autumn spent looking at her new phone, how distantly polite she was with Jack.

The Mothers had said we could not have cell phones until we were thirteen, but Autumn had received hers at the beginning of the month because her dad had messed up the contract's start date. Tom had given it to her anyway, as my mother put it, "without check-ing with Claire, as is custom in his kingdom." That night, when I received my first cell phone, I told Autumn we could text instead of using the cup and string strung between our windows. She'd smiled at that, but it hadn't seemed like she was planning to text me the way she had been texting her new girlfriends all week.

At the end of the night, when we were dropping Jack back at his house, he looked at me with pity before getting out of the car. I don't think he meant to, but I could see it on his face. He didn't believe that Autumn was—or ever had been—my friend. The daughter of my mom's best friend, who was around a lot? Sure. But he thought I had deluded myself into believing this hot girl was my friend.

I made it my mission to prove that Autumn *was* my friend. For the next two months, Jack was flooded with invitations to my home, where pictures of Autumn and I, arms slung around each other, covered the walls and where my mom could tell him story after story of all the adventures Autumn and I had together.

I succeeded in proving to him that Autumn and I had been friends, but I failed to prove to him (or honestly, me) that she and I were *still* friends. On the last day of school before winter break, Jack finally said something. I cannot remember what I had been telling him, only that it had been about Autumn.

"Finn. Dude. I mean, I get it. I'd eat broken glass for seven minutes in heaven with her. But does she even talk to you anymore?"

"We aren't guys who get invited to parties where they play spin the bottle or whatever," I said.

"And that's why she doesn't speak to you anymore," Jack said.

I didn't bother telling him that she did speak to me occasionally.

"We'll probably hang out over break," I said and shrugged.

Jack, always generous with me, did not tell me I was dreaming. And as it turned out, it wasn't a dream. It happened.

Autumn had come out of her trance, and it was as if she could see me again. The relief was so deep that it hit me on a physical level. I slept better in those two weeks than I had in months.

I was back in the game. Our relationship still wasn't where I wanted it to be, but I was holding the line again. I could make my move.

The locker room conversations hadn't reached the level of smut that they would in high school, but I'd heard an eighth grader bragging about following a group of hot seventh graders at the mall. I recognized Autumn and her friends in his description—he called Alexis by name—and I was shocked how he said they smiled and winked at him, then walked into the fancy underwear store when they knew he was following them.

For the first time, I questioned if I knew Autumn as well as I thought and then made assumptions about her life without me that were wrong. It wasn't the last time. I later assumed that Autumn was drinking and having sex freshman year based on a combination of hearsay and envy.

But back in seventh grade, I thought I'd figured out the kind of guy Autumn was into. I needed to be more masculine, like the older jocks. I was already good at sports, but I'd get better. I didn't have a real dad in my life to emulate, but I could learn more about *dudes*. I thought it would be months, though surely not years, before I would have my chance to impress Autumn.

Then the miracle happened. Autumn came back to me that

Christmas. We were friends again. Every day, we were together, talking and laughing like old times. I wasn't going to miss my chance to show her that I could be who she wanted.

We watched *When Harry Met Sally* with The Mothers over the break. Obviously, I'd loved the friends-to-lovers rom-com, and when Autumn told my Mom, "It was romantic at the end," I made my plan.

I would kiss her at midnight on New Year's Eve. I would show her that I could be bold, that I could be manly. My plan was, after we'd run outside and banged our kitchen pots to greet the new year, I'd throw them down, grab her romantically, and kiss her. I assumed that I would know how to do something like that instinctively.

I was so exuberant at midnight that I'd almost exhausted myself whooping and yelling, the way Mom's boyfriends had in other years. When I realized that I was about to miss my chance and everyone was going to go back inside, I'd reached out and grabbed her arm.

"Wait," I said. Talking hadn't been part of the plan, but it was already a couple of minutes past midnight.

"What?"

I had meant to take her in my arms and hold her, but I'd caught her above her elbow, and it would have to do. I leaned in, and her eyes widened.

Her lips were as soft as I had imagined. Again, I had assumed my romantic instinct would take over, telling me how to kiss her like people do in the movies. But I pecked at her, like I had kissed so many cheeks before, mostly The Mothers.

Still though, I was kissing *her*. My body was full of wonder and hope. I watched her face as I pulled back, waiting to see her reaction.

She was stunned, and then she said, "What are you doing?"

My fantasy came crashing down. This hadn't been my chance. This had been my test, and I had failed it. She'd let me back in, and I'd tried to make out with her like I was her equal. I should have waited. I should have worked out more. I should have been her friend when she had time for me over winter and summer breaks, and then, when I was cooler and taller and her friends liked me, maybe, *maybe* then I would have had a chance to be her boyfriend.

But I had ruined everything.

She was disgusted with me. It was clear on her face.

I wanted to hold on to her, to keep us together. It was only after she tugged her arm away that I noticed my hand ached from holding on to her.

I did not mean to hurt her.

My mother called for us.

Autumn pulled away and ran, ran away from me like she never had before. She never looked back, never waved for me to follow her.

Inside, the four of us had cake. It was dry in my mouth. My mother asked why we were so quiet and we both said, "I'm tired," at the same time. We startled and looked at each other and away again. I did not protest when she left for next door soon after.

It was not until New Year's Day brunch at her parents' house when I saw the light bruises on her arm that I recognized how terrible my big move had been. I'd assaulted her. I could see myself in her eyes, desperate and grasping, pathetic without being pitiable. It was all I could do to not bolt off the couch and give her the space she must have so desperately wanted from me.

At school, Jack asked about my break. He'd called twice over the holidays wanting to hang out. I'd told him both times that I was with Autumn, that we had plans the next day too. When he asked, there had been curiosity, even hope in his eyes, like I would have good news about Autumn.

I started to tear up. It wasn't an all-the-way cry, because I was fighting it, but it was close. It was one of the worst moments of my life.

We were in the locker room, right before second period. Jack looked around, panic in his eyes. I expected him to abandon me. Instead, he laughed loudly, punched my arm, said, "Oh yeah? Let's take this outside," and hurried me out.

There was a quiet place that he knew about behind the dumpsters. Other kids seemed to too. There were a couple of cigarette butts and lots of candy wrappers on the ground. He listened to me talk for the whole period. I laid it all bare, and afterward I felt marginally better.

We sat shoulder to shoulder, huddled together against the cold.

I said, "I don't know what to do. She was my best friend."

Jack shrugged. "I don't have a best friend either."

After that, I left Autumn alone. Until Valentine's Day.

There was this fundraiser. For two dollars, a red or white carnation would be delivered with a card to the person of your choosing. The banner said, "White Carnations Are for Your Friends!" leaving us to figure out for ourselves what red ones meant. I sent Autumn two carnations, one white and one red, one with my name and the other signed "Your Secret Admirer." I overheard The Mothers saying that Autumn had received a total of four red carnations signed exactly that way. No one sent me anything.

At the end of February, Mom came and sat on my bed.

"Heeeeeey, kiddo!" For her sensitive talks, Mom always tried to catch me at the end of reading in bed, right before I turned out the light.

"What is it?"

She sighed and put her hand on my foot.

"You know Claire and I always hoped that you and Autumn would be friends, but we wouldn't force it on you."

I had no idea where she was going with this.

"If you and Autumn have grown apart, we understand, but I wanted to know if *you're* okay with your friendship with Autumn. You've seemed down lately."

I thought it was painfully obvious how I longed for Autumn. The idea that anyone could not see it stunned me.

Perhaps that's why I snapped, "What friendship, Mom?" and returned to my book.

She must have been surprised, because I'd read a few sentences before she spoke again. "Sometimes brothers and sisters go through phases when they aren't friends, but they still love—"

I dropped my book and stared at her in horror. Her face went through a series of emotions like they were projector slides: surprise, amusement, joy, and then sadness. Deep sadness.

"And sometimes," she continued, "really good friends go through periods when they aren't that close, and that's okay. They still care about each other. Later, maybe they become close again, or maybe they become something more than friends. Maybe."

I tilted my head to show her that I was listening.

She said, "The thing to do is focus on what makes you feel good about yourself, like school and soccer. You have your new friend Jack. You can remind yourself, 'Autumn is where she wants to be right now, and that's okay. I'm still great, and I'll be around if she needs me.' Hmm?" She squeezed my foot again.

"Okay," I said. "A bit after-school special, but thanks." I shrugged and let her hug me.

After she left, I turned out my light and thought about her advice.

It made sense, because it wasn't that different from what I had thought before, though I had overshot the goal. I needed to get cooler. Soccer was the best path forward to looking more manly. I'd show Autumn that I wasn't a loser without friends; Jack and I would make more friends somehow.

I'd met my father twice before at that point, and he was very tall. The pediatrician said that I would be tall too, that it was only a matter of time. Time was what I needed to become a better version of myself. While Autumn ignored me, I'd transform myself.

So though it hurt whenever I was near her, I ignored that and stared at her out of the corner of my eyes like an addict desperate for a fix. But I gave Autumn time, and I gave Autumn space, and I worked on myself.

The next Valentine's Day, I sent one anonymous red carnation to Autumn, and I sent one white carnation to Jack signed, "Paola."

He whacked me with it at lunch as he sat down beside me.

"Thanks," he said, "but don't think this means I'm going to put out."

"I just felt sorry for you," I said.

By the end of lunch, the table was littered with white petals from hitting each other with it. The other guys we hung out with, more for numbers than their conversation, were annoyed with us, but it was probably the most fun I ever had for two dollars.

four

———

FANTASIZING ABOUT HAVING SPENT A different sort of night with Autumn in that tent and then mulling over all my mistakes that have kept us apart did not improve my mood. My head aches. I'm even more exhausted, and the guilt is back. Autumn doesn't want me thinking about her that way. I need to get control of myself.

I roll off the bed and head to the bathroom, unable to stop myself from glancing out my window at her closed curtains as I go. I strip down and get into the shower, switching the water to as hot as possible and staying under the stream for as long as I can stand. Then, quickly, I turn the dial all the way to cold.

You are here, in this moment, right now, I tell myself as the frigid water batters my fevered skin.

The reality is, what you imagined will never happen, and what you remembered is already done.

In this moment, Autumn is your friend.

Don't fuck this up.

But be ready for when she leaves again.

Once I am shivering, I turn the water dial to the middle. I wash away the fantasy of her beneath me and the memory of her head under my arm.

———————————

My cell rings as I'm putting on clean boxer shorts. I answer automatically, assuming it's Autumn without looking at the screen.

"Hey," I say.

"Hi!" Sylvie says.

My stomach drops.

"Oh. Hi. Wow. Where are you?"

"London. I have a long layover until my flight to New York, so I'm going to go sightseeing, and I'm trying to squeeze in a lot, so I'll be busy. I wanted to talk to you one last time."

She means one last time before she's back in the States, but it feels like she means one last time before I break up with her, not that she knows it's coming.

"Yeah," I say. It's been getting harder and harder to pretend there will be something for us after Sylvie returns.

"So?" she says. "Are you looking forward to seeing me tomorrow?"

"Yeah," I say again, and it may be the biggest lie I have ever told. "When are you arriving?"

"Around four or so... You'll be at the airport, right?"

That hadn't even occurred to me. Of course she expects that. But

I can't hug and kiss her in front of her parents, then break her heart in private.

What can I say? "Probably. I'll let you know."

"You don't know?" There is suspicion and hurt in her voice. At times, it seems like she's putting the pieces together. I don't know if it's cruel or not, to let her suspect. Is it better for her that way? I don't know how to do the cruelest thing the kindest way.

"Sorry, I—"

"What did you do last night?" Sylvie asks, cheerful again.

"Oh, Jack spent the night."

"Sounds fun!" She tells me about her plan for the ten-hour layover in London, including taking a minicab to a nearby picturesque village, sitting alone and drinking a pint in a pub, then walking along the Thames before catching another cab back to Heathrow. Sylvie has done that her whole trip: every hour accounted for so that she can experience as much as possible. It's one of the things I love about her. She never does anything by halves; she never lets an opportunity pass her by.

Autumn would like that about Sylvie too. She appreciates passion. If they weren't both so convinced that the other hated them, they'd be a good influence on each other. The moment Autumn stepped outside the airport, she would lose her sense of direction and her passport, both, perhaps, never to be seen again.

Early on, before I realized how the summer would go, I told Sylvie that Jamie dumped Autumn. We were sitting on her porch before Sylvie left for the airport. I was in the habit of occasionally updating her with public information one might pass on about a mutual acquaintance. It helped to keep up the story of my platonic feelings for Autumn. My lie. Because if I never talked about the other girl whose life so constantly collided with mine, Sylvie, rightfully, found that suspicious too.

Sylvie had a lot of questions about the breakup. As I sat next to her and her bags, I told her all I knew was that Aunt Claire said Jamie had broken up with Autumn. Sylvie was surprised, much like everyone else seemed to be. She asked twice if I was sure about that part. I mean, we'd all heard Jamie brag about how he and Autumn would be together forever.

At the time, I'd suspected Jamie of taking Autumn's virginity and then dumping her, but I didn't say so or act too worried about Autumn. I wasn't about to reignite Sylvie's jealousy over nothing.

But then, it wasn't nothing. Autumn was so depressed about Jamie that The Mothers asked *me* to try to talk to her. Suddenly, Autumn and I were hanging out every day.

At first, I told myself it wouldn't last, so it wasn't worth mentioning to Sylvie. Then after about a week, I let it slip that I'd missed her call because I was watching a movie with Autumn. Hanging out with Autumn again had felt so normal, even after all these years, and her name had just slipped out.

Sylvie interrupted me. "You and Autumn are friends again?"

I hadn't heard that tone in her voice for a long time. "We were never not friends," I said, and there was a pause on Sylvie's end.

34

"So," she said, "anyway."

And that was that. Sylvie never asked about her again. I've managed to not mention Autumn, despite how much we've been together this summer.

In those early days of the summer, when Autumn and I started hanging out again, I hadn't planned to break up with Sylvie. What would have been the point? I was still in love with Sylvie, and when I originally fell in love with her, I'd already been in love with Autumn for years. So emotionally, for me, nothing had really changed.

But over the past few weeks, it's become clear: I love Sylvie, but I can't say that I will be in love with her every day for the rest of my life. I adore so much about her and understand her foibles, but I'm not devoted to her. She's a partner but not a part of who I am.

My devotion to Autumn is engraved on my very being. I am in awe of her. I will sit in the stands and cheer her on in life as her most ardent admirer. I know I will always love her in the same way I know I'll always need oxygen.

Sylvie is taking time off before starting college. She needs some more time to figure things out, so I'm glad. But our situation won't get easier when I'm down in Springfield with Autumn and Sylvie is still here in St. Louis.

"How about I call from my layover in Chicago, and you can let me know if you're going to be at the airport when I arrive tomorrow," Sylvie says.

35

"Okay," I say. I'm worried about her acceptance of my dereliction of duty. Does she know what's coming? Is she hoping that by being agreeable, she might convince me to stay? Is she clueless, so happy to see me that it doesn't matter if it's at the airport or after? Do I want her to suspect or not?

"Well," she says, "I should go. Hopefully, I can sleep during the flight."

"What time is it for you?" I ask, a go-to question of our stilted conversations of the past few weeks.

She answers, but there's an announcement in the background, and I can't quite make out her words. "Oh. It's..."

I'm surprised when I glance at my alarm clock. Where did the afternoon go?

"Five o'clock. Anyway."

"I love you," she says.

"I love you too," I say, and it's not a lie. It's just not the whole truth.

She hangs up.

———————

As many times as I've asked myself how Autumn and I ended up this way, I've wondered the same thing about Sylvie and me.

If I hadn't made the varsity soccer team, everything would have been different.

Jack and I had worried one of us might not make it on the junior varsity team. When the lists were posted, I searched for my name

36

on the JV list and was devastated to not see it. Still, I was happy for Jack.

Then I heard one of the taller, older guys say, "P-hen-e-ass Smith? Who the hell is that?"

"It's Phineas," I said. "Call me Finn."

There were a few chuckles, though I wasn't sure why—until I saw my name. On the varsity list.

Jack told me later that my ability to brush off the snarky comment from that junior, my new teammate, made me seem cool. There had been chuckles of appreciation according to him. I wasn't sure about that though.

I was terrified by the unexpected development, despite Jack's enthusiasm.

"You are going to be cool, and you'll make me cool by association. You get that, right?" Jack told me as we waited for my mom to pick us up after tryouts. Jack had not one but two parents as affectionately neglectful as Autumn's father, and my mom was often his ride for activities we did together.

"I don't know about that," I said. I was as tall as the seniors and juniors on varsity, but they seemed eons older. Also, I was used to being one of the best on our intramural teams. Surely, on the high school varsity team, I would be one of the worst. I'd probably spend all season on the bench.

"Finn, it's high school. It's an ecosystem, and you just shot to the top of the food pyramid!"

I rolled my eyes.

"You mean the food chain."

"Whatever. You're going to date a cheerleader," Jack said gravely.

I laughed aloud at the thought.

The varsity soccer team practiced on the north field, near the student parking lots. The junior varsity team practiced on the south field, closer to the circular drive where parents dropped off and picked up kids. Even though Jack and I were on different teams, our schedules were still the same, and my mom would drive us to and from practice every day for those last weeks of summer.

It turned out, compared to the older guys, I was still pretty good. I wasn't the best on the team, but I no longer worried that I would spend the games on the bench.

At the end of the first practice, my teammates all walked to their cars. One guy asked me if I needed a ride, which was nice, but I told him I was all set and walked across campus to where Jack would be waiting for me. I was excited to tell him that practice hadn't been as hard as I thought.

I was walking next to the gym building, not really paying much attention, when a door opened next to me. I almost ran into a girl carrying a cheer bag.

"Oh!" she squealed.

"Alexis!" I said in my surprise. "Sorry."

She blinked and looked at me. We'd never actually spoken

before. I wasn't sure she even knew who I was. Three other girls with similar bags joined her.

"You're...Finny, right?" Alexis said.

"Finn, actually," I said, but I took it as evidence that Autumn had talked about me to her friends.

"Right. Well, no harm done. Wanna walk with us?"

And that was why, when I met up with Jack at the circle drive, I was accompanied by four pretty girls.

"Uh, this is my friend Jack," I said as we approached the wall where he was sitting. "Jack, this is Alexis, Victoria, Taylor, and..." I realized I didn't know the last girl's name, and I blushed.

"I'm Sylvia—Sylvie," she said.

We all joined Jack on the low wall, waiting to get picked up. We didn't talk that much, but the next day, as I trudged from the north field to the south, I saw the girls by the gym door again. It was only as I approached and saw them watching me that I figured out they were waiting for me.

"You ready?" Alexis asked when I reached them.

"Y-yeah?" I said, and we all walked together.

After that, I expected them. It wasn't much. They hung out with us while we waited for our rides. We didn't really talk, because we didn't have anything to talk about. It was like we wanted to hang out with each other without knowing why. Well, I knew why I wanted to hang out with them; they were Autumn's friends. I thought.

One afternoon when my mother was running late and the girls

had already gone, Jack claimed to be in love with Alexis based on her being so pretty and nice.

"They're all pretty and nice," I said. "We don't actually know anything about any of them other than that."

"It's a good start," Jack said. "And Alexis is my kind of pretty. Actually, I thought maybe you would be into her?" He checked my face. "That's kinda why I brought it up?"

"Oh? No." I didn't see why he would think that.

He looked relieved that we weren't into the same girl, but he remained suspicious.

"Yeah, well, who do you like then?" he asked.

"I mean, I don't know any of them, dude," I said. "That's what I'm trying to tell you. I don't know if I like any of them."

"Okay, whatever. I know you've jerked off to one of them at least once by now. Which one was it?"

"Come on..." I began, and Jack punched my shoulder.

"See! Which one? Victoria, right?"

"Sylvie, you pervert."

"Really?"

"What?"

"I didn't think she was your type."

I laughed. "What is 'my type'?" and he gave me that blank look, that "Autumn" look as I'd come to think of it.

Maybe he thought I would be into Alexis because she had brown hair, brown eyes, and was about Autumn's height. Victoria's figure was closer to Autumn's shape. Sylvie, blond with a willowy ballerina figure and tall enough to look me in the eyes without raising her face, is Autumn's physical opposite in every way. Except that they are both beautiful.

"I don't know," I told Jack that day. "Sylvie seems like she's... herself? And I like that." Sylvie hadn't gone to our middle school, and I wondered what Autumn knew about her, thought of her. Since Autumn wasn't a cheerleader, maybe she hadn't met her yet.

"Okay," Jack said and went back to talking about Alexis. My interest in anyone besides Autumn, on any level, was enough for him.

I was so happy that summer. I thought that my plan was finally coming to fruition. Autumn's cool friends liked me. She and I didn't talk that much those summer weeks because we were both busy, so I didn't notice that Autumn never mentioned them anymore.

What I should have noticed was that Autumn's "friends" didn't seem to talk about her anymore either.

five

————

It's FIVE THIRTY, AND I'M still in my boxer shorts, still thinking about all my misjudgments. I sit on my bed, holding my phone, even though Sylvie hung up long ago. I look over at Autumn's window. Her curtains are still closed.

Attempting to sound offhand, I type into my phone, Hey, whatcha up to?

I don't expect a reply so quickly, so I'm happy—until I read it.

Writing.

Just the one word.
Autumn is where she wants to be right now, and that's okay.
I get off my bed, pull a T-shirt over my head, and grab some pants. I clean my room to kill time and then head to the basement and put on a load of laundry. Back in the living room, I take down the rest of our tent, fold the blankets, and slide them into the linen

closet. Autumn left half a glass of water on the coffee table. I finish it and wash and dry all our glasses.

I wish I had a dog. It would be good to have a dog that needed an evening walk. Autumn has always wanted a dog.

I go back upstairs and pick up my book. I'm not the voracious reader that Autumn is, but I almost always have a book I'm reading, slowly and steadily.

Autumn, though, I've seen her finish a novel, pause staring off into space for a minute like she's receiving instructions, and then open another book. It's as if her job is to read and she's behind on her quota.

In elementary school, when she was particularly excited by a book, she would read it as we walked home, trusting me to make sure she didn't run into anything. I remember being next to her and watching her cry as we walked, silent tears rolling down her cheeks, her gaze never wavering from the page. I also remember walking next to her as she laughed so hard that tears spilled out of the corners of her eyes.

I never get angry or sad or exhilarated by books the way Autumn does. It's more of a break for me, some time spent as a detective or a spy before I go back to my real life. I usually forget a novel shortly after I've finished it. Books are Autumn's real life. She is made of the stories she has read.

The best thing about Jamie breaking up with Autumn is that I don't have to worry about him pressuring her into becoming a teacher.

Autumn would be miserable as a teacher. I know this because my mom is a teacher, and I see the sacrifices Mom makes because she loves teaching. Autumn would not love teaching. She might not hate it, but I know it would never be a passion. Writing is her passion. Autumn would grow to resent her students because they would take her away from writing. I can see so clearly how she would feel trapped.

When she changed her plans and started looking at colleges with creative writing majors, I was relieved, but not only because I thought she would be happier. I had started to wonder if maybe I didn't know Autumn as well as I thought, that maybe she *did* want to be a teacher. But once she had switched back to envisioning a writing career for herself, it reconfirmed that I knew who she was deep down inside.

I don't think Jamie ever understood Autumn.

Jamie.

I remember punching the wall in my room after graduation when I thought she was waiting for him to whisk her off to make love somewhere romantic.

Autumn had loved reading *Wuthering Heights* in English class junior year. She always finished books before the rest of the class, ignoring the reading schedule. Autumn had gone on and on about Heathcliff's passion during class discussions, often infuriating our classmates by spoiling the plot because she forgot the rest of us hadn't finished the book yet.

I sat behind her in that class and stared at the back of her head as

I hung on her every word. I'd tried to like it too. *Wuthering Heights* is about childhood friends in love. I wanted the plot to reveal that Autumn and I were meant to be together. But all I could see was how Heathcliff's obsession with Cathy had turned him into the worst version of himself.

So after I punched the wall all those weeks ago, I rubbed my bruised knuckles, checked the wall for divots, and thought, *There's some Heathcliff passion for you, Autumn. Now Jamie can get you pregnant, and I'll give myself a concussion on a tree when you go into labor.*

Autumn brings out the worst in me, and it's not her fault.

Jack thinks it is though.

I owe it to him—my only other real friend, if I'm being honest with myself—to consider what he said to me when he left today: Either Autumn and I are the two stupidest people in the world who somehow don't realize we're in love with each other, or she's fucking with me.

I don't know where to begin with that though. It's like he told me to consider the possibility that she murdered someone.

Autumn has her flaws. She's offhandedly arrogant about her looks. She lacks tenacity or drive for anything that isn't reading or writing. When she's in a bad mood, you must tread carefully. She can, in the blink of an eye, casually strike with a few cruel words that get right to the heart of your insecurities.

But she almost always apologizes quickly. She'll flinch after the words leave her mouth and tell you she's sorry. I'm not saying it's okay. It happens mostly when she's depressed, and if her mom is any indication, depression is going to be a lifelong thing for her. I'm simply saying that Autumn's base motivations are defensive, not cruel.

If Autumn knows I adore her, what would she get from torturing me with her presence all summer? She's not insecure about her looks. If she wanted attention from a guy, she could...go somewhere public? And sit with a book until someone sat down next to her? It wouldn't take long.

The girls had always insisted that Autumn's friends were our rivals, and though Jack and I agreed Jamie was an obnoxious showboat, we didn't see this competition with them that they did.

Could Autumn have seen it that way though? Autumn has never liked Sylvie in particular. She's never said so to me, but it's clear.

Sylvie has never liked Autumn. She has said so to me clearly.

Would Autumn purposely blow air over the coals of my long-burning love for her to torture Sylvie? Could her heartbreak over Jamie be so deep that she'd take pleasure in hurting Sylvie through me?

It doesn't sound right, doesn't sound like the Autumn I love, but it sounds more likely than any theory of Autumn simply wanting to hurt me.

Autumn knows I have an old crush on her. Maybe, maybe, maybe, Jack is a little bit right, and she is messing with my head to mess with Sylvie?

It seems too vicious for Autumn.

But I promised Jack that I would think about it, and I have.

I've been lying here with my thriller open on my chest staring at the ceiling.

I try to read.

I don't care that the ambassador from the fictional country was poisoned.

Autumn said to me once, "When you're reading a book and you can't focus, ask yourself, 'How much is the writer's fault, and how much is mine?' Be honest. That's how you'll know if you should set it aside forever or for a few hours."

I can't tell if it's the book or me, so I set it back on the nightstand. Autumn's curtains are still closed.

I get off the bed and reach for the light switch.

It isn't fully dark yet, but Autumn's house sits in the shade of mine. I'm pretty sure her lights are not on. I would see a glow between the curtains.

What kind of stalker am I that I've stared at her window enough to come to that conclusion?

I can read her moods by assessing a variety of factors: the time she's taken with her appearance, her level of concentration while reading, how forthcoming she is with different topics. At school, I could pick out her laugh in a crowded hallway. In class, I could predict her feelings about books assigned and events studied.

Even when I could have escaped her or avoided thoughts of her, I chose not to. For example, I've used Autumn in my mnemonic devices for countless vocab words in school. She is comely, hallowed, and impervious. My love for her is vehement, protracted, and interminable.

Sylvie caught me at it once. We were studying for the SAT and

47

running flash cards together on the couch. The word was *pulchritu-dinous* (I *pul*led her to me after *Chri*stmas).

"Autumn—beautiful!" I said, my brain too focused on studying to remember to keep my secrets.

"What?" Sylvie looked at me over the cards.

"Beautiful, right? That's what it means?"

"Yeah," she said. "But you said—"

"Oh! Autumn, like my birthday! Fall leaves and stuff. You know how I like the leaves changing color."

Sylvie knows I love fall leaves. It's my favorite season, my birthday, etc., etc., but I honestly don't know if she believed me.

No, that's not true. I know that Sylvie didn't believe me.

She had looked at me for a long moment. She didn't seem angry. She seemed resigned. She flipped through the stack of cards in her hand to find one in particular.

"Mendacious?" she finally quizzed me.

"Dishonest. Next word?"

She let us move on.

I hate myself for interrupting her, but I take my phone out and type, Can I come over? and send it before I can second-guess it.

I head downstairs to the kitchen and eat the leftover pizza. I recycle the box and pour a Coke. There's an inch of rum left. I look at it and then put it back on the counter. It won't help me. Maybe Autumn will want it before The Mothers come home tomorrow.

I check my phone even though I'd have heard her respond.

I sit down at the computer and watch a few clips of the Strikers game I missed. I can give them website traffic at least.

I glance at my phone again. This summer, she's always texted me back quickly.

What if, this morning, she woke up in the tent before I thought? What if she woke up as I lifted my arm off her, then lay there wondering why I had been touching her, why I was still lying close to her and not speaking? If that was the case, she would have—or could have—heard me say many, many, incriminating things to Jack outside the tent.

For fuck's sake, talk to her, kiddo!

Tell her you're sorry. Tell her you know she doesn't feel the same way. Tell her you're working on it. Tell her that you just want to be there for her.

That isn't the speech I should be working on tonight.

I have to figure out what to tell Sylvie, because I can't tell her the truth.

Before Sylvie took me back after our breakup sophomore year, she asked, again and again, if I was really, really, really sure that I no longer had romantic feelings for Autumn.

I lied to Sylvie, again and again, because I loved Sylvie, I missed her, and I desperately wanted her back.

I even used the idea that had so offended me when my mother shared it: I told Sylvie that Autumn was my first love, but now, we were like brother and sister. Finally, she believed me. Or rather we both pretended to believe me.

I cannot tell Sylvie, "I can't be with you anymore because I am in love with Autumn. She doesn't want me that way, but it isn't fair to you now that she wants to be my friend again."

Because Sylvie would say that if I still loved *her*, I should stop being friends with Autumn.

I can't tell Sylvie that I'm choosing friendship with Autumn over our nearly four-year relationship. She's worked so hard to value herself again after what happened before we met.

It strikes me how backward my plan sounds: give up a girl who adores me, who I love well enough, to be a disciple for a different girl who will never fall for me. Jack has always said I'm irrational when it comes to Autumn, and maybe I should have taken him more seriously, because he was right earlier today.

I'm in way over my head.

six

——

IT'S ONLY AUNT CLAIRE AND Autumn's house. I go over there all the time. It wouldn't be weird to head over, ask if she's eaten, because we still have cash from The Mothers and a little rum—just a little!—or whatever. It'll be clear that we don't have to keep hanging out if she doesn't want to.

Then, depending on how she acts, I'll know if she overheard anything this morning, if I need to explain myself.

No matter what, I will tell her how I feel...eventually. But it can wait. I've waited this long. The thing to worry about now is what I will say to Sylvie. I escape the guilt of thinking about Sylvie by getting off the couch and heading out.

Aunt Claire always locks her back door. My mother often forgets to lock ours and she often loses her keys, so she keeps an extra key hidden. Aunt Claire doesn't keep a key hidden, but Autumn often loses her keys and forgets to lock the back door, so I'm betting that she forgot to lock it today.

She forgot to lock it that day she snuck Jamie over freshman year. I saw them go inside from my window, then closed my curtains. But to my horror, Mom asked me to run next door and ask Autumn if they had eggs. As I crossed the lawn, I prayed that she'd left the back door unlocked. She had, but it hadn't saved me from intruding on them.

Today, I knock gently, but there is no answer. I try the doorknob, and it turns. *It's Aunt Claire's house.* Autumn hadn't been surprised or confused to see me that day I came over for eggs. The only awkward part had been when Jamie emerged from the hallway, making eye contact with me while Autumn was looking in the fridge. I could tell she didn't want me to know that Jamie was there. We both knew her parents wouldn't want Jamie over while they were out.

I even pretended I thought that no one had been home to save her the embarrassment.

Jamie, on the other hand, made his presence known, staked his claim. I wanted to say something, but then Autumn was handing me the eggs for Mom. Should I have exposed him? Would Autumn have realized back then that his ego was more important than her wishes?

Autumn hadn't minded me inviting myself in. She hadn't minded that day or a million times before or after. That's what matters. It's always been that way with The Mothers and our houses. Still, my heart is beating hard. Where is she?

I expected her to be watching a movie in the living room or eating in the kitchen, but the rooms are empty and the lights are off.

I turn to the stairs and listen to the creak and groan under my feet as I climb. Surely, she can hear me? Has she gone out?

I knock and push open her bedroom door, half expecting the room to be empty. But deep in the darkness, in the far corner of her bed, I see her shape.

"Autumn?"

"Hey," she says. Her voice is calm, yet it shakes.

My shoulders tense. What happened?

"I came to check on you."

"I finished the novel," she says. She's crying. She's more emotional than with other books she's read, and if she means her own novel, surely they would be happy tears? These don't look like happy tears.

Still, it doesn't matter why she's crying, because she's crying. Instinct takes over, and I cross the room, pulling her into my arms the way I have dreamed of so many times before, with so many different tenors of emotions and desire.

But there's only one thing I want right now: to stop the pain that is making her fingers curl around my shirt. It's been so long since she let me see her vulnerable like this. We were so young the last time.

Autumn's sobs reverberate in my chest as she presses her sweet face against me, and it is proof I am awful. I am taking such pleasure in comforting Autumn. Just as I have been all summer, ever since Jamie made me the happiest man alive by breaking Autumn's heart.

My Autumn.

No, Phineas, not yours.

She's in her bathrobe, but I try to push that thought aside.

She starts to quiet. Her breathing slows. I want to stroke her hair, her back, kiss the top of her head. I can't. I won't. *Autumn*.

I feel her shoulders slump, followed by the faintest of whimpers. She's done crying. I could move, but I don't. I hold her gently, careful to make sure she's in control, and she can pull away with the slightest of movements.

"Do you want to tell me what's wrong?" I ask. *I'll be around if she needs me.*

"It's like they're dead," she says.

Of course. Jamie and Sasha. The two people who kept her anchored through her ups and downs the past four years. She had her time and space to be numb, but now, finally, she is truly grieving the end of their friendship. Still, I give her the opening to explain it.

"Like who is dead?"

"Izzy and Aden."

I only have time to think, *Who?* before she says, "My main characters."

Her novel. The one she's finished. I don't understand why that has made her cry like this, but I'm so relieved that I laugh and say aloud to myself, "I thought something was really wrong."

She raises her head off my chest, and I let one of my arms fall away as she faces me. In the dying light, her tear-filled eyes are luminous. Her lovely face is pink and puffy. She looks so sweet and so absolutely devastated.

"Something *is* wrong!" Her voice quavers and her lips quiver. "Can't you tell I'm upset?"

I laugh. I can't help it. I laugh because she isn't crying about something from the real world and because I'm so happy that she finished her novel. Her devotion to her writing is beautiful, like the rest of her.

Then she punches me. It isn't very hard, but it hurts a little, and it makes me laugh again.

"Stop laughing at me," she insists.

"Sorry," I say, trying to swallow my mirth. "It's just really obvious that you're upset." *And you're just so wonderful that it makes me terrible*, I do not say. "And I meant I thought something was really wrong. Like Jamie had called you."

"Who cares if Jamie called me?" she says.

I feel my grin widen again, but I can't help it.

"Who cares about Jamie?" she says and begins to cry again.

I use the excuse to pull her close. Who cares about Jamie indeed?

"You don't understand," I feel her moan above my heart.

I take a deep breath of her scent.

"I know," I say.

I understand this much: Autumn lives in this world and the fictions of her mind or those written by others like her. Whatever it is that puts us together as people, be it God, genes, or destiny, Autumn was made to tell stories. She's going to be an amazing writer. She's always been amazing. Whatever this novel is about, it's going to blow my mind. I know it.

"But I can't wait to read it," I say. I'm smiling again, and I know she can hear it in my voice. She knows me almost as well as I know her.

"You can't read it." We're leaning into each other like two sides of a triangle. She's still sniffling.

"Why not?" She said something before about how I might take elements too literally, how I'd draw parallels to her real life. Maybe there's stuff in there about Jamie or her dad, or rather his absence. Maybe there's something about Sylvie? That seems unlikely.

The thing is I know that she wants me to read it. She knows what she wrote is good, in the same way she knows that she's pretty. She knows it's good, but she's terrified that it's not as good as she hopes. At least that's what I assume, because that's what she said about the final draft of her four-part poetic drama about the faerie-dragon wars she finished when we were almost twelve.

"Not all dragons want to wipe out faeries, only some of them, and the other dragons are finally joining the faeries' fight," Autumn explained to me as if these were current events.

I wasn't enthused by faeries, but I figured I wouldn't hate her story. When I read her superlong poem, though, it was so much better than what I had expected. She surprised me. It didn't sound like something a kid had written, and I told her so afterward. I told her how I found myself caring about that dragon prince way, way more than I had expected or even wanted to. It was the truth. She was triumphant, and it was wonderful to see.

It's turned dark now. Her breathing is quiet. She could move if she wanted to. Why hasn't she moved?

"Okay," she says. "You can read it after dinner." She lifts her head off my chest, and both of my arms fall away.

"All right," I say. I don't need to tell her that I ate dinner a while ago. Meals don't have time or meaning for us this summer. I hop off the bed and hold out my hand to her.

"Um, I need to get dressed?" she says.

I drop my hand.

"Oh." I try to laugh. "I forgot. How about you meet me in the car?"

I guess I can't be too bad of a guy if my concern for Autumn's emotional state could make me entirely forget her state of undress.

seven

Outside, with the moon and streetlights, it's brighter than inside her house. I get in my car and start the engine, turning my headlights on so that her back porch is illuminated like a stage. It isn't long before she makes her entrance. Autumn's wearing jeans and a T-shirt, casual and untouchable. She carries her laptop. Is she bringing it now so that she doesn't lose her nerve later? Autumn shades her eyes as she heads to the car.

"So where are we going? Tacos? Burgers? Chicken?" I ask as she sits next to me in the passenger seat. The flush is gone from her face.

"Oh?" she says, as if she had forgotten that dinner involves food.

"This is a celebratory drive-through run," I tell her. "We'll stop at that gas station that sells those candies that you like, the one that looks like hair gel in a tube and the one that comes in the paper packets that looks like laundry detergent."

She doesn't laugh. "Okay."

"I mean, it's great that you finished your novel, even if you feel like you've"—I try to choose my words carefully—"like you've lost your main characters?"

"Yeah," she says with a nod. She turns and faces forward, looking out the windshield. "I didn't know it would hurt this much."

"You'll still have to edit it, right?" I take the car out of park. "And when it's published, they'll live forever within other people, you know?"

She gives me an annoyed scoff.

"What?" I ask.

"You can't just say, 'When it's published,' Finny."

I catch a glimpse of her face before I turn in my seat to navigate down the long driveway. She's gazing out the dark window.

She sighs. "It's probably never going to be published. That's simply a fact."

"No, no, no." I wait for a car to pass before I turn onto Elizabeth Street and continue, "That's not a fact. A fact is that you're good. A fact is that you're going to let me read it." I'm starting to feel giddy. It must be an aftereffect of holding her.

She sighs again. I risk another glance. Autumn is curled up in the seat, leaning against the window. I want to tell her that it's not safe to ride with her feet off the floor, but I don't want to be bossy, and anyway, I'm a good driver.

"So where are we going?" I ask.

There's a pause before I hear her quiet voice next to me.

"Tacos," she says.

"As you wish," and I get the laugh I knew the movie reference would win me. When she lifts her head, I roll down the windows to let in the night air the way she likes. Autumn puts her hand out the window and rides the currents. The wind whips her hair around, and I gorge myself on her scent, filling my lungs to capacity.

There have been nights with her this summer when I only turned the car toward home because I was afraid I would be too tired to drive safely if we didn't head back. I love her next to me. I love hearing her react to the random madness of local radio stations. I love holding her hands beneath mine on the steering wheel, showing her that she will be able to drive if she trusts herself.

"And then what?" Jack asked me. "Then what?"

Eventually, I'll have to tell her that it can't always be like it's been this summer or how it will probably be this fall if I'm being realistic. I don't want to be like all the asshole guys who can't see past her body, but I can't only be her friend. Not if I am this close to her. Not if my feelings are so much more than a friend's. I'll have to tell her by Christmas though, or I'll go mad.

But tonight, she needs me. For a while, I have this excuse: her current fragility, the coming adjustment of us both going to college, and then, and then, and then—

I can't think about it right now.

"Care if I put on music?" I ask.

"Yeah, sure," she mumbles, and I reach with one hand for a CD in the glove box. There's this song from a band I discovered that I want her to hear because, well, to be honest, there're a few songs on this album that make me think of her. The opening song reminds me of this summer with her, the nervous energy of us being out at night in my car, even if we aren't together in quite the same way. It's safe to put on this CD and pretend it isn't a message to her, because I'm filling the silence and she's still in her head.

I shouldn't be enjoying this moment so much. I've done nothing to earn it. Autumn is trusting me to be the friend she needs, yet here I am, whispering the lyrics, pretending I'm singing them to her.

Sometimes love is heavy, but tonight it is making me light and free. I'm grateful to have this time with her. It's almost enough.

"I really liked that," Autumn says when the song ends.

I blush, even though I know she didn't get the message. The next song starts.

"You missed the exit," she says.

"Oh, whoops," I say, because I missed it on purpose.

"Don't forget you promised me candy."

She's starting to sound a bit more like herself.

"I wouldn't think of it. First, tacos, and then all the high-fructose sludge and powder you desire. And theeen"—I turn to look at her—"we go home so I. Can. Read. It."

She groans. Out of the corner of my eye, I see her put her face in her hands. She makes another noise and looks up and away. We're turning around and getting back on the highway after the exit I "missed," and I glance at her while at the stop light before the on-ramp.

Autumn stares stoically out the window like someone nobly

facing execution. I stifle my laugh and decide to stop teasing her. Well, about her writing.

This is what Jamie never understood. Autumn needs her friends to tease her and stop her from taking herself too seriously. Otherwise, she gets lost inside her mind. But that doesn't mean not taking *her* seriously. She's in agony over letting me read her work—I won't let her go back on saying I can read it—but she doesn't need me to needle her about it.

"You know, someday, when all your teeth are gone, you'll regret being such a sugar goblin," I tell her as we speed down the ramp, back onto the dark highway.

She laughs in the way I hoped. "I'm not a sugar goblin," she insists, but she knows it's true. "I'm not going to lose my teeth," she adds.

"Eh." I shrug.

She huffs next to me, and I let myself smile but I do not laugh.

"Oh, so now you're going to dental school?" she asks.

"I might have to if you maintain your rate of sugar consumption," I say, and I receive another playful whack.

The glowing lights of the taco place greet us.

"Okay, but—" Autumn says suddenly, as if we hadn't been silent for the past minute.

I pull the car into the drive-through.

"You're majoring in premed," she says, "and you've been eating greasy fast food with me nearly every night all summer. Admit that we're both terrible and wasting our youthful bodies on trash food."

Keeping my foot firmly on the brake, I turn to her in my seat.

"I admit it," I say. "But I go running three or four times a week. You're naturally thin, but—" I lean in so I can meet her eyes in the dark. "You are lazy, Autumn."

"That is true," she says primly, happily, and I have to laugh.

Damn, she is cute.

We look at each other.

The car behind us blares its horn. We're holding up the line.

"Oops!" she says and laughs, then uncurls in her seat and stretches.

I pretend that navigating the car two yards forward takes my full concentration. We've hit a late rush. We aren't even to the menu yet. "Do you want what you always get?" I ask, still staring straight ahead.

"Yup."

I hear her settling back into the seat. That's the thing about being in this car that makes me want to make every trip last as long as possible—it's close, intimate, but I'm safe from losing my mind. It's like driving takes up enough of my frontal lobe activity that I can keep perspective.

I release the brake, and the car inches forward.

"It'll catch up with me someday," Autumn says.

Involuntarily, I look at her, then look forward again as I hit the brake softly.

"What will?" I ask.

"My diet or lack thereof? Right now, I can eat whatever I want.

I won't gain an ounce. After I've been pregnant or am older or whatever, I bet I'll have to think about calories or even exercise on purpose, like you."

It's always fascinated me that girls can be so comfortable with the idea of constructing an entirely new human inside their bodies. I guess if it were something my body was capable of, it would be easier to imagine, let alone be casual about. My point is her train of thought would have surprised me anyway, but her confidence that someday she would be pregnant, that made me pause.

Someday, someone would get her pregnant.

"Maybe, but that won't be for a while, right?" We're finally approaching the box to order.

She laughs. "Yeah, I'm not immaculately conceiving."

The employee asks for our order, and I'm saved from the urge to make a joke about helping her raise a little Jesus II.

Because I would help, stupid as that sounds.

———————

With our tacos in tow, our mission is half complete. I turn us back toward the highway and the odd little gas station that sells Autumn's arcane candies.

She finished her novel.

We're eighteen, almost nineteen; our birthdays are coming up.

She is as extraordinary as she is beautiful.

"Do you want the windows back down?" I ask. *I'm so proud of you*, I think.

"I need to finish at least one taco first," she says, chewing. "I'm really hungry."

"What did you eat at home?"

"Um."

"Autumn?"

"I was writing!" she cries.

"It's eight o'clock at night!" I glance at her. "All you've had to eat were those two pieces of toast and that taco?"

"But I have six more tacos right here," she says. She finishes the first and unwraps another.

After a minute, I ask, "Would you have eaten if I hadn't come by when you didn't answer my text?"

"What text?"

She shifts in her seat, and there's light from her phone as she opens it.

"Oh!" she says. I'm glad she's surprised that she didn't notice. "Sorry."

"Not a big deal. It's good I came by before you passed out and hit your head on something."

"Oh, har-har," she says, but I mean it.

This, this right here, is why I need to wait until Christmas break to tell her that what I feel for her is more than physical attraction, that I need some space. First semester, I'm going to need to make sure Autumn remembers to get to the dining hall before it closes.

When Autumn is depressed or stressed or writing, she gets so inside her head that she forgets about her body. I can't imagine not noticing that I'm hungry. I can't imagine living so outside the physical world the way she does.

Autumn would probably say that she can't imagine having a body like mine, one that runs in a confident rhythm or that can take aim and hit the desired mark.

"Do you want to steer on the way back?" I ask as I pull into the gas station parking lot. The light inside glows warmly, and I park in one of the spaces illuminated by the windows.

"I'm too tired. I'll crash. Even you couldn't save us," she says.

"I'll get your candy. Stay here and eat."

I should probably tell Autumn that the "nice older man" inside, who always smiles and says hi to her, also leers at her when she's facing away. I don't think he's dangerous, but it's gross. He's fifty at least. I'm eighteen, and I have a better handle on my hormones than him.

"I'll be right back."

Autumn nods and chews another mouthful. She looks content. I know this summer could never mean as much to her as it does to me, but I want her to remember it fondly. I don't want this creep saying something to sully the memory.

Autumn's sludge tubes and the little powder packets are at the bottom shelf of the candy aisle with the other sugar oddities. For example, this must be the last place on earth that sells candy cigarettes. I wonder if we've been the only ones buying this candy here all summer and if, after we've gone, this shelf will sit untouched for months.

I get sodas despite my earlier teasing, because I know it'll make

66

Autumn happy. I will go to dental school and rebuild her teeth if she needs it.

The older guy is there. I see him see me as I wait in line. I see him look for Autumn behind me.

As I set my items on the counter, he says, "Alone tonight?"

I look at his face, because I'm not certain of his tone. He's raised one eyebrow and gives me the sort of smile he makes when he thinks no one sees him eyeing Autumn.

"No, she's with me." I emphasize the words so that they imply what I wish were true—that I am hers.

As he's ringing up the items, his gaze moves out the window to my car. "So how is it?" he asks, like I have something to share.

"I don't need my change." I grab our stuff and leave. Tomorrow, I'll buy the whole stock of Autumn's weird candy so that we never have to come back here again.

"Hey. Yay!" Autumn says as I slide in next to her.

I drop her loot in her lap and restart the car. I glance at the counter as I pull out, but the man is busy with another customer. He'll never see her again.

The CD is still playing. If she hadn't liked it, she would have found something else on the radio. We're quiet together as another song plays that makes me think of her. I want to drive with her like this for the rest of the night, for the rest of our lives. The road stretches out in front of us, seemingly unending.

After the song finishes, I ask, "Are you certain you don't want to practice driving tonight?"

"Nah," she says. "Aren't you going to eat?"

"Maybe later."

I wonder if she notices the way I loop the long way along North County, the way I drive the speed limit. I hope she's absorbing the words from the songs, like my love could be a protective spell, even if she's unaware of it.

Christmas might be too soon. She can't keep track of her phone or her keys. How is she going to keep track of her drinks at parties? I'm going to have to stick around to make sure whatever guy she falls for treats her right. This time, if I see something, I'll say something.

Autumn is where she wants to be, sitting next to me, her friend, and I'll be there if she needs me.

"Have you been thinking about what you'll focus on in med school?" She's leaning her temple against the window again. The floor of my car is littered with taco wrappers.

I turn the music down. "I won't figure that out until a couple years into classes," I say. "It's not like I know that much about the human body yet." I pause, because I want to share something more with her. "I've been thinking about the brain a lot lately."

"What about it?" She sounds dreamy, but I can tell she's listening.

"Well." I pause to make sure I'm saying it right. "I'm driving, so on one level, I'm thinking about visibility, speed, and car spacing, and I'm making adjustments with the steering wheel, but I'm not really thinking about any of those things. I'm really thinking"—*that you're so close to me*—"about our conversation. Meanwhile, my brain is also telling my lungs to breathe and my heart to beat, but I'm not

68

thinking about any of that either, not at all. My brain makes sure my body is doing all this, while I'm thinking about"—*how much I adore you*—"whether I'm explaining any of this well."

I've run out of air. I guess my brain isn't doing so hot after all.

I breathe deep and plunge back in. "One organ is responsible for all those things, and it's so small. Most people don't realize how small their brain really is, probably because we talk about how big the human brain is compared to other animals. But you can hold it in one hand. And it's responsible for everything that we consider to be 'us.' Your novel came from your brain, Autumn, word by word, and I wish I could understand how your brain is able to do that."

Autumn is silent. I can't end there. It implies too much.

Then she says, "Or how a brain can know things logically but still send illogical signals and emotions? Tell you to do stupid things?"

"Yeah, exactly." I steer the car off the highway. "It does all these things right and gets all these things wrong. It records all this information and still misses so much." I shrug. "I'm looking forward to learning something about how it does all that." I glance at her.

She smiles at me, making my heart beat faster.

I turn up the music. The album has started again at the first song, and maybe, on some level, her brain understands that I'm playing this song for her.

eight

WE HEAD INTO MY HOUSE without discussion. She's withdrawn again. I want to reassure her that I'll love her novel, but I know it won't help. I gesture to the rum on the counter.

"Do you want me to pour a little in your Coke?"

She wrinkles her nose.

"I'm never drinking rum and Coke again." She adds, "Don't laugh at me. I might actually mean that."

"I just thought you might need some liquid courage." I nod toward the laptop in her arms, cradled like a baby. She hugs it closer.

"Do I have to be here while you read it?" Autumn asks.

"Do you want to go home?" I feel myself frown. I'm not sure which I want more: for her to stay or for me to read it.

"No," she says quickly.

"I'm not sure what other option you have then."

Autumn sighs, frustrated by the confines of reality, then marches to the living room. I follow, and she slumps on the couch and opens her computer. A few clicks, and she sits back, then looks over at me. I sit down next to her.

She pushes the computer into my lap and says, "There's the title page. Scroll until you're done. It's pretty short. Barely a novel."

"You don't have to let me read it," I say as I finger the keyboard, because I feel like I must. As much as I want to read it, I'm starting to worry that she's not ready to share it.

"No. It's time."

I glance at her beautiful, scared face, then begin to read.

"Just don't think about it too much," she says quietly, but I'm already falling under the spell of her words.

She's taken a lot from our childhood. That's obvious. That must be why she's worried. It isn't like she took us as kids and wrote it all down though; sometimes the character of Izzy seems like Autumn, but then I see flashes of me in her and pieces of Autumn in Aden. They do the things we did, like using our fingers to draw on each other's backs at night, and the things we didn't do but wanted to, like building a tree house.

I glance at Autumn, curled up with a book in the far corner of the couch. I want to tell her that I'm honored to have glimpses of our lives in her book, but I know she'd want me to keep reading.

Izzy has a great, present dad and a runaway mom. Aden's parents love him but are troubled and emotionally distant, hence his spending so much time next door. Between Izzy's dad's constant presence and the occasional support of Aden's, the two of them have enough parenting to get by. It's true, and it's not true.

Autumn isn't good at drawing, but Izzy is, and she makes Aden comic books of her stories. In reality, I did the drawings for Autumn's stories, and we made them for ourselves. True and not true again.

It's like time traveling but to a parallel world. Like a kaleidoscope, the story shifts in my vision. It's us. It's not us. It's us. It's not us.

And then comes the part that is not us, cannot be us, because Aden is kissing Izzy, and she is kissing him back. I feel my mouth pinch, but I don't frown. Distantly, I'm aware that Autumn has switched from reading to watching a movie, and my brain, ever ready to multitask when it comes to Autumn, takes note of her occasional glances at me.

My main focus, though, is on Autumn's novel. Of course she is worried that I will misunderstand this part. As Izzy and Aden's romantic relationship begins, I start to see Jamie in Aden: the random gag gifts, the way he stakes his claim over Izzy so publicly. But I still see me. There're the obvious details, like Aden plays soccer and has blond hair. But it's more than that, much more.

It's the way Aden sees through Izzy's insecurities and appreciates her strengths.

It's the way Aden grins at Izzy when he says, "I like how you take it for granted that I'll teach you to drive."

I get up for a glass of water.

I take a swig of rum from the bottle.

I return to the living room and sit down.

It's like she's taken slivers and slices from her life and the lives of people she knows, put them in a blender, and then very heavily seasoned it all with fiction.

There's a big soccer game where Aden blocks a last-second goal from the other team, preventing overtime, and Izzy runs out on the field and jumps on him even though he's covered in mud. Sylvie jumped on me after I blocked a pass like that a couple of years ago. Autumn wasn't there, but I guess she heard about it. Sylvie got in trouble with the cheer captain for muddying her uniform and losing poise or something.

But in the novel, Izzy isn't wearing a uniform, because Autumn was never a cheerleader. Izzy is and isn't Autumn. I see flashes of her friends Brooke and Sasha in Izzy too.

Izzy and Aden hang out in the rafters above the stage in their school's auditorium, which is entirely the sort of thing that Autumn would wish she could do.

Aden isn't only me. He's also Autumn, and he's also Jamie and maybe other friends that I don't know well.

But the way that Aden loves Izzy? That is me.

The way he asks her if she's okay with a look and understands her silent replies? That's me.

The way Aden tells Izzy to ignore the teachers telling her to consider an education major because she's too good a writer not to try is me. That's always been me.

Autumn stands and stretches, but I keep reading. That's how

73

good the story is. I don't think most people's first drafts are this good, are they? She's a great writer, and she's only going to make it better.

I stand up and realize Autumn is gone, and I head to the kitchen, get the rum, and settle back on the couch.

I'm finishing this tonight.

nine

———

I SIP THE RUM AS I go, reading faster now that my brain isn't keeping track of Autumn's movements in the background. As the story is narrowing to its finale, it's easier to rush.

The ending surprises me. I'd predicted a coldhearted end to their tale. Autumn has shown that it's easy for her to drop friends, and I expected the same from Izzy and Aden.

I close the laptop and set it on the coffee table. Her novel is even better than I expected, but I can't focus on the story.

Writers write what they know. I knew that.

But if Autumn has depicted my love in such perfect nuance, then it means she knows. It means she's always known, always understood how I feel about her.

All these years, I had convinced myself that I'd fooled Autumn into thinking my feelings were puppy love at worst or teenage hormones at best. But she knew the truth. She observed my love and served it up to me, fictionally requited.

Jack said, "I'm leaning toward she knows you love her, and she's fucking with you to make herself feel better."

She knew. All summer, she knew.

All these years, she knew. Since middle school.

She could have told me my feelings were obvious and it made her uncomfortable or that she needed space. That would've been enough. I would have understood. She wouldn't have had to spell out why.

Instead, she vanished on me.

I was dumb for kissing her that New Year's Eve, but I didn't deserve the ice that took years to thaw so that she'd simply smile at me again—especially not if she knew I was in love with her and missing her all semester. If she knew that I loved her, then she must have known how it would twist me when she magically came back to me that Christmas only to abandon me again.

The rum is gone; the book is done. Why am I still sitting here?

This new knowledge sits like a boulder on my chest. I make myself get off the couch with great effort.

I drink a glass of water before I go to find Autumn. I want to be clearheaded when I confront her.

I check my mother's room first, but of course she went to my bed. Because she's always known, and she's using me to make herself feel better.

As I turn the doorknob, my brain freezes. I don't know what I'm going to say to her.

The light from the hall falls across her face, and she winces.

76

"Autumn." I'm so angry at her, yet her loveliness hits my body like a punch.

She makes a noise and blinks at the light. I push the door so it's mostly closed and the light isn't directly in her face.

"Autumn," I say again.

"What?" She sits up, pushes the hair from her face, and looks at me, bleary eyed and beautiful.

"Why did you have to leave me like that?" is what comes out.

"I was tired. You were reading."

"No." I'm not going to hold back. I say it. "After we turned thirteen. Why did you have to leave me like that?"

Autumn goes still. I can tell that she is fully awake and understands.

She has no answer.

I know that now.

Finally, she says, "I didn't leave." We both know she is lying. "We just grew apart."

I'm not going to let her do this to me anymore.

"We did not *just grow apart*, Autumn."

"I didn't mean to," she says. "I'm sorry." Tears shine in her eyes. She looks sorry.

But that's not enough. Not enough by far.

"I already know why you did it." She doesn't have to explain that part. I know she's never wanted me like that. I don't need to hear her say it. "I just want to know why you had to be so cruel about it." It's time to face what Jack has been telling me all these years.

She stiffens. This time, I'm not going to shrug it off.

"Okay, I was stupid and selfish that fall. And I'm sorry. But everything would have gone back to normal if you hadn't kissed me out of nowhere without even asking. Do you have any idea how much you scared me that night?"

Scared? A vision of her face as she pulled away from me floats before my eyes. She was disgusted. No, she—

"I scared you?"

Autumn's tears have started to spill over. "I wasn't ready." She drags the heel of her hand across her cheek like a small child. "And I didn't know what to think."

She wasn't ready?

I scared her.

This is too much to take in. I sit down at the foot of the bed. I'm facing my window, her window, and I can't bear that, so I look down at my hands.

She wasn't ready? And I scared her.

I'd clenched her arm. I'd tried to be romantic, but I'd missed her cues.

I deserved the way she treated me the following year. I'm lucky she gives me the time of day now, that she thinks of me fondly enough to put parts of me in her novel. Autumn brings out the worst in me. All along, I knew that, yet I'd still blamed her.

I hadn't overshot the mark with Autumn that night. I shouldn't have taken the shot at all.

If I had waited, given her space. If I'd trusted the Autumn I knew instead of the tall tales of locker room jerks...

78

I feel the mattress shift as she scoots across the bed.

"I'm sorry. I hate myself for hurting you."

She tries to get a good look at my face in the dark, but I can't bear to see her yet. I woke her up to confront her cruelty only to discover that I am the one who owed her the bigger apology.

"I'm sorry too," I say. We're both so many years late.

"For what?"

She must still be part asleep.

"I'm sorry for kissing you."

"Don't say that." She sounds sadder than I've ever heard her sound before. "Don't say you're sorry for that."

Do I owe her an apology for something else?

It turns out I don't really know who Autumn is, and I don't know who I am either. A dark laugh escapes me. No matter how I try, I always seem to end up hurting her.

"I never know what to do to make you happy, do I?"

She answers so quickly that it surprises me.

"You make me happier than any other person ever has."

The conviction in her voice is unmistakable.

"Do I?" Like Jack said to me: her story doesn't make sense.

"Every day," she says.

We sit.

Autumn wasn't ready for me to kiss her.

Autumn doesn't want me to apologize for kissing her.

I make her happy.

These three new facts roll around in my head, bumping against each other until suddenly they line up together in a way that makes sense.

Except it can't be true.

Do I know how to make Autumn happy?

Before, I kissed her without asking.

"What if I kissed you right now?"

She takes a quick breath, and I am already dead.

Autumn says, "That would make me happy."

I'm almost not sure what to do next.

You aren't facing her, my brain gently nudges me.

I turn on the bed, tucking a leg under me, waiting for her to stop me, to clarify what she said, because there's no way she meant it.

Autumn raises her face to mine, and her expression steals my breath.

I reach out a hand, ready to pull back at any moment. Gently, I rest my hand on her hair, just above her neck. She relaxes against my touch, and something breaks inside me.

Greedily, I pull her toward me. As I lean in, I hit her nose with mine. I'm about to apologize when she turns her face, and her lips are so close.

All apologies, every apology, is forgotten, and my lips are on hers.

I am only my lips. No other part of me exists.

Autumn.

I'm kissing Autumn.

The urge comes to push her back against the bed and feel her beneath me, and I begin to think actual thoughts again.

Don't fuck this up, Finn.

I rest my hand against her hip so that my thumb can stroke that little spot that divots inward below her ribs, the glorious shape of her. Autumn sighs the sigh from a thousand of my fantasies.

I'm kissing her, and she's leaning into me.

This is real.

This is happening.

Autumn.

Her hand is on my shoulder, and I think she might push me away, but instead she pulls me closer, even though we're as close as we can be sitting like this.

She wants this. She wants *me*.

Autumn puts her hand on my knee, and I stifle a groan.

"Ow," she says.

Her head shifts and I realize my grasp has tightened in her hair.

I pull back.

"Sorry," I say and begin to take my hands off her.

"No. Don't stop," Autumn says. Her hand is still on my shoulder. She pulls again, says, "Lie down with me."

Autumn stretches out on my bed. She holds out her arms to me.

"Oh God," I say.

She wants—

She said "with," not "on," but her arms—

I pull myself over her, leaning on my right elbow. One of her breasts is pressed against me. When I look at her face, her eyes meet mine. Her arms close around me, and she raises her lips toward mine.

I'm kissing her.

She's kissing me.

It's strange to feel as if I don't have a body, but that's what it's like. I'm simply a soul existing ecstatically in the universe. Time and space are meaningless, temporary, inconsequential to me.

And then I crash back into myself. My body, her body, the actuality of the moment: they all hit me at once.

She is kissing me passionately.

Autumn is kissing me.

I cup her face in my hand.

I've wanted to touch her face so many times; every smile, every frown has tempted me. The lines of her face have haunted me as much as any other part of her body.

Her body.

Autumn holds on to me tightly, pressing against me. She moans softly as our lips part to inhale and exhale. If our brains weren't so good at balancing needs, we probably would have suffocated by now.

I hope I'm kissing her right. It seems like I am. Maybe my instincts can finally be in charge and my frontal lobe will relax before I overthink this and find some way to mess it up.

Autumn is kissing me with the same intensity that I am kissing her, fast and hard. I try to slow down, worrying that perhaps my fervor will become tiring. But Autumn shifts to match my pace like we are dance partners and the music has changed. She doesn't loosen her grip on me. Her sounds of pleasure are dizzying.

How did we get here? Unscrambling the last few minutes is too much for me right now. I need to be in this moment while it lasts.

Her.

Her.

I want to touch her breast.

No, Finn.

I try to bring my focus back to her lips—Autumn's lips!—kissing mine again and again and again.

I try to be grateful for the breast that is pressing against my chest, but the other one is also right there.

Do I know how to make her happy? Because I can't tear myself away from her mouth to speak. My left hand trails off her cheek and down her neck, around her shoulder.

Slow, Finn. Slow.

I try to signal what I'm doing so that she knows. No surprises, no mistakes. My thumb is at the bottom of the swell of her other breast, her ribs beneath my fingertips.

Slow.

I'm moving my hand, and then—

I'm holding Autumn's breast in my hand.

After all these years of trying not to look at them yet having their silhouette branded in my mind, Autumn is beneath me and in my hand and under my lips and hips.

She sighs the sigh from the tent this morning, the one that I wished I had inspired, and I am gone again. I am only sensations. There is no other reality, only Autumn.

"Finny."

I feel my name against my mouth at the same time as I hear it.

Again, I am crashing back into time and space.

I remember that my body is kissing Autumn.

The signal comes through.

Stop.

I raise my head and look down at her.

"Yeah?"

"I want—"

The light is still dim, but I can see her face a little better. She is flushed and her eyes are sparkling, wet. She looks apprehensive again.

I'll say it for her if she can't. "Do you want me to stop?"

"No!" she cries, surprising me. "I want the opposite of that." Autumn bites her lip after blurting out the words, and she squirms nervously underneath me, setting off a series of feelings in my body that make it hard to process what she's saying.

Because surely, she can't mean what I think she means.

The opposite of stopping is—

"You want me to keep going?"

"Yes," Autumn says.

My body screams for the same conclusion.

My instincts want to be in charge again, but this time, they are very wrong.

"I–I don't have—"

Autumn must assume that I have condoms, which I don't. Does

she really want to do it with me after making out once, after waiting for so long with Jamie? *No mistakes. No misunderstandings.*

"I don't care," she says. There's a firmness to her voice, a deep certainty.

"Autumn, no." I should sit up and let us both cool down, but I don't move. Autumn is nuzzling me. *Nuzzling me.*

"Please, Finny," she says and kisses my neck in a way that melts me. "Please, Finny."

In all my fantasies, there's never been an explanation for why Autumn and I make love. I always jumped into the story after having magically seduced her under innumerable, varied circumstances.

And there have been many fantastical circumstances.

Never, not in any classroom, back seat, backyard, or rooftop scenario, has Autumn ever begged me.

"Please," she says as her lips travel along my neck and jaw. "Please, please."

The barrier inside my mind is crumbling.

Her lips are back on mine, and I am lost to desire.

Surely, she'll tell me to stop.

I slide my hand over her shirt, and she pulls it off. She doesn't tell me to stop when I reach for her bra's clasp.

Autumn's bra is off, and the feel of her skin and the shadowy shape of her body leave me in thoughtless wonder. She pulls on the button of my jeans.

She means it.

Autumn makes a frustrated noise as her fingers slip and the button stays fastened.

She wants me.

All my reason and logic have been lost to that undeniable fact: Autumn wants me.

Now I'm the impatient one.

I push her hand aside and do it myself. I pull away from her enough to scramble out of my jeans and boxers and toss them off the bed. There's a muffled thud as my phone in my pants hits the floor, and I look back at Autumn, who's raising her hips to slip out of her own jeans.

I am all hands again, trying to help pull them past her knees and almost pulling her into my lap instead. Autumn giggles, and I kiss her feet as they reemerge from the denim.

And then I've taken off my shirt and I'm looking down at her.

"Oh, Autumn." *My friend. My dream. My love.*

The trust in her eyes is intense. I cannot deserve that look; this cannot be happening.

She starts to pull off her panties, the last clothing between us.

I've lost the will to tell her that we can't, even though I know this is all happening so quickly that we probably shouldn't. I help her. I toss her underwear to the floor.

If this is a mistake, we're making it anyway.

She opens her arms for me to return to her embrace. I have to say it while I still have thoughts in my brain.

"Can I tell you that I love you first?" I won't miss my chance to tell her, even if she knows it must be true. I'm already risking so much.

"Yes."

I fall over her, catching myself in time to lower myself gently, positioning myself between her legs, the animal instincts back in control.

"I love you," I tell Autumn, saying it for all the times I couldn't before and all the times I may never be able to again.

And then I'm saying, "Oh God, I love you," because she's there. I'm there. Autumn isn't telling me to pull back or stop. She's nuzzling me again, her breath hot on my collarbone. "Oh God, Autumn."

Slow, Finn.

No mistakes.

I can tell from the way her breathing changes, the way that her grip on me tightens, she is in agony mixed with ecstasy.

Slow. Keep your head in the game, Finn.

Slow.

She's trying to relax beneath and around me. I can feel it.

Autumn wants me to keep making love to her, even though it hurts. I don't know why I can be so certain after all the mistakes in our past, but then again, the situation is irrefutable.

Autumn seduced me.

The absurdity of the realization would make me laugh, but she whispers in my ear, "It's okay, Finny. I'm okay."

Autumn rests her cheek against mine. She sighs happily.

I hope that I am still gentle enough after that, because I am consumed with the rhythmic sway of her breasts against my chest, the way her thighs grasp my waist as if she's afraid I will escape.

It's her name I mean to say at the end, but I do not make it past the first vowel.

ten

———

Autumn whimpers, and I feel one of the many reasons we shouldn't have done this spilling from us. I move, but I am without regret, because I will always at least have this memory of us.

I'm coming out of my trance and need to know she's still okay.

"Autumn" is all I can get out.

"I love you too," she says. "I forgot to tell you." She begins to cry, but not like before, not like when she was grieving the end of her characters. Still, they're tears, so I file what she said away for later and focus on her.

I lean down and kiss her face again and again.

"It's okay. Don't cry," I say, because all the other things I want to say can't seem to find their way out. *You are safe.* I kiss her eyes. *You are cherished.* I kiss her forehead. *I'll be whatever you need me to be after this.* I kiss her cheek. *Whatever you want me to be.* I kiss her other cheek. "Don't cry. It's okay."

"Will you hold me?" Autumn asks, and it is honestly the greatest idea I have ever heard. I slide over, and she's quick to wipe her eyes and rest her head on my shoulder. I wrap my arms around her, and it is glorious.

"Like this?" I hold her gently but tightly.

"Yeah," she says, and I'm never going to move again.

I breathe in the scent of her hair and feel light-headed.

I've never known euphoria like this.

A choir of birds is singing a tribute to this beautiful new day, to her body, to my joy. In the morning light, I can see the shadows of her eyelashes on her cheeks, the swell of her hip under my blanket.

I'm so happy that I could die.

"I can't believe that just happened," I hear myself say. My eyes start to involuntarily close, and I'm glad when she speaks to help me stay awake.

"Did you mean it when you said you loved me?" she asks.

"Of course I did." I'm so tired and so happy that I don't think about what a silly question it is. I shift slightly beneath her to savor our skins against each other before we drift off. My eyes have closed completely when she continues.

"You weren't just saying that because it's what the guy is supposed to say?"

My eyes are still shut, and I'm thinking, *What guy?* when I realize she means me. I'm the guy. The guy who was supposed to say—

My eyes open.

Is she pretending to not know?

Fully awake now, I replay her question in my brain.

She is pretending to not know.

Why is she doing that?

I roll out from under her and sit up on my elbow. I need to see her face.

"Come on, Autumn," I say. "I know that you know I've been in love with you for forever. You don't have to pretend." Whatever she wants from me after this, my one rule is nothing left unsaid between us.

"What?" she says.

It's very convincing, but I know how good of an actress she can be.

"It's okay." I sigh. I can't help but feel a little exasperated even now. "I've always known that you knew."

But Autumn's getting upset. She sits up and pulls the covers around her protectively. She frowns at me. The birds are still singing.

Why is Autumn upset that I knew that she knew I loved her? I'm not mad at her for knowing it.

At least not now. I'd forgotten about my reaction to her novel last night.

"What do you mean by 'forever'?" Autumn asks.

"You know," I say. "Forever. Since we were like what, eleven?"

"Fifth grade? The year you punched Donnie Banks?"

There. She knows what I'm talking about.

"Yeah. You remember what Donnie Banks said?"

"He called me a freak."

"He said, 'Your *girlfriend* is a freak,' and he knew that you didn't want to be my girlfriend and that I did." *Because everyone knew that. Everyone. Including Autumn.*

Right?

"You liked me like that back then?" Her confusion is real. But if she didn't know in elementary school, what happened to us?

I sit up all the way. I need to think clearly.

"But isn't that why you stopped hanging out with me in middle school? Because you got tired of me wanting to be more than just friends?" That's what happened. I was there.

"No," Autumn says. "I had no idea you wanted anything like that."

It's the truth. Somehow, some way, she hadn't known.

"But after I kissed you, you knew?" Because Autumn knows I love her. I read her novel. It was there.

"No," Autumn says. "I didn't know why you had kissed me, and it freaked me out. I thought maybe you were experimenting on me."

Experimenting on her? Am I hallucinating after all? My gaze wanders briefly around my bedroom. Everything else seems normal.

If Autumn didn't know that I loved her in elementary school or in middle school—no. No. She had to have known.

"But this doesn't make any sense," I tell her. "If you didn't know, then why did you leave me?"

She drops her eyes. Is this it? Have I caught her in a lie? My stomach twists. I'll love her even if she turns out to be cruel. That's my curse.

"It just felt so nice not to be the weird girl anymore," Autumn says. "I liked being popular. We did kinda grow apart that year."

She's blushing with embarrassment, and I feel my mouth hanging open.

"I'm not saying it's not my fault. I'm just saying I didn't mean for it to happen."

Oh, Autumn.

Autumn caring what people thought about her was never something I had considered. It seems incongruent with her character. I always defended her in elementary school but not because she'd never shown any sign of being bothered by what the other kids thought or said. Maybe a couple of times, there'd been things that happened that had made her cry, but I'd believed her when she said she was upset about the injustice or the principle of the matter.

When Autumn was finally appreciated by our peers, she seemed to take it as a matter of course, that things had finally settled as they should. She'd never said anything during the early days of middle school about being excited about becoming popular overnight. She'd seemed distracted, not elated.

Autumn is a good actress but not that good. For example, at the moment, she's trying to hide her embarrassment and failing. Autumn is a good liar. Autumn is not a good liar. It's true and it's not true.

"You really didn't know?" I ask to be sure.

"No. I really, really didn't," Autumn says.

I believe her, and it's more than I can handle. My nervous system decides that in order to keep functioning and engage in conscious thought, it can't hold me up. I lie on my back and stare up at nothing.

Autumn didn't know that I loved her.

I'm staring at the blank ceiling above me, but all I see are a

93

thousand memories being rewritten with this new information. It's like the DNA of my entire relationship with Autumn has mutated. Every time I'd inwardly flinched at how pathetic I must seem to her, she hadn't known or noticed.

"And all these years I was terrified that you could tell that I still...you know," I say.

"Still what?"

Because even after all this, she still needs me to spell it out. "Still wanted you."

"Really?"

I can't even answer that one.

All my agonies had been caused by figments of my imagination. That night I'd had to call Jack to sober drive Sylvie and me home, I found Autumn eating leftovers on her front porch. She was bummed about her parents and had been quietly patient with my inebriation while I thought I said the most obvious, drunkenly lovestruck things to her. The next morning, I lay in bed, sick as a dog and writhing with mortification.

But it had all been in my brain. None of it had been real. Autumn hadn't known. Autumn hadn't heard the love that had screamed so loud inside my mind.

That semester when we were partners in gym, I regretted so many of the things I said after class, and the moments I'd given in to the temptation to touch her seemed especially egregious. I was certain that I was always on the verge of being cast off by Autumn again, because I was doing such a terrible job of hiding my love for her.

But she hadn't known.

It hadn't been proof that I'd overstepped her boundaries when she said that Jamie wouldn't like it if we hung out. Jamie probably would have been a dick about it, and if Autumn had actually loved me back then—

What had she been thinking all these years, this girl that I loved and thought that I knew through and through?

"What about Sylvie?" Autumn asks, and I can't help my laugh. It all seems like such a madcap Shakespearean comedy of mistakes. Is this irony? Maybe Autumn can tell me.

"The only reason I started hanging out with the cheerleaders after soccer practice was because I thought they were still your friends. I thought that maybe I'd have a chance with you then, that maybe I'd be cool enough for you to see me like that. Then when the first day of high school came, you didn't even say hi to me at the bus stop. And I found out that not only were you not their friend anymore, but you hated them. And then you started going out with Jamie, and Alexis was asking me why I was leading Sylvie on, and I didn't even know what she was talking about…"

That had been an awful conversation. It was after a soccer game, the first one I'd really gotten to spend time out on the field, and Alexis had pulled me aside as I'd come out of the locker room. I was exhausted and soaking wet. She was going out with Jack by then, and it had kinda freaked me out the way she'd grabbed my arm possessively. She looked furious.

"Why are you doing this to her?" she hissed at me.

95

"Who?" My brain went to Autumn even though it made no sense.

"Oh. My. God." Alexis whispered, "Sylvie, you monster."

My feelings for Alexis after the past four years are like how a lot of people describe their feelings for their siblings. I love her because I have known her for so long, but she drives me crazy, and most of the time, I don't like her that much.

Alexis was exaggerating that day, but there is always a grain of truth to her wild hyperboles.

I was kinda into Sylvie at that time.

Sylvie talked to me at the bus stop. No one else did. The fact that Sylvie was as pretty as Autumn, though in a different way, provided a welcome distraction. Sylvie felt safe to look at.

When Alexis made her case, I could see her point. And I felt responsible. Besides, I'd seen some guy kissing Autumn on those steps where she'd been hanging out. My plan had failed.

So I asked Sylvie to a movie, and we had fun. Real fun. She was the only other kid I'd ever met who listened to NPR while getting ready for school in the mornings. I liked that she read biographies and kept a shelf of her favorites. She was beautiful. She was nice. She wanted to be with me.

Sylvie has been good for me. I've enjoyed almost every minute with her. She has made me a better person in so many little ways. I hope that someday I'll be able to fully explain this to Sylvie, but for now I say to Autumn, "Don't think that I never cared about Sylvie, because I did." *I do.* "She's not really what you think." *She's so much more.* "And she needed me to take care of her when you didn't anymore." *Because she's like you: complicated.* "I loved her, but I loved her differently from the way I've always loved you."

I still love Sylvie, and there's so much I'm not saying out loud despite not wanting to leave things unsaid.

But there is so much Autumn and I need to talk about besides Sylvie.

"Oh, Finny," Autumn says. Her voice has so much emotion in it that my heart flutters.

I fill my lungs with air to steady my nerves. I look at her out of the corner of my eyes. It's an old trick: looking at Autumn without really looking at her.

Autumn is watching me, still sitting up in my bed. Her hair is glowing around her face like an aura. The sheet has fallen away again. I cannot trust myself to look her in the face. I'll lose my nerve.

"You said—" I start. I need to know. She was crying when she said it and, amazingly, unsure of how I felt about her. "You said that you loved me too." Perhaps in her vulnerability, she said more than she meant.

"Yeah," Autumn says, "I do." Her voice is trembling but certain.

"Since when?" *Since last night? Last month?*

"I dunno," she whispers. "Maybe since forever too, but I didn't admit it until two years ago."

Maybe forever too?

I cannot resist anymore. I look directly up at her. Autumn has this soft, sublime smile on her face that breaks into a sigh as she collapses back on to my chest.

She loves me.

She really, truly loves me.

I'm holding her so tightly that I order my body to relax so as not to hurt her.

Autumn.

My Autumn.

If she wants to be.

"So…" I don't know how to ask this. Autumn loves me, but I am trying to make sure there're no more misunderstandings.

"What?"

"It's you and me now, right?"

I feel her laughter against my chest before she speaks.

"Phineas Smith, are you asking me to be your girlfriend?"

Isn't that all I'm ever doing? I think wildly. My heart is beating fast. To me, this seemed like a formality, but perhaps my history of misunderstanding Autumn is catching up with me again.

"Well, yeah. Is that weird?"

"Only because it feels like we're already so much more than that."

I relax again. "Yeah, I know," I say to her as I tell my brain to stay calm, that asking Autumn to elope to Vegas is absurd. "But it'll have to do for now."

For now.

I close my eyes.

"You still have to break up with Sylvie," she whispers.

My eyes open again.

"I know. I'm going to. Tomorrow."

"You mean today," she says.

My stomach drops. Of course, it's morning. I'm such a fool.

"Oh. Right." I hug Autumn to me. "We should get some sleep, I guess."

"Yeah, I guess," Autumn says.

We cuddle up close, and soon, Autumn is snoring softly.

But I don't sleep. There's too much to think about.

eleven

ONE OF THE THINGS THAT might be ironic—I really must remember to ask Autumn to explain irony to me—is that now I have something to tell Sylvie.

Sylvie will accept that I'm choosing Autumn over her if it's for more than friendship. That's what makes this so hard.

I try to be careful with my words. I try to only say what I mean and exactly what I mean. People think I'm hard to read, but I never understand that. I'm not secretive. More often than not, I simply don't share information unless I'm asked.

The first time Sylvie asked me about Autumn, we didn't actually talk about her.

It was the last day of freshman year.

Jamie had crossed in front of us as we left campus. He was carrying Autumn over his shoulder as she shrieked with joy and pretend panic, and their court of grungy offbeat friends trailed behind them singing an obnoxious song at the top of their voices.

"What's with that?" Sylvie said.

Jamie's little parade had passed us, and we'd started walking again. Sylvie and I were headed to the fast-food place near campus, and I had a sinking feeling that was their celebration plan too.

"Eh, that guy is always showing off," I said. I watched as Jamie spun Autumn around and set her down.

"No," Sylvie said. "What's with you every time you see her with him?"

"What are you talking about?"

"Autumn Davis and Jamie Allen." Sylvie tugged on my arm, and I looked at her. "Come on, Finn. You were just glaring at them."

"I don't like him." I shrugged. "I told you before: Autumn's an old friend from when we were kids. Sucks that she likes such a show-off." I shrugged again. Up ahead, Autumn and her friends were waiting at the crosswalk for the light to change.

"I mean," Sylvie said, "aren't they all kinda, 'Woo-hoo, I'm so quirky'? She wears a tiara every day and seems to like the way Jamie tosses her around in public."

"Autumn was born strange," I said. "She's being herself. Jamie does things for attention, and you know how I feel about that."

That was a low blow, aimed as much at Sylvie as it was at Jamie, and we were silent for a bit.

Some weeks before, egged on by some older guys and someone Victoria was dating, Sylvie had made out with Alexis on a Ferris wheel, and we'd had our first really big fight.

I'd told Sylvie I wouldn't have cared if she made out with Alexis because that was what she wanted to do. It would have been hot if either of them were really into it. That Sylvie had done it to impress some dudes we'd never met before grossed me out. And I had told her so.

"I can't be with you if you're only looking for attention."

The rest of the way to the burger place, Sylvie and I were silent. Autumn and her friends were already there when we arrived. Sylvie went to the bathroom. I ordered for us and sat down facing away from Autumn and her friends.

When Sylvie came back from the restroom, she looked like she'd been crying.

"Syl—"

She held up a hand to stop me.

"I need to tell you something later," she said.

We ate, and I was glad when Autumn and her friends left so they couldn't see how awkward Sylvie and I were together. Afterward, we walked to the park and sat on a hill, and Sylvie told me about Mr. Wilbur.

Sylvie explained how in seventh grade, this teacher was interested in helping her develop her many talents. He'd offered to personally tutor her, talking about how he would prep her to finish high school early so she could start college classes at sixteen. Sylvie's parents had thought this was evidence of how intellectually gifted she truly was.

Wilbur had taken his time with his motives. He claimed disappointment again and again in Sylvie's progress, asking her why she refused to work as hard for him as he worked for her. He isolated her from her friends and had her drop her other activities to focus on her studies. And then came the comments about her needing to cover up, how he was a man after all, and she was so pretty. It wasn't until midway through the second semester of eighth grade that he'd finally told her that she'd disappointed him academically and tempted him sexually too many times. She owed him, he'd said.

Luckily, someone had walked in.

"We got caught," Sylvie said, then frowned and corrected herself. "Someone walked in, and *he* got caught."

"Yeah, they caught him," I agreed. "You didn't do anything wrong. You were rescued." I wanted to say so much more, about how strong she was, how her intelligence wasn't a lie he told her but a fact he exploited.

Sylvie shrugged. "A bit late anyway."

We were sitting on this hill that overlooked the lake. It was too hot to be comfortable, but neither of us said anything about it. I was horrified to find myself frozen, unable to offer comfort or support. I simply sat there next to her and listened.

"So," Sylvie continued, and for the first time in nearly an hour, she looked over at me. "I see this therapist once a month, and the point of me telling you all this is because you were right."

My brow furrowed in confusion, and I blinked at her.

"About the Ferris wheel. I told Dr. Giles about our fight, and I talked with him about why I did it. It's just—"

"Sylvie, it doesn't matter."

"No," she said. "It does matter. I need you to understand this. Wilbur was awful to me, but his approval was like getting high. He had me so desperate for his validation that it was such a rush when it came. I don't know. Dr. Giles says sometimes I miss that feeling. I"—she rolled her eyes here—"'act out,' but maybe he has a point."

"I think I understand," I said. It was all I had to offer her. I'd hurt her to protect my old wound with Autumn, never wondering if she had her own. I was appalled at myself and amazed by her strength and dignity.

"The thing I'm trying to work out with Dr. Giles," Sylvie said, no longer looking at me, "is when I'm being me and when I'm being the way Mr. Wilbur made me think about myself. The Ferris wheel thing...I am working on it, okay?"

"Sylvie—" I started.

She held up a hand like before, and I fell silent.

"Wilbur tried to steal my high school years from me. No friends, no parties, just him and some community college classes as he fooled my parents into thinking he was preparing me for Harvard. I switched schools, and I'm doing all the high school things: cheerleading, student council, dance committees. I want to have fun, wild times and make normal teenage mistakes."

"I'm sorry you went through that. I'm sorry I said—"

"Let me finish, Finn. My ambition? That was always me, not Mr. Wilbur, though he exploited it. So when I say that I want to do all the high school stuff, I mean it. That's the plan, and that's really me."

She glanced at me, and I nodded. I could see that.

104

She continued, "And part of that is, you know, having a high school boyfriend. But Dr. Giles says that I can't be with someone who makes me feel insecure."

"I'm sorry," I said. "I didn't mean to—"

"What I need to hear, Finn," Sylvie said, "is that you want to be with me. That I'm not the convenient choice for you because you can't be with the person you actually want."

She looked at me, calm and measured, ready for my response, whatever it would be.

"You are so strong," I said, because it was true. I was trying to unscramble what I could say that was honest. It *was* convenient to be with her. Autumn didn't love me. But I genuinely wanted to be with Sylvie. I told her, "I want to be with you. And everything you've told me just makes me respect you more. I love you, Sylvie." I'd never used the L word around her before, and I felt a moment of panic, but she smiled softly.

"And?" Sylvie said.

"I don't know what more you want me to say," I lied.

"That you don't want to be with anyone else. That you only want to be with me," Sylvie said.

I put my arm around her. I didn't do public displays of affection much, especially that first year. She leaned in.

"Sylvie, you are one of the most beautiful girls I've ever seen in my entire life. And the smartest. You're so driven. Before meeting you, I'd never realized how attractive ambition is to me." I kissed her forehead before continuing, "I want to do all the high school stuff with you, Sylvie—all the dances, events, and traditions that you want. We'll go to parties and make stupid mistakes that turn into hilarious stories." I went on like that for a while, making promises about all the stuff we would do together over the next three years as I held her close. I ended by saying, "I love you, Sylvie," again and kissed her until we were breathless.

At the time, I thought that she hadn't noticed what I had not said, but I was wrong.

———————

Autumn stirs in her sleep. For my own protection, I shift her head off my shoulder and onto a pillow. I glance at the clock. It's seven in the morning. Today I must tell Sylvie that I'm choosing Autumn over her, like she's always feared.

I lie on my side and let myself stare at Autumn's face until finally sleep comes.

———————

She pummels me awake several times, and perhaps the noises I make as the blows land wake her too. Each time I'm falling back asleep, I reach for her, her face, her hands. I try to whisper, though I'm not sure the words ever leave my mouth, "I love you."

twelve

I wake.

My phone.

It's ringing, inside the pocket of my jeans, on the floor, where I tossed them when Autumn and I—

She stirs next to me. I hurry off the bed and try to stop the ringing before it wakes her. I see the name I expect. I decline the call. When I look up, Autumn is watching me.

"Hey." I'm not so sorry to see her awake.

"Was that her?" Autumn asks.

I set my phone on the nightstand. It's one thirty in the afternoon.

"Does it matter?" I ask. I want it to be only us, as much as possible for as long as possible.

"Yes."

"It was."

Autumn looks down. Her pink lips purse. I drop my jeans and climb back in bed.

"Come here." Pulling her to me is a relief.

Autumn snuggles against me, and when she shifts her face, she breathes in deeply. It feels like she's breathing in the scent of me the same way I have with her. I'm struck again by my new reality. She loves me. Autumn is in love with me, definitively. It's so much more than I ever could have imagined.

All these years I'd fantasized about Autumn physically, I never let myself think about what it would be like to be her boyfriend, not consciously at least.

I've always been a vivid dreamer though. I could control my thoughts when I was awake, but at night, my brain dwelled on its secret obsession. It was a frequent, recurring dream over the years that Autumn and I were a couple. Always, like my conscious fantasies, there was no explanation of how we got there. We would simply be together.

No matter what the dream with Autumn was about—whether it was set in deep space or in a version of McClure High School with upside-down halls—I always felt such a sense of relief when I dreamed that we were together. It was like the dream was my reality, and when I woke, I was in a nightmare where Autumn and I were both dating other people and weren't even friends. I'd denied my feelings to Jack, to Sylvie, to myself, but my brain had continued to stubbornly insist that Autumn and I were supposed to be together. I'd thought that it was my lust and jealousy mixing to give me the delusion that an error had been made and the matchups that kept us apart were all a big mistake.

But.

Here we are.

"Do you feel guilty?" Autumn's voice is feather light, like she's trying to gently blow the words from her mouth.

The guilt is mine alone. I need her to understand that.

I need her to understand that I had to do this. I had to be with her if the chance was there. My love for her is part of who I am.

"Yeah," I say. "But I also feel like I've been loyal to something bigger." It's only the start of what I want to tell her, but I'm interrupted by a beep I should have expected.

I'm going to ignore it, but Autumn says, "You should see who it is."

"I don't want to," I say reflexively.

"It could be The Mothers, and if we don't answer, they'll think we're dead and come back early."

I would still put the odds on it being Sylvie confirming her flight details before she boards her plane from Chicago, but Autumn has a point. I don't want The Mothers interrupting our time.

I roll away from Autumn, sit up, and pick up my phone.

ORD > STL Flt#5847 4:17pm Dinner after Y/N?

I'm glad that my back is turned, because I can't help the tiny smile that cracks my face. It's such a *Sylvie* text: the militaristic shorthand, the assumption that I'll recognize the Chicago airport code. Part of the reason Sylvie underestimates herself is she doesn't

109

recognize that most people don't possess her efficiency or candor. Sylvie assumes everyone else knows exactly what they want from life and is strategically plotting to get it as soon as possible. Autumn is the only other person I know like that.

Glad u r safely stateside. Up all night. Need rest. See u alone? 7?

I turn off the sound on my phone.

I lie back down, and we settle in close, facing each other.

"It was her again?" Autumn asks, because she knows.

"I told her that I won't be meeting her plane. I'll see her after she has dinner with her parents."

"Oh. When?"

"We have a few hours." Four hours fifty-one minutes and counting. "Go back to sleep."

"I'm not tired."

"Me neither." It doesn't matter what we do as long as I can look at her.

Perhaps Autumn feels the same, because she stares at me, and I do what I've longed to do a thousand times: I reach out and brush the hair from her forehead.

Autumn's eyes drift closed as I stroke her temples and her hair. She looks so happy. How is it possible that I'm making her smile like that with just the tips of my fingers? There isn't anything else I can blame the smile on: no music, no other sensations.

There must be a catch.

After four years of saying no to Jamie, why did she say yes to me?

I almost laugh because I realize she didn't say yes to me. She proposed it. I gave in to her request, despite the reasons it was a bad idea.

Autumn trembles under my touch, like the feel of my fingertips is more than she can handle.

"Do you regret it?" I ask, because surely something will go wrong.

Her eyes open. "No," she says. Before relief can hit me, she continues, "But I wish it had been your first time too."

Autumn looks away from me, and I freeze.

Without betraying Sylvie, I need to explain to Autumn how significant last night was for me.

I let my hand fall away and concentrate on my words.

"The first time, we were both so drunk neither of us can remember it. And then it turned out that she couldn't do it unless she was drunk. And if she was drunk, it felt wrong to me. It didn't happen often or even go very well when it did. So, I mean, in a lot of ways, it was a first for me."

I hope I don't have to say more, but Autumn says, "What do you mean 'she couldn't do it unless she was drunk'?"

"Someone hurt her once," I say. It's true that Sylvie was hurt, but it's not true to say that she was hurt only once.

"Oh," Autumn says.

It's a bit of a bummer to not really remember the first time I had sex, but that isn't why last night felt like a first time for me. With Sylvie, most nights ended with me telling her she was too drunk

111

for me to keep going. There were nights she was sober enough to consent, but we had to stop in the middle. Success was rare, and I lived in fear of hurting Sylvie.

Autumn lays her hand over mine, and suddenly, I remember all the things that I still need to tell her. I twine my fingers with hers.

"I wanted something better for you," I told her. "That's why I made you promise not to do it when you were drinking, but really, the idea of you ever doing it with anybody made me mad." I need to warn her about the effect she has on me. "Do you remember how you told me that you were going to do it after graduation? And then the day after, you were sitting on the porch, and you said you were waiting for Jamie?"

"Yeah?"

"I came up here and punched the wall," I admit. "I'd never done that before. It hurt."

"You thought..."

"Yeah." Also, I need to warn her how selfish she makes me. "Then, after I found out you guys had broken up, it was hard to see you miserable over him when I was so happy. I wanted to pick you up and spin you around." Like I'd watched Jamie do so many times.

Rather than responding to my hypocrisy, Autumn says, "You were sad that time Sylvie broke up with you. I was so angry at her for hurting you that I thought about pushing her in front of the school bus."

I almost laugh at Autumn's hyperbole.

"I was sad," I agree, "but it was my own fault. I told everybody

112

that I didn't like it when they made comments about you, and Sylvie got jealous. She asked me if I had feelings for you." She asked directly that time. "And I told her to drop it and kept trying to change the subject. She could tell."

I'd tried what had worked before, saying true things in a way that hid what I didn't want to say. Again and again, I tried to get Sylvie to pretend that I'd told her what she wanted to hear, but that time, she wouldn't play along. Sylvie dumped me, as I deserved. She was cool and brisk.

Sylvie said, "Finn, even if you weren't being purposefully obtuse, that would still be a problem. I'm tired of the charade." That had hurt because I hadn't thought of my relationship with Sylvie as a farce.

Part of me wishes I could tell Autumn how much I missed Sylvie those weeks. I missed talking with her about politics. I missed going on runs with her when no one else would go with me because it was too cold. I missed calling her to say good night. I missed our evenings at the library together, working side by side, not talking.

Finally, I lied to Sylvie. I lied again and again. Sure, I'd told her I had a crush on Autumn. But I said losing *her* had made me realize that I hadn't really been in love with Autumn at all. I told Sylvie that she was the only one I wanted to be with, and after that, she seemed to believe me again.

"Why did you get back with her?" Autumn asks, surprising me.

"You loved Jamie all this time too, didn't you?"

"Yeah," she says, and I'm amazed that I still feel a flicker of jealousy.

"Then why don't you understand? I wanted—I tried to love only her."

Autumn's face tells me that she understands at least that much, so I continue.

"When I told you last month that I was going to break up with Sylvie, it wasn't because I thought I had a chance of being more than just your friend. It was because loving you from a distance was one thing, but it wouldn't have been fair to her if I were in love with my best friend."

Abruptly, Autumn sits up. She hugs the covers around herself like bandages on a wound. I don't understand what's happened. I confessed to punching blameless walls and rejoicing in her heartbreak, and she smiled sweetly at me. Why is she upset now? I sit up too.

"Autumn?"

Her hair is hanging over her face. "What if you see her and realize this was all a mistake?"

"That will not happen."

"It could."

"It won't."

"If you love her—" Autumn says, but I can't let her go on.

"But if I have the chance to be with you—" It's surreal to me, but somehow, after everything, she still doesn't understand how uncontrollably in love I am. "God, Autumn. You're the ideal I've judged every other girl by my whole life. You're funny and smart and weird. I never know what's going to come out of your mouth or what you're going to do. I love that. You. I love you."

After all these years of feeling like I was holding back the most eloquent words of love, my big speech sounds weak to me, but I try to let all my emotion show in my voice.

Her brown hair parts over her face, and her huge eyes peek up at me from under her eyelashes.

I don't know how I'm still breathing.

"And you're so beautiful," I hear myself say.

She ducks her head again, and I laugh aloud.

"Now, I know you already knew that," I say. I'm laughing because I've seen her shrug off that exact compliment so many times.

"It's different when you say it." She speaks so quietly I can barely hear her.

I laugh. "How?"

"I don't know," she whispers.

Sweet Autumn.

"You're so beautiful." I reach for her face and tilt her chin up. I need her to see me say this. "Last night was the best thing that ever happened to me," I tell her. "And I would never think it was a mistake unless you said it was."

"I would never say that," she whispers.

I smile and lean my forehead against hers. I close my eyes as I reply. "Then everything is going to be okay. We're together now, right?" I need to hear her say it. No more mistakes.

115

"Of course," Autumn says, and I can't help my laugh again.

She pulls away.

I explain, "I never ever thought this would happen, and then you say, 'of course,' like it's the most natural thing in the world."

"Doesn't it feel like it?" she asks me.

It does, and it doesn't. Being with Autumn feels natural, but it also feels supernatural. I think about the way her novel captured and displayed my love for her so perfectly without her having consciously known all that was in my heart. I think about my recurring dreams of having returned to the right timeline, where she and I have always been together.

"How did we ever get here?" I wonder aloud. How is it possible that two people could simultaneously seem to be both destined and not destined to be together?

Again, I have that feeling that there must be a catch, that fate will not allow me to be with her; but when I look back at Autumn and see her quietly and calmly watching me, waiting for whatever I say or do next, I realize that it doesn't matter.

My face must change because she smiles and clambers into my lap. We wrap our arms around each other and settle in. After a moment, she says, "You know, I never thought this would happen either. When Jack told me—" and then she stops.

I move my face away enough to look at her.

"Oh. I didn't explain that part last night."

"What part?" I hope I don't sound as panicked as I suddenly feel. What did Jack tell her?

"It was a couple of weeks ago, after the horror movie we went to with Jack, remember? You went inside to get pretzels or something, and he was all, 'It took Finn forever to get over you last time. Are you messing with his head?'" Her Jack impression is decent, but she's still talking. "I was like, 'Whaaat?' because I had no idea that you'd ever felt that way. But Jack said you were over me, that he was only worried. So for the past couple of weeks, I've thought I'd missed my chance with you."

I don't say anything in reply. My head is too full of opposing thoughts and feelings.

"Finny?"

"Sorry," I say. "I was trying to decide whether I should kill Jack for telling you I was into you or if I should kill him for telling you that I wasn't into you. Tough call."

"Noooo," Autumn says. She kisses my cheek. "Don't be mad. He was looking out for you. It was sweet. He loves you."

"Yeah," I admit. Jack was protecting me, but there's no way he believed that I was over Autumn. I'm wondering now though. "What would you have done if he'd told you the truth, that I was"—I try to remember how Jack put it before—"bonkers in love with you?"

Autumn rests her head on my shoulder. I can't believe this is real life, holding her like this.

"Hmm," she says. "I think I would have had a hard time believing him."

"Really?"

"I mean, yeah. I'm not exactly your type."

117

"I—" I decide to skip over the whole "type" comment. "Let's say Jack convinced you. I'm certain he could have eventually. Then what?"

"I guess I would have…" Autumn trails off and begins again. "I guess I would have flirted with you?"

"How?"

"I have no idea," Autumn says. "But when I gave you my nov—Oh." Before I can react, she's sliding off my lap and looking at me with frantic eyes. "With everything that happened last night, I almost forgot you read my book."

She's looking at me like I've turned into a wild animal she does not trust.

"Autumn, it was great," I tell her. She's still looking at me dubiously. "Really."

"It's a first draft," she says. "It can't be great. But if you liked it okay, that's a good start."

"I loved it," I say.

She shakes her head, brushing off my praise.

"Why were you so nervous to share it with me?"

"Because." Autumn picks at the blanket in her lap. "It's all of me, dissected and splayed out. I'm not nervous about how you interpreted Izzy and Aden's relationship anymore, but last night, I thought it might be the end of our friendship. Because you got over me. After I abandoned you."

"But I didn't," I say. "I couldn't get over you."

She looks back at me.

118

"I'm glad you didn't," she says, and a smile cracks her worry briefly. "So you liked the book. Obviously, you're biased."

"You remember how furious I was last night? I thought you'd recorded my devotion in perfect detail and then dropped it in my lap without considering my feelings. And I still loved it as a story. You're a good writer, Autumn. You've always been good."

Autumn shrugs and looks away, but her smile is back. "Thanks," she whispers.

I can't take it anymore. I lean over and kiss her deeply. A few minutes are lost to that, and then I gasp as I feel her fingers close around me.

"We can't double our chances of you getting pregnant," I say, even though I'm kissing her neck now and doing nothing to stop her hand.

Autumn pulls away and puts her other hand on my shoulder.

"Don't worry," she whispers. "I know what to do." Autumn pushes me down on the bed, and for some unknown period of time, I am entirely at her mercy.

thirteen

"How much longer do we have?" Autumn asks.

I don't want to think about it, but I glance at the clock anyway. We've kissed and dozed the afternoon away.

"In an hour, I should take a shower," I say. When she went to the bathroom earlier, I quietly checked my phone and saw the text from Sylvie, confirming I can pick her up at her house after seven.

Autumn presses her back into my chest, and I stop stroking her arm to hug her. I raise my head and kiss her cheek. We've been lying like this for a while.

After Autumn charmingly tortured me with her hands and then triumphantly ravished me with her mouth, I tried to return the favor. I needed more coaching, but Autumn's enthusiasm remained throughout.

Again and again this afternoon, Autumn has looked at me like she's trying to believe I'm real. It was such a strange mirror of my own feelings.

Over and over, Autumn has told me she loves me. She's said it breathlessly between kisses. She's growled it before biting me softly on the shoulder, making me gasp in surprised pleasure. She's said it smugly after destroying me, while I was still trembling in her hold.

It's starting to settle into my brain as fact. Autumn loves me in return.

"Tomorrow," Autumn whispers.

"What about it?" Tomorrow is going to be wonderful, and the day after and the day after, because I am hers. Tonight is the only concern, and that's mine alone.

"What if you waited until tomorrow?"

I tighten my grip on her and bury my face in the back of her neck.

"No, it's the right thing to do." I kiss her shoulder. Somewhere in the back of my brain, I'm still amazed that she wants me to touch her.

Autumn rolls over, and we settle in, facing each other.

"Tell me a story," she demands.

"What kind of story?" I try to hide the amusement in my voice because she's being very solemn.

"About us," she says. "Something true. Something that happened when we didn't know we loved each other."

"Hmm." I think I understand what she's asking, and I wonder if she has stories of her own. "Do you remember that tiara my mom got you one year for Christmas? She said, 'Finny picked it out.' I bought it. I saw it at a store and knew you would love it. I gave it to Mom and asked her to say it was from both of us."

Autumn's mouth is hanging open.

"Oh, Finny," she says. "You could have told—"

"No," I say. "I couldn't have. We hadn't gotten each other Christmas gifts for years. It would have been weird."

"Oh, Finny," she says again, but this time, she's agreeing with me.

"Now you tell me a story," I say.

"Well," she begins, "remember the Valentine's Day right after that? You were sick, and I brought you that note from..." She stalls at that part, but I don't need her to continue.

"I remember." The agony I'd felt that day stayed fresh for the rest of that winter. I had obsessed over that embarrassing conversation for weeks.

"You were so hot," Autumn moans, looking away from me, and I blink in surprise. She scrunches up her face and closes her eyes against the memory. "You were shirtless and sweaty and flushed and—" She breaks off into a frustrated growl. When she looks back up at me, she says, "But you saw me checking you out, right? You had to have. It was so obvious." She's smiling like she expects me to agree.

"I thought *you* had brought me a Valentine. I was confused and happy and then a different sort of confused when it was from Sylvie." I find myself faltering again. "I thought you could see my mistake, and I felt so sick and gross in front of you, and you were so beautiful like alwa—"

"You thought that I—How could I have—Finny, no," she says.

We're staring at each other in amazement.

"I wish I could go back in time," she says.

122

"Why don't you just go back to telling me I'm hot?"

Autumn laughs. She tells me about both loving and hating going with The Mothers to my soccer games. She says my muscled legs in my running shorts drove her to distraction, and it blows my mind that she'd lusted after certain parts of me from a distance the same way I had after her.

As if picking the thoughts from my own head, she tells me she was always secretly aware of any movement my body made when I was near—at the bus stop, on the couch as we watched television, at the holiday dinner table—just as I memorized every detail about her.

I stroke Autumn's hair and her arm as she talks, and I watch her face as her eyes close in pleasure, then open to look at me as she speaks.

"I want another story," she says.

I try to remember my most intense memory of longing for her. I move my strokes down her back and she sighs. I'm getting this right. I'm learning the rest.

"Last Halloween," I finally say. "I was watching you the whole night. I couldn't stop myself. You were—" I sort through all the vocab words I'd used her to help me remember. "You were splendiferous that night, Autumn. Like, if I'd had one of those new phones that take pictures? It would have crossed my mind to try and take one. Not that I would have!" She's smiling at me as I confess how horrible I am; I guess I should be glad she thought *Wuthering Heights* was romantic.

"I wasn't even wearing a sexy costume." Autumn giggles.

"You were radiant," I tell her.

I was particularly moonstruck that night. Her pale skin and the dark shine of her hair have always had the power to hypnotize me. That Halloween, she was particularly bewitching, her laugh dazzling and her every movement like an alien ballet.

"I couldn't keep my eyes off you," I confess. "Before you ran into me, I looked away so you wouldn't see me staring, but I misjudged your speed and we—"

We both laugh at the memory.

I can see her reaching back in her mind. "You were worried Jamie and I would have sex that night."

"Yeah, well, that's because, if I had been in Jamie's position—"

She bites her lip as a smile creeps up. "I guess we know now what would have happened," she says.

"Well, I can't imagine how we could have possibly reached that point."

Autumn's gaze shifts like she's watching a movie I can't see.

"Say that when we collided," Autumn muses, "my drink spilled on me instead, and I said, 'Come up with me and stand guard while I change my shirt.' I'd have wanted to have a moment with you, and I bet you'd have done as I said."

"Sure," I say, encouraging her to continue.

"And then upstairs, you'd have finished your drink while I changed shirts."

"Maybe?"

"Yes," Autumn tells me. "Because you would have been nervous, right? You said the Halloween magic had you enthralled, and you weren't driving for once." She doesn't wait for me to agree with her. She knows she's correct. "You would have downed that drink while staring at my door, trying not to think about me taking off my shirt on the other side. And when I came back out, I would have smiled at you, a little drunk too, and gazed up at you for a little too long..."

Suddenly, I can see it exactly as she describes, as if it had happened that way. Autumn's lips curling up as I look down at her face in the shadowy hallway, the thumping hum of the party beneath us somehow making it more intimate, secret. I feel the tempting circumstances she's painted us into, and in this version of events, neither of us would be able to resist each other.

"If you'd kissed me, Finny, I would have been astonished, but I would have pulled you right back into my room and—well, like I said before..." She smiles.

"I don't think we would have gone all the way," I say as I return her grin. "I'm not reckless. You know that. And besides, would you have been ready?"

"It was never about not being ready with Jamie," she says. "It didn't feel right with him, but I didn't know that until I kissed you. If we had made out that Halloween, you're probably right. We wouldn't have done *it*." Autumn giggles. "But we'd get in some state of undress before we came to our senses and realized that we'd be missed or caught."

"And what about that?" I say. "The party is still going on, we're in your bed, and..."

She grins, but I want to hear this story!

"Okay then. Hold on." Autumn's eyes get that distant look, and she mumbles, "We recognize we have to stop before we get caught, and as we detangle our limbs, we make a few whispery, alcohol-fueled confessions. There isn't time for much. Neither of us would be brave enough to say the L word, I think. We'd fix our clothes and hair, but we'd know we couldn't be seen going back downstairs together."

I'm fascinated. This is what she's thinking in her head when she gets that look?

"We'd agree that I should go first," Autumn decides. "Since it's my house, I'd be missed first. I'd sneak back to Jamie and pretend to be more drunk than I was, and you would wait and sneak back to the party a few minutes later." She looks at me again in this reality. "Do you think we'd get back in our places in time? That our excuses would be believed?"

I'm pleased that she wants my opinion. I think about our class-mates, the layout of her house, and my memories of that night.

"Someone would have seen something," I decide. "But nothing big enough for anyone to say anything about it until the next day."

Autumn nods and continues, "We'd have to pretend to act normal and try to avoid each other for the rest of the party. We'd probably both drink more to disguise our emotions, both try and fail not to watch the other across the crowd." Autumn is back in the story she's writing to please me. "Before the night was over, I'd be wondering if our encounter had really meant anything to you or if you'd just been drunk." She looks at me for confirmation.

126

"Yeah. Same," I say.

"In the morning, I'd pretend to be sick…nah, I'd probably be sick in the morning and use the excuse to get my friends who stayed the night out ASAP. Where would you have been?"

This question is easy. "At home. Alone. I would have called you the moment I saw Jamie's car leave."

Autumn smiles, pleased either by my contribution to the narrative or by my obsessive nature, I'm not sure which.

"Okay," Autumn says. "Over the phone, through the pain of our blinding headaches, we'd stammer confirmations of last night's heartfelt whispers, offer more detailed explanations of our true desires. One of us ends up over at the other's house and…" She motions with her hand to our current situation, and we smile. "I mean, that's about it."

"But remember, someone saw something the night before," I prompt.

Autumn yawns.

"Well, of course we'd each have to break up to be together. The story of whatever suspicious thing was seen at the party would get spread and exaggerated. There's no avoiding that chapter. We'd be the center of a scandal, ostracized for being cheaters. Or I don't know… Everyone likes you, so maybe it wouldn't have been that rough for you?"

As glad as I am that Autumn would have broken up with Jamie for me and faced whatever consequences came next, I'm still distracted that she continues to deftly avoid saying Sylvie's name while we've

127

both casually referenced Jamie. This is why I must break up with Sylvie today. Can't she see that?

"I wish all that had happened," I tell her. "I wish we'd had that time together and today was another regular day for us."

Autumn's gaze finds mine again, and she repeats my words to her. "Everything is going to be okay. We're together now, right?"

"I love you." How many times have I said that? Surely it will be annoying soon?

"I love you too, Finny," Autumn says and pokes my nose. "While we're talking about unsaid things, you haven't secretly been wishing that I call you Finn?"

"Nah," I say. "Finn is how I think of myself, but that's what I like about you calling me Finny. It's special."

"Even though The Mothers call you that too?"

I poke her nose, and now I'm the one repeating her words. "It's different when you say it."

"Finny." Autumn kisses me again and then again hungrily. A few minutes later, she breathes in my ear, "We have time, don't we? Can we just—"

We have just enough time, but it's getting harder to resist making love to her again, so I decide to buy condoms tonight.

Afterward, I ask her if she wants to join me in the shower. Autumn blushes and hides her face in her hands. We're lying on our sides, tangled together still.

"Autumn?"

She says something behind her hands.

"I can't hear you, beloved."

I'm surprised by the term of endearment. I've never used it before in my life, but it's fallen from my mouth naturally, and I wonder if it's going to become a habit.

"I'm too shy," she says. "I can't take a shower with you."

"We're...already naked?" We've been in my bed together for hours.

"But there's water in a shower!" Autumn says, and I decide that this is one of those times when her brain is wired differently.

"Okay," I say. "Showers are a level of intimacy we can work our way up to."

"Might take a while," she says into my bare chest.

I can't hold back a small chuckle. I run my fingers down her back one last time, and she shivers in a way that almost tempts me to stay after all.

"We have forever," I whisper into her hair, and then I wonder if forever is too much for her.

Autumn raises her face and grins at me.

"Okay," she says. "You're right."

We lock our lips together deeply, then I kiss her forehead and climb out of bed. She doesn't follow me as I gather my clothes. She stays in bed and watches me. I give her a quizzical look.

"I can't get dressed in front of you," she says. "That's too awkward."

I pause, trying to decide how to ask my first question, but then I laugh and say, "I love you, Autumn."

And somehow, she isn't tired of hearing it yet.

fourteen

WHEN I COME BACK FROM the shower, Autumn's confidence in our future is gone. She's sitting on the center of my bed, curled up tight in her rumpled clothes and finger-combed hair. She looks wild and elven—and scared.

"It's going to be okay." I wish her brain could accept the truth that mine has; we've made it back together.

"Can't you wait until tomorrow?"

"I want it to be over." I can't explain how hard it is going to be to break up with Sylvie. It wouldn't help Autumn's confidence. But the certainty of our future together drives me, and when I get back to her, she'll understand. I'll show her every day, for as long as she wants me. "I want it to be just us."

I fidget, but the fact of the matter is the time has come for me to go. I'll be back in a few hours. It's fine. She's nervous because she's the one having to wait for me, but there's nothing to be worried about. I look at her, still sitting with her knees under her chin.

"Walk me out?" I'm trying to sound casual, but all the dread about seeing Sylvie, how I'm going to hurt her is coming back.

I have to tell Sylvie.

Autumn holds my hand and walks beside me, down the stairs and out of the house. The sky is gray with thick clouds, and the wind has picked up.

The sinking feeling inside me will be there until I get back to her, but she needs to see my resolve. I'm doing this for us, and somehow, amazingly, she still doesn't understand the depth and breadth of my passion for her.

At my car, I say to her, "I promise you, I'll come back as soon as I can. It may take a while though."

"Please don't go," she says.

Oh, beloved.

I take her in my arms and hold her close to me.

"I have to do this," I tell her. "You know that, Autumn."

She's quiet, but she leans into me.

"Here's what we'll do," I say with my chin resting on her hair. "When The Mothers get home, you go to bed early, and when I get back, I'll sneak in your back door and come to your room, and then I'll hold you all night." Or do more than that if she wants. When she's ready again, I'll be ready with condoms.

She pulls away enough to look at me. "Okay," Autumn says, like we're making a sacred vow. I wish we were.

I can't help kissing her quickly, but when she moves in to kiss me again, I lose myself in wonder. Autumn wants me. Autumn loves me.

As Autumn leans back against the car, she pulls me with her, and I press into her, once more seduced into more than I had planned. I want her again, right now, caution and ethics be damned. Autumn kisses me desperately, and I am breathless with love. If I'm not back inside, skin to skin with her in another minute, I will lose my mind.

I feel her tense before my brain registers the sound of the car door slamming. She peers over the car roof behind her, and I look over her head. The Mothers are home early. Aunt Claire has a quiet smile. Mom seems to be trying to hide her face.

"Do you think they saw?" Autumn asks.

"Definitely." We aren't even ten yards away, but they are pretending to be completely unaware of their children, who they have not seen for two days, making out in the driveway.

"Oh God," Autumn says.

I can tell she's in misery over the coming tide of discrete smiles and little comments. The thing is, when we were babies, The Mothers daydreamed about us getting married so they could be grandmothers together. But really, The Mothers will be happy for me. It's been impossible to hide how much I wanted this.

"I think my mother has a special bottle of champagne hidden away for just this occasion," I say. I'm only partially joking. Mom has labeled some of her alcohol, like for when George W. Bush leaves office and stuff. One expensive one said, "Finny-Autumn

Day or NYE 2010." At the time, I was glad she'd made alternative plans for it.

"Oh God," Autumn says again. She buries her head in my chest. Finny-Autumn Day has come after all.

I look down at Autumn, my beloved. I will make that name a habit. It suits her.

"I'll be back to help you fend them off."

"Okay," Autumn says, and it's time.

With space between our bodies, I lean down and kiss her before I go, because I can, because it's not the last time.

I open the car door. The sinking feeling in my stomach is increasing with every moment, but I'm buoyed by the knowledge that I'm going to come back to Autumn and hold her and kiss her and lie beside her as she fights dragon-faerie wars in her sleep. I smile at her. She looks so somber.

"After this, things are going to be the way they were always supposed to be," I tell her. I can't put it off anymore. I sit down and close the door between us. "It will all be over soon," I mumble as I start the car. I don't let myself look at her again until she's in my rearview mirror. I turn onto the street and drive down the hill as the rain starts.

fifteen

I only look at my phone because I know it's Mom calling. I haven't even turned off our block yet. Autumn must have already made her excuses and bolted.

"Technically, Mom," I say instead of hello, "it's raining and I'm driving, so I shouldn't have answered."

"My advice worked, kiddo!" Mom says. "I get one minute to gloat. And it's barely raining."

I'd forgotten what she said before leaving for the weekend: "Talk to her." She'd had a better view on the situation than I did.

Neither mother has ever said anything about us dating in all these years, not directly. That's the thing about being raised by women: you learn about layers of communication from an early age. Without ever saying it, The Mothers have told me many times that they wished, for my sake, Autumn loved me back. It never occurred to me that maybe they were trying to tell me that she *did* love me back.

"This was not the outcome I was expecting," I admit to Mom,

trying to share enough to get out of the conversation while saying as little as possible.

"It's been quite a summer," she says, and I can't help but laugh.

"Yeah."

"Claire and I are at our place having some champagne," Mom says, and I have to stifle another laugh. "Autumn has escaped to her room, and we'll leave her alone for now. I promise." Mom pauses. "Should I nudge Claire toward staying late or at our place tonight?"

"Uh, yeah. Sounds good," I say, blushing. I'd thank my mother for intuiting my clandestine plans and assisting them, but it's too much for me.

"Okay then," she says, relieving me. "I'll let you do what you need to. I love you. I'm proud of you."

"You always say you're proud of me for the weirdest things, Mom," I tell her. "I love you too. Bye."

———————

I'm going to get two errands done at once by going to that gas station: buying the whole stock of Autumn's favorite candies and some condoms. I figure the creep's shift won't have started yet.

I'm wrong though. I park in the same space as the night before, and I can see him through the window. Does he live here? It's truly raining now. I'd planned to call Jack on my way to Sylvie's, but I don't like to drive and talk on my phone when it's raining. I pull out my phone and scroll for Jack's name.

"Hey?" He sounds confused, probably because he told me to

call him after I broke up with Sylvie, and he knows it's too early for that.

"Hi," I say. "I'll be at Sylvie's soon. I was calling to tell you that you were right."

"Of course I was right," Jack says. "About what?"

"Autumn and I are the two stupidest people on earth."

"Wait," he says. "Huh?"

"She loves me." I'm so giddy, my voice sounds ridiculous even to my own ears. "We talked about so many things last night, and she had no idea. She never knew. She apologized for middle school, but it wasn't all her fault. It was mine too—and we're together now." I stop short.

There's silence on the other end. I almost think the call dropped when Jack says, "Are you sure?"

"All the way sure." I laugh. "I'm serious, dude. We spent all day—trust me. She's in love me, I swear."

"Okay. Huh," Jack says. "Um, well, I'm happy for you? And while you're happy and distracted, I guess I'll share my news. Alexis and I have been hooking up again."

"Oh, come on, Jack," I say.

"It's only for the rest of summer!" he insists. "I'm not agreeing to indentured servitude again. It's just physical."

"It's a good thing she's headed to Carbondale, because otherwise you two would end up accidentally married."

"Well, when you break it off with Sylvie, Lexy might cut me off," Jack says. "Especially if you tell her that you're going out with Princess Autumn Fucking Davis."

"Don't call her that," I say.

"My point is that's what they call her. I'm only warning you."

"If Alexis cuts you off because I'm with Autumn, I'll be doing you both a favor," I say. "And I already know how rough this is going to be with Sylvie. You're supposed to be celebrating with me and are failing miserably."

"I'm happy she apologized," Jack says.

"She did so much more than that," I say. "Trust me."

"I'm happy that you're happy," Jack says. "Are you at Sylvie's yet?"

"I'm making a quick stop. Picking up a few things." I finally get out of the car and bolt for the door. My hair gets soaked immediately.

"Don't put it off too long," Jack says.

"This is an essential errand," I say as I head for the candy aisle. "Then I'm on my way to Sylvie's. I probably won't be able to call you later."

"Why not?" Jack asks. "You should come by after."

I'm loading up my arms with the sugar sludge and powder as I answer.

"I'm gonna be with Autumn." I scan the aisles and realize this place keeps the condoms behind the counter, so I'm going to have to talk to the creep. "I should probably go. I'll call you tomorrow."

"Okay, Finn." Jack sighs. "Later."

I hang up. Yup, there they are behind the counter.

I should not have assumed this guy wouldn't start his shift this early. The pay is probably terrible, and the hours are likely long. I'll simply ask for the condoms and hope he won't say something gross.

I approach the counter and wait. The creep is making jokes with the customer in front of me. He doesn't notice me until it's my turn and I drop the load of sugar onto the counter.

He looks behind me like he's hoping to see her, and his face falls. I look at the shine of his forehead, not his eyes.

"And some—a twelve pack of condoms." I try to keep my voice casual.

I hate that this guy intimidates me. His behavior oozes everything I hate about stereotypes of my gender, yet somehow, there's a part of me that wants to be man enough for him. It's probably rooted in my dad not being around, but the point is guys like this one make me feel disgusted yet inadequate.

He rings up Autumn's candy before grabbing the condoms from the shelf behind him. He glances at me with a smirk, trying to catch my eye. I need to tell Autumn the truth about this guy.

I'm so in my head I don't even hear him speak to me.

"What?"

"Big plans tonight?" He taps the box of condoms with his index finger.

"You are so gross," I hear myself say, and for a moment, the creep and I are both surprised. "Sorry," I say, even though I'm not. "Stop leering at teen girls. Meet someone your own age."

The man's shiny forehead is suddenly cut by a bright red-purple vein. His mustache wiggles with his fury.

I throw down my money and head out. I vow to always carry cash with me for the rest of my life in case of a similar situation.

The man shouts something after me, but it doesn't matter what because I'm already sliding into my car. I pull out of the parking lot. I have places to be.

sixteen

SYLVIE'S HOUSE ISN'T AS NICE as a lot of people from school would expect. I don't mean to say that it's not a perfectly good home, but Sylvie carries herself like she lives in a mansion. It's not a bad thing. I love her poise. I admire the way she finds high-end stuff on sale and handwashes her silk dresses and cashmere sweaters.

It's not that Sylvie pretends to be rich. It's more like she's dressing for the adult she wants to be. It's part of how she took control of her life after Wilbur, I think. And even though she doesn't know what dream she wants to pursue, she knows that she could be a senator or CEO.

Sylvie and I make a great team. I never thought, *I want to marry her*, but I couldn't see myself breaking up with her either.

I love Sylvie, and the thought makes the ache in my chest intensify. I pull to the side of the road.

It's not a "but not *in* love with her" situation. I am in love with Sylvie, but I cannot be with her anymore, and that hurts. It also hurts to know that I am going to hurt her. The fact that this is all my choice doesn't make it any better. I need to get off the side of the road and drive the rest of the way to her house, but I don't. Not yet. I tap the CD player and start the song I played for Autumn last night. Last night, when everything was different between Autumn and me.

If only I'd told her that I loved her years ago, I wouldn't be here now. Because she loved me. She loved me this whole time.

Only two things will get me through this.

The first is that I want Sylvie to be with someone who loves her the way that I love Autumn. She deserves that.

And the second is that Autumn is waiting for me. I cannot fail her. Until I have ended this relationship, we can't really begin ours. I want to hold Autumn without guilt.

I have to do this, and I have to go home.

By the time the song ends, I'm driving again. I'm nearly to Sylvie's modest two-bedroom ranch where we studied and made out and tried to make love a few times. She must have been waiting for me by the door because she's dashing through the rain toward my car before I've parked in the driveway.

I unlock the passenger door, and before I know it, she's in the car, closing her umbrella with a shake and shutting the door.

Sylvie.

She brushes her blond hair from her face and looks at me.

"You fucking asshole," she says.

seventeen

PART OF ME HAD HOPED that Sylvie also felt we were drifting apart and suspected something so that I didn't completely blindside her, but I didn't expect this.

We stare at each other with only the sound of the rain between us.

"What do you know?" I ask after a moment.

"Everything," she says, which can't be true. I didn't even know everything until last night. And Jack wouldn't have called her before I arrived.

"Like what?" I hadn't known I could feel more guilty, but apparently there's no end to that well.

"Are you kidding me?" Sylvie is as surprised as she is furious. "Every time you and Autumn went to Blockbuster this summer, I got at least two emails about it from people who saw you. You didn't even try to hide it."

"Until recently, we were only friends," I begin to explain, but she's right. It's no defense.

"Shut up and drive somewhere," Sylvie says. "I haven't told my parents that you're breaking up with me tonight. They think you have some romantic gesture planned. I needed to yell at you before I figure out how to disappoint them again."

"They won't be disappointed in you because of what I did, Sylvie," I say.

Her seat belt clicks into place. "I'm not looking forward to explaining this to them, okay? But I have Dr. Giles for talking about my fear of disappointing authority figures. You don't get to give me pep talks anymore. Not after the lies you've told me."

"I—I—" I cannot say I never lied to her. I lied to her years ago when I told her that I wasn't in love with Autumn anymore, and I lied by omission all summer.

I suggest we go somewhere that we can sit and talk, but she says she won't be able to yell at me if we go to a coffee shop.

"Why don't you focus on driving and listening, okay, Smith? Because I have a list of questions I need you to answer."

Then Sylvie Whitehouse pulls a handwritten list out of her purse and smooths it on her lap. It would make me laugh with love for her if it didn't also make me want to cry for the same reason. I wish she and Autumn could be friends.

"First of all," Sylvie says, and I swallow my emotions and pay attention. "When was the first time you cheated on me?"

"Last night," I reply, but that question takes the longest to answer, because she does not believe me.

It takes so long to convince her that nothing physical happened

144

with Autumn until last night that I drive us over the river and into the rural plains outside East St. Louis. The rain comes down harder, and lightning strikes flash across the sky, stealing our words from us. It feels jarringly intimate.

"So you did…whatever it was that you did with her last night, Finn."

I don't need to look away from the road to know she's rolling her eyes.

"But that doesn't mean that you were faithful this summer," she continues.

I drive, and we argue about the definition of cheating.

Our argument would have lasted longer had Sylvie not been on the speech and debate team, but we would have ended in the same place. Because she's right.

This didn't start last night.

From the phone call all those weeks ago when I told Sylvie, "I'm about to eat breakfast," and didn't disclose that it was with Autumn, I was betraying Sylvie.

I told myself that I wasn't talking about Autumn during our phone calls for Sylvie's sake, but that wasn't true. I didn't tell Sylvie that Autumn and I were friends again because I didn't want to explain we were platonic friends. When Sylvie called from Europe and asked what I'd been up to, I'd say, "Watched a movie," and leave out "with Autumn," let alone "with Autumn in my bed, and when she fell asleep before it ended, I muted it and lay beside her."

After I'd decided that I was breaking up with Sylvie, I considered answering honestly, giving her a chance to suspect something, but when she asked what I was up to, I would say, "Nothing," instead of "Autumn and I parked near the airport and watched planes take off while she ate so much candy her teeth have turned green."

"You're right," I say as we cross the bridge back into the city. "I lied to you all summer. I'm sorry."

"So you get that this isn't only about last night?"

"Yeah," I say, "I get it." We're back in Missouri. I turn north, toward home. It's still raining, but the thunder is far away.

"My second question," Sylvie says. "Were you ever in love me?"

"Syl," I start, but I don't know where to begin. I stay on the highway, passing all the exits that could take us home.

"Were you ever in love with me?" Sylvie repeats. Her voice is firm, but she's saving her anger. "I don't want to hear that you cared about me or about any other kind of love besides romantic. No more lies by omission."

I take a deep breath. "I am in love with you, Sylvie." I wait for her to protest. There's only the sound of the rain and the windshield wipers.

"I believe you," Sylvie replies.

I'm so surprised that my mind shuts down. I wait for her to say something so I know what to think next.

"I can't ask you to apologize for loving her more than me."

"I don't love her more than you," I interject. I can see her

146

body shift in her seat out of the corner of my eyes. "It's not about more."

"What's it about then?" Her question almost twists into a laugh.

"Our souls." I know how ridiculous I sound. But I owe Sylvie the truth, even if it's proof of what a fool I am.

"Your what?"

I take a deep breath.

"Whatever our souls are made of, hers and mine are the same."

"Wh—Are you—" Sylvie is so rarely without words that I instinctively glance over at her. She is pink and angry. "Are you quoting *Wuthering Heights* to justify cheating on me?"

"No," I say. "I can't justify that." I grit my teeth and swallow the lump in my throat, because it's time to tell the cruelest truth. "I'm quoting *Wuthering Heights* to explain why I'm choosing Autumn over you."

The wipers are too loud against the windshield, and I turn down their urgency. The rain is slowing. The streetlights are on. I occupy myself with adjusting the air so that the windows don't fog.

"You should let me out," Sylvie says and clears her throat.

I glance from the road to her face. Tears stream down her cheeks. Her calm voice had disguised what the streetlights reveal.

"I'll take you home," I say quietly. The suburban road is empty. I turn on my blinker to make a U-turn.

Sylvie says, "No, I mean let me out here."

I make the turn anyway. Sylvie unbuckles her seat belt.

"Syl," I say as I drive toward her house, speeding up a bit. "Don't be ridiculous. I've been enough of a bastard already. I'm not letting you walk home in the rain."

"I just want to get away from you!" she screams.

I glance at her, but I'm not sure what happens after that. The road is wet, and the car is sliding. I try to brake and turn, but we're going too fast toward the ditch. We're spinning.

This could be it. This could be how I die.

We hit something.

Suddenly, everything is still.

What happened? I'm still alive. My face hurts. I touch my upper lip, and my hand comes away with blood. The airbags didn't go off. Did I hit my face on the steering wheel? Why is there glass?

I look to my right to—

Sylvie!

Where is she? Did she get out?

And then I see her.

On the other side of the low median we hit, sprawled across the wet asphalt.

She's crumpled. Surely broken.

I am...okay. I can move.

Get to Sylvie. Tell her to lie still.

Make the call.

Get Sylvie to the hospital.

Go home to Autumn.

148

With a plan in place, I climb out of the car and run across the rain-soaked pavement to her.

I fall to my knees in front of Sylvie, putting my hand to the ground. It's wet—

jack

one

"Phineas Smith is dead."

"Lexy," I say. It's too fucking early for her to call. It doesn't matter if we're sleeping together again. "Stop being a drama queen," I groan into the phone and roll over in bed.

"Jack. I'm not kidding."

"Lex, I don't care how pissed you and Sylvie are at him—"

"Finn died last night, Jack." She raises her voice. "That's what I'm telling you. He died. He's fucking dead."

I sit up.

"Bullshit." It's still too fucking early for Alexis to be calling me because Finn finally dumped Sylvie. The sun is hardly up.

"Finn's dead, Jack," she says. "I just got back from the hospital with Sylvie and her parents. There was an accident. Sylvie has a concussion, but Finn died."

"Bullshit," I say again, because it has to be. No. No?

"Yeah. Finn's gone." Alexis is crying. She's actually crying.

"Fuck," I say. "No. How?"

This can't be real.

This really can't be real.

Surely she's going to say that he's in a coma or clinically dead and on a ventilator, but there's still a chance? There's got to be some hope?

"What? I can't understand you, Lex."

I strain to listen. Outside, birds are singing. The sky is clear after the rain.

"How the fuck did Finn get electrocuted?"

It's like pounding my head against a wall, the way I'm trying to find the comfort or hope that's supposed to be in every bad situation. There is none.

Finn is dead.

I try to make it right.

Okay, I say to myself. *Finn is strong. He'll learn to live with—*

But no.

There has to be some way this can be undone.

But no.

This is death.

I hung up with Alexis a few minutes ago. I'm supposed to be getting ready to go by her place, but I'm sitting on my bed.

"Finn's dead," I say aloud.

We have to go back in time and fix this, I think.

Time travel is not an option. Except every problem in life has a solution. If you think hard enough, work hard enough, there's a solution. Right?

I need to tell Finn that he can break up with Sylvie over the phone. That's the solution.

But it's already done. He's gone.

My mind spins, trying, trying, trying to find a way out of this maze. There's got to be a way I can think this into not being true. Death is so final. Over. Done. Finn.

———————

"I'm going to his house," I say into my phone as I pull out of the driveway. My voice is shaking.

After I hung up with Alexis, I was frozen, staring at everything and nothing, trying to make sense of it. Then I called for my mother to come to my room like when I was a kid waking up after a nightmare. I didn't trust my legs to work.

Mom sat next to me on the bed and held me, and I told her the news. It's been years since I've held on to her like that, like I'm drowning. With six other brothers in the house, it took a serious injury to get one-on-one time with Mom. She stroked my hair, and as my sobbing slowed, I remembered the last time I'd needed her like this, when I'd cracked my shinbone in sixth grade. It had seemed like an eternal wait in the emergency room before I'd been given pain medication, though my mother had sworn it was only twenty minutes.

There's no medicine for this pain.

Eventually, Mom asked about Finn's mother, and I said I didn't know how she was. That got me out of bed. Mom was hesitant to approve my plan, but after I used her line back at her about Finn not being lucky enough to have a big family like *ours*, she told me to go ahead.

I pull the car out of the driveway and hold the phone against my shoulder with my cheek so I can use both hands to turn. Finn would tell me that using both hands doesn't make up for talking on the phone in the first place.

"But everyone is coming over here," Alexis says.

"I'm gonna check if his mom needs anything. I'll be by later. Are Vicky and Taylor there?"

"Yeah, b—"

"Lex, I'll be by. I should do this."

"Why?"

"I—He was my best friend, Lex. And she's been important to me. You know that." Alexis and I talked about deep stuff at least sometimes.

"Sorry, what? Jack, I gotta go. Everyone is arriving. I know. I can't believe—"

I hang up. Finn was right about Alexis and me.

Our last conversation.

It hits me again.

I won't be able to tell Finn that he was right about Alexis.

He'd called me to tell me that I was right about Autumn, or really, that I was wrong. He had a funny way of seeing it.

That had been last night—no, evening?

The day before that, I'd woken up in a blanket fort Finn had built for Autumn. They'd been snuggled into each other like litter-mates, Autumn snoring like a freight train.

Is she in love with him too, or is she an honest-to-God sociopath? I'd wondered as I watched them together.

I'd not put the odds in Finn's favor. So when he called to say she loved him back, I asked if he was sure.

"All the way sure," he said. He sounded so happy.

He's dead now.

Finn's dead.

But he can't be.

My breath quickens. I pull the car to the side of the road and rest my head against the steering wheel.

What if it was mistaken identity or a mix-up at the hospital?

Alexis said Sylvie saw him herself. Saw him dead.

Dead.

Finn.

This is a new world. Finn is dead.

I am numb.

Finn's driveway is a pain to get up and down because of the hill, so I park on the street and cross the lawn. His house looks the same as always, though his car isn't there.

Finn isn't going to be inside or upstairs or on his way home.

Finn is never coming home again.

With that thought, all the never-agains come crashing down on me, and I'm frozen in place, standing on the grass he'll never complain about mowing. He'll never kick another soccer ball or play a new video game. Finn will never tell me another story or joke. He'll never study for another test, eat another burger, roll his eyes at me, or watch that new superhero movie we were looking forward to in December.

It's all done.

Finn's story is over.

His whole life.

That was it.

Not even nineteen years, and he'll never, ever do anything else ever again. Finn won't go off to college or celebrate his birthday. He won't get another haircut or get the oil changed in his car. He won't bite a hangnail on his thumb or buy another CD. Finn Smith has done everything he will ever do.

He won't get to be with Autumn.

The memory of his joy last night hits me again.

The thing is I've always hated Autumn. The first time I met her, she was ignoring Finn on his birthday. Then she kept ignoring him for, I don't know, the next four years? It was only in the past two years that when he talked about her (when I'd tolerate it), it seemed like she'd warmed back up to him. Somewhat.

Then, suddenly, Autumn breaks up with Jamie and starts spending every minute with Finn. I was pretty sure that was proof she was as evil as I'd always suspected. But I had fun hanging out with him and Autumn those couple of times. I've always understood why Finn was so into her. I'd just never understood why he'd hung on so long when it was clearly never going to happen, and I was preparing myself to spend my first semester of college getting Finn through another Autumn abandonment.

So I hadn't really processed what Finn told me over the phone last night. It had seemed impossible, what Finn claimed had happened between them, but he'd been so sure, so happy. He was so certain that she loved him.

And he's dead now.

I can't ask Finn what made him certain. I can't ask him anything anymore. He's never going to have a thought to share because his brain is no longer thinking.

I was afraid that Autumn would break Finn's heart. Now I wish she had the chance. I wish he was inside, devastated by Autumn or perhaps severely injured in the accident. No matter how horrible, I wish Finn was able to feel something, anything.

I'm still standing in Finn's yard staring at the grass he'll never mow again. I don't know how long it's been when a woman's voice says, "Jack, right?"

It's Angelina's friend, Autumn's mother. Finn always called her Aunt Claire or something?

"Hi. Sorry," I say, though I'm not sure what for—being here or that Finn's not. "I was coming to see Angelina. If she needed...if I could do...something."

159

I feel like I'm pleading, but I'm not sure why.

She hugs me, and I start to cry in front of his house, in front of this woman I barely know, and she pats my hair like my mother did earlier this morning.

"I know," she says. "I know. I know. I know."

I can tell that she does understand in a way my own mother hadn't. She knows how unfair it is. How Finn is the last person who should be in some freak accident. How everyone loved him.

Then it's like a valve has shut off. My crying stops. I'm trying to get my breathing under control as she steps away from me.

She says, "Look at me," so I do. She stares into my eyes like she's trying to find her way inside my brain. "It's going to be like that for a while, okay? You'll be fine one minute and crying the next. You aren't losing your mind. This is too horrible to take in all at once. Do you understand?"

I nod, even though I only sort of do.

"Okay then." She pauses and looks me over for a moment before she says, "There is something you can do for Angelina, or rather for the two of us. I need to go to the hospital with Angelina. I can't let her do that alone. Can you stay with Autumn for us?"

She studies my face, and I slowly realize what Angelina is going to the hospital to do.

The body.

His body.

Finn.

Alexis said Finn had been declared dead on the scene. He hadn't

160

heard the zipper as the body bag closed over his face. There had been no sirens when the ambulance drove him away, because there was no more rushing, no more worrying over Finn. Unlike Sylvie's parents, Angelina would have been told to come when she could. I wonder who told her that: a policeman at the door, a phone call from the hospital? Did they explain to her how to find the morgue?

"Yeah," I say. "Sure." It sounds easy enough, and I'll do anything she tells me if she says it's for Finn's mom. I follow her around to the back of the house. I'm focused on Finn's body, his body that used to run next to me across the soccer field, now an item to be claimed like a piece of luggage.

Again, my mind wonders if it won't really be him. But then there is the problem of where the real Finn is and that Alexis said Sylvie saw him when she regained consciousness.

Finn is dead. I need to stop trying to find a way out of it.

As I walk into his house, a house he'll never walk into again, I'm overwhelmed by the smell of Finn. Not that he smelled bad but the way that everyone has a smell. It's part their shampoo or whatever and part them. I can smell Finn here in this house, though I'll never smell the whole of Finn again.

We ran together a lot, and not only at soccer practice. Because we both liked to run, the smell of his sweat mixed with his old-man deodorant was as familiar as our ribbing each other when we raced. I would give anything in the world for another run, another sniff of sweaty Finn.

I wasn't prepared for how the air of his home would affect me, let alone the pictures on the wall or the staircase where I slipped once and Finn diagnosed my sprained ankle. I should have expected it to be difficult to be here.

But I remind myself I am here for Angelina, and for the first time, I wonder why Autumn can't be alone.

I get the answer when I see her.

I guess I don't have any lingering doubts about Autumn's feelings for Finn. Her face is so swollen from crying that she almost doesn't look like herself. She's curled in a ball on the corner of the couch, chewing on her fingernails, staring at the floor like she's sleeping with her eyes open.

"Autumn?" her mother says.

Autumn's head turns robotically in our direction.

"I'm going to take Angelina to the hospital," her mother says.

Autumn winces.

"Jack's here. He came to see if we needed anything. Isn't that sweet?"

"Hi." Autumn's voice sounds terrible, so hoarse it's barely a rasp. Everything about her is flat and emotionless, like a garden statue that decades of rain have left with only the impression of a face.

I'm not sure what I'm supposed to do, but sitting on the opposite end of the couch seems appropriate. Her mother heads upstairs. When I look over at Autumn, she's staring at me.

"Hi," I say, since I'd not said it before. She continues to stare, and I start to feel uncomfortable.

"Who told you?" she finally asks. It sounds like it must be painful for her to speak.

"Alexis. Sylvie's parents called and asked her to come to the hospi—" I stop, but my reference to Sylvie doesn't seem to have upset her.

"How is she?"

"Alexis?"

Autumn laughs, coughs, and winces. "No," she chokes out. "Alexis is probably hosting an unofficial wake and making this all about herself." Her face tightens in a way I can't read. "I was asking about Sylvie."

"I don't know." I wonder if I should have called Sylvie and seen if she needed anything before coming here.

The stairs behind us creak, and I hear Angelina's voice from the back of the house.

"Autumn, Jack, I love you both so much, but if I see your faces right now, I'll cry. I have to go. I have to go. I have to go..." Angelina repeats, and Autumn's mother mumbles in soothing tones until the back door closes.

Autumn takes a shuddering breath.

I'm not sure why I came here except that it felt more appropriate than going to Alexis's house, where there'd be people who knew Finn but also hadn't.

Not like Autumn and I knew Finn.

I look over at her again.

She's back to staring at the rug and speaks without looking at me. "You can turn on the TV if you want."

"Thanks," I say. "Maybe in a minute."

Autumn returns to chewing on her nails. Her hair is a disheveled mess, and I can faintly smell her sweat. I don't know if she loved Finn anywhere close to as much as he loved her, but she loved him. I believe it now.

I'm trying to decide if I should say what I'm thinking. Nothing feels real, so it's hard to think clearly. Finally, I decide it's what he'd want me to do.

"You know," I say, "Finn called me last night on his way to pick her up."

Autumn looks up at me, startled.

"I thought you should know that he was really, really happy."

For the briefest of moments, joy lights her face, and then it burns out again.

"Yeah?" she whispers.

I clear my throat to get the tremble out. "He was so happy."

"I was afraid he would change his mind when he saw her," Autumn says. I can barely hear her.

"That—no—There's no way."

I don't know how to explain this to her. I don't know Autumn, not really, and this is such an intimate but vital thing that I need her to understand, for Finn's sake.

I push past the catch in my throat. "Nope. No way. Autumn, he's been in love with you for as long as I've known him."

Autumn looks at me with interest but not like she believes me.

I try again. "Like, fairy-tale love? Cartoon character with hearts floating all around him? Or a movie montage with the best song?

164

That's what you were to him." I'm sniffling, but I need to finish. "You were the biggest, most impossible dream for him." I press the tears away with my fingers before they can fall.

"You're sure?" They sound like the last words she'll be capable of speaking.

The tears I'd been fighting retreat as quickly as they'd overpowered me, like her mother had told me they would.

"Absolutely," I say.

Her shoulders relax slightly, and a little bit of tightness leaves her puffy face. I try her mother's technique.

"Look at me," I say, trying to sound firm.

She raises her eyes but not her face.

"Finn loved you," I say, confidently. "He was coming back to you. You can be certain of that."

"Okay," she says, but I don't hear it. Her voice is gone, and I only see it on her lips. Maybe a fraction of a percentage of her devastation has been eased. There's nothing I can do about the rest of it.

Eventually, I turn on the TV, and we sit in silence.

I wonder how long it takes to formally ID a body and sign papers.

Finn Smith in a morgue. His stupidly long legs and mop of blond hair will never be sweaty from running again. His body is cold.

The body that is Finn and not Finn, because Finn is gone.

I cry for a little bit, discretely brushing away tears and a few sniffles. I'm trying to be quiet, because I'm embarrassed. I stare in the direction of the TV and think I'm doing a pretty good job of hiding my emotion, but right as I've caught my breath, Autumn croaks.

"You were a good friend to him." She was waiting for me to finish. "I'm so glad he had you. You were a better friend than I was for the past few years." She coughs and strains to speak, then makes a sound like a laugh but maybe not. "The last third of his life," she finally gets out.

"Are you okay? Are you sick too?" I ask. "Or is that from crying?"

Her eyes get this faraway look, and it scares me somehow.

"I was screaming for a while," she says. "I was trying to make it not real by not believing it, and screaming worked...for a while."

I don't know what to say, but she doesn't seem to expect an answer. It seems like she's watching the TV again, but it also looks like she's been drugged. We're silent after that.

When their mothers return, I hug Angelina and stay a little while. She looks like she was in a car accident herself, but she's able to talk to me calmly for a few minutes before I go. Autumn's mother walks me to the front porch, and she thanks me for staying with Autumn.

"Ms. Davis, uh, is Autumn okay? I mean, none of us are okay, and I'm worried about Angelina too. It's just—" Suddenly I feel terrible for asking.

"Autumn will be okay, and so will you. We all will be." She looks at me the way she did when I arrived, but this time, I think she's trying to convince herself too. "Life can be and often is fiercely cruel," she continues. "You and Autumn have learned that a little younger than most, but you all, including Finny, would have had to

166

learn it eventually." Her voice falters. She takes a deep breath and gives me a weak smile. "Angelina and I already knew that about life. She—we've—losing a child is the worst, but we'll survive, because we must. We all will, including Autumn. Including you."

I nod because she needs me to, not because I agree.

"The arrangements still have to be made, but I'm sure we'll see you at the wake, Jack," she says before going inside. "Thanks again."

two

———

As I DRIVE TO ALEXIS'S house, a strange thing happens. It's like I'm watching myself. It's not an out-of-body experience; I can't see myself, but I don't make choices or feel any emotions. Everything I do is automatic and remote.

It isn't until after I've parked that I see that the street is crowded with cars. I've parked a few houses down from my normal spot.

I don't recognize the girl with the tear-streaked face who answers the door and points to the basement before heading to the bathroom. I guess she doesn't recognize me either.

In the basement there is, indeed, a strange, sad party of sorts going on, with so many more people than I would have thought. There is crying, and there is alcohol and weed mixed in with the crying, even though it's only noon, even though Alexis's parents could theoretically come home from work early and catch us all.

I wish I could tell Finn how seeing the foosball table makes me want to fall to my knees and sob, because he would think it was funny and make a joke about the times he kicked my ass on it. But if I could tell Finn anything at all, then it would be a meaningless foosball table. We'd never think of that table again after next year. Now I want to both kiss that foosball table and set it on fire so no one else can touch it since Finn's gone.

Before my thoughts can spiral, Alexis comes up to me and throws her arms around my neck as if we still love each other.

"I can't believe it's true," she says, as if only a few hours ago, she wasn't the one convincing me.

I pat her back with one hand as I scan the space. The feeling of living outside myself lingers. People are gathered in little knots around the room, speaking in low voices. Ricky from the soccer team is putting his hand on the shoulder of a girl who never gave him the time of day before.

"How are you doing?" Alexis asks me.

Jasmine steps closer to Ricky, and I think about Finn telling him to tone it down, we didn't need to hear all his thoughts on her body.

"Jack?" Alexis asks. She takes a step back, and my gaze pans the room before coming in for her close-up.

"It doesn't matter," I hear myself say.

Alexis nods. "Yeah, it really puts everything in perspective, doesn't it? Remember how I said my life was over when I was wait-listed for WashU? That seems so stupid now."

"Yeah," I say, as if she's responded to what I said. She's clearly been using the WashU line all night.

All day.

169

Light from the high basement window filters into the room, illuminating dust motes in the air. This nighttime atmosphere in the afternoon has an absurdity to it that suits this horrible situation. Nothing feels as it should.

Alexis is saying something to me, but all my focus is on trying to figure out how this moment can feel like déjà vu if Finn is dead.

"Yeah?" I say.

Alexis starts to reach for me, then seems to understand that I'm not up for pretending to be a couple. I note how easily she switches modes.

"Why don't I get you a beer?" she says.

After Alexis hands me a drink and goes off to play hostess elsewhere, I try to find a place to sit down, preferably alone.

My sense of detachment is gone, replaced entirely by a quiet horror. I've hung out with Finn and Sylvie so many times in this underground room. Is that the source of this new yet familiar feeling?

A few people greet me warily as I walk past. At least two people whisper, "his best friend," but I don't join any groups. I find a beanbag chair in the corner, far enough away from the nearest group that they don't feel the need to include me. I wipe the condensation off my hand holding the beer and take a sip. Talking with Alexis has brought back a snippet of dialogue from our phone call.

"Sylvie could see he was dead when she came to."

I try to focus on the golden light. I try to watch the dust motes and think about how, as a kid, I theorized that they were tiny planets and cosmos swirling in and out of existence. I figured our Milky Way was dust motes in some giant's world, our existence from the big bang onward as brief to those who observed us as the dust motes' dance seemed to me.

"What do you mean, Lex?"

"I probably shouldn't explain."

The girl who let me in upstairs crosses the room, and the dust motes swirl again like tiny, synchronized swimmers of air.

It's still the day of Finn's death.

"The electrical burns went all the way up his arm. That's what killed him, they said. From his hand through his arm to his heart, and that side of his face was—"

If Alexis said that Finn was pronounced dead right after midnight, did he die before midnight? I think again about the paramedics arriving, packaging him up, and delivering him to the hospital without urgency.

"Sylvie told me that when she saw his face, she wished she had died too."

I scan the room for Sylvie. Alexis said Sylvie, by some miracle, only had a concussion and was allowed to go home. She isn't here though. I think about finding Alexis and asking her if hosting this party is a better idea than being with her best friend after she almost died, but I know it's pointless, like everything with Alexis.

I won't be able to tell Finn he was right. But if he was alive, I'd probably still hook up with Alexis until I leave for college and over Christmas break, if she was up for it.

It seems so obvious now; it matters which people you spend time

171

with, and it matters how you spend your time, because you don't know how much you have.

I gaze around the room again. People are laughing or crying or talking, and they're all going to die. Maybe not today. Maybe not tomorrow. But they will die. Everyone they love will die too, and no one can stop it.

There was a book Finn and I read in class the year we met about a boy who sees an apple change, but he doesn't understand how it changed, only that it changed somehow, and later you find out that he's seen in black and white his whole life and was perceiving the red of the apple for the first time.

I'm looking around at all these people in the basement, and it's like I'm that boy in that book, except I'm seeing everyone as a future corpse.

All these people drinking and milling around, they are simply meat packed around skeletons. The tiniest amount of electricity—just the right amount!—runs through each of us, but it will stop someday. We will rot or be burned, but we will be disposed of in some manner.

We are all dead bodies that haven't died yet.

The apple was always red; the boy just couldn't see it.

I take a deep breath and look down at my own chest. I imagine my pink lungs under my white ribs, taking in the air, pushing it out, taking it in, pushing it out. I feel my fleshy heart beating, beating, working to deliver the oxygen from my lungs to my blood. I even feel my arteries pulsing, pushing, working.

I am alive.

I've always been alive.

But today I feel it.

I take another breath and hold it until my body begs for more, and then I let it out so that I can take another.

After a while, someone puts a song on repeat from the one depressing album Finn liked. I think about finding out who so that I can either punch them or hug them. He has that now, no alarms or surprises, like the song says.

Sudden pain strikes my toes, and I look up.

"Oh, sorry."

It's the crying girl from upstairs. She steps off my shoe and closer to her friends, who've congregated near the beanbag chair. She isn't crying anymore, but I still don't recognize her.

"I'll live," I say to no one in particular and flinch.

She doesn't notice my choice of words and turns back to her friends. Jacoby, Melissa, and Seth—I know them. Seth was on the team at least.

"Anyway," the girl I can't remember says, "I know that it's such a small thing, him having that pencil. But it was so nice of him, and it really was a terrific pencil."

"No, I get it," Seth says. "Everyone knew Finn was the nicest guy." They all murmur agreement.

Jacoby adds, "Yeah, he really was."

I want to ask him how they can talk about Finn being dead so easily, as if he's been gone forever.

"I should've saved that pencil to remind me to be nicer to people," the girl says somberly.

What right did you have to cry? I want to ask her. *Why are you here?*

Alexis's voice cuts through the conversations from across the room. "He loved her so much."

Is she speaking louder than everyone else, or do I pick her voice from the crowd because of its familiarity?

"They were the longest running couple of our class, right? Yeah." Alexis nods.

So that's going to be the story.

I don't know if Sylvie told Alexis that Finn was breaking up with her last night. Part of the reason I'd been pushing him to do something about it was because whenever Alexis and I hooked up, she asked questions that made me wonder if she knew something was up with Finn and Autumn.

But it doesn't matter now. Alexis is going with the happy couple story, and that's what will be repeated. By the time Sylvie is out and about again, that will already be gospel.

"No, he would never," Alexis is saying.

I take another sip and discover the beer I don't remember drinking is empty. I get up and walk past Alexis and the group she's talking to as I head to the recycling bin.

"I mean, I used to be friends with Autumn Davis. Whether she would flirt with him? That's a different story."

174

I suppose I could defend Autumn, but how? By interjecting that Finn had always loved a girl who was not his girlfriend?

Alexis's stance is starting to make sense to me.

Finn probably did one shitty thing his entire life, and it was cheating on Sylvie the day before he died. What could be gained by anyone knowing that Finn and Sylvie were breaking up that night? It's probably easier for Sylvie this way.

As I head back to my lonely corner with a new beer, I hear Alexis saying, "Ask anyone. Finn lived for taking care of Sylvie. That's probably why—"

I try to block her out as I settle back into the beanbag chair. The same knot of people hovers nearby. They aren't talking about Finn anymore. They're sharing stories about other people they know who have died, as if their grandparents' deaths mean anything compared to Finn dying.

In a flash, I figure out who she is, the girl who is no longer crying.

Last week of school, Finn and I were talking in class before the start bell. I asked him to loan me a pencil. When he gave it to me, he told me that he needed it back because it was "Maddie's pencil."

I'm not sure what my face did, but he hurried to explain.

"We've sat next to each other in trig all year, and most days, she's lost her pencil by last period. And you know how Ms. Fink is about not being prepared for class. I tried carrying an extra pencil for her, but sometimes I'd loan it out and forget to ask for it back."

Again, my face must have reacted because he rushed to finish.

"I told her to buy a box of pencils and give one to me, and that

175

would be her pencil in my bookbag that I would never loan to anyone else. She'd lost all those other pencils, but I still have this one, and there's a fifty-fifty chance that she'll need it today. If it was anyone but you, I would have lied and said I didn't have another pencil."

"Because this is Maddie's pencil?" I said.

"Exactly," Finn said.

If it had been anyone else, I would have asked how hot this Maddie person was, because, you know, why else would it have been his problem that she didn't have a pencil at the end of the day? But this was Finn, so of course he went out of his way to help someone simply because they sat next to each other in class.

Her comment about saving "that pencil" makes sense in another way, because of course he made sure she left with it at the end of the school year. It was her pencil.

Maddie, Jacoby, and Melissa aren't talking about death anymore. I could interrupt and tell them that Finn *did* loan out Maddie's terrific trig pencil to me once. So clearly, if she has the right to cry, then I should have the right to scream. Scream like Autumn had.

Or I could get up and tell Alexis, tell everyone, that Finn didn't live to take care of Sylvie, he lived as himself, and he was someone who took care of the people around him.

But it isn't Maddie's fault that I can't cry like her or scream like Autumn or even tell all my Finn stories like Alexis, who is busy making sure no one hears about the one shitty thing that Finn ever did.

"Autumn always had a thing for him, but she was like a sister to Finn," Alexis says.

I would laugh, but I can't. All I can do is sit here, sip my beer, and listen to people who barely knew Finn talk about him as if they were friends.

Finn isn't here, and for a moment, I'm envious of him.

three

Coach and some guys from the team are going to be pallbearers, and he asked us to all meet at the start of the wake to talk about how the funeral will go the next day. It feels like a huddle during a game, except we're standing in the parking lot of the funeral home, not on the field, and we're in khakis and suits instead of shorts. We hang our heads like we were getting a lecture after a bad play, though Coach's voice is gentler than I'd ever known it.

"Coffin is closed," he says. "No one asks why. In fact, no one says much of anything in front of the family, 'kay? I picked you boys for a reason. Make me proud."

There are nods and mumbles.

"No one is late tomorrow. Get here early. All right. See you then."

We start to disperse, but Coach calls my name, so I kick at the ground until the others are gone.

"How are you holding up?" he asks.

I've discovered this will be a thing going forward. I was briefly an adult after graduation, but I'm back to grown-ups checking in on me, telling me how the world works.

"I'll survive. We all will," I say, because I've been finding it a helpful mantra.

"That's good to hear," Coach says. "If tomorrow is too much for you or—"

I look up from the asphalt. "I wanna do it."

"I'm just letting you know, it's okay if you change your mind." He claps me on the shoulder. "See you inside."

My parents have come with me, and they're waiting by the car. I'm their seventh son, their last. My parents don't like each other much, but we're Catholic. Or they're Catholic. Point is, as far as my parents go, they love me, but they've done it all before and don't have the energy to have much of a relationship with me. Plus, if they leave their carefully constructed confines to spend time with me, they may encounter each other, which they've both ruled is not worth it.

So it's nice and awkward to have them both with me. I'm grateful, and I'm resentful, and meanwhile "Finn is dead, Finn is dead" is beating in my head like a drum. This knowledge pulsates through my body like it has the power to change the way my organs are arranged within me.

The parking lot is full. At first, I think there's another wake or funeral going on. The place is small and has two rooms. Both of my grandparents' funerals were here. I know it well.

But both rooms are for Finn. A line of people snakes along the wall from one room into the next like they're waiting for a ride at

Six Flags. A harried-looking employee in black asks if we are family, then directs us to the end of the line.

Like I said, I can see pretty much everyone I've ever known here. People who I didn't know even knew Finn and people I've never seen in my life, all waiting to say goodbye, to say *sorry, so sorry*.

I wish Finn could see this.

The thought opens a new wound, because I wish Finn had known that this many people cared about him.

He always blew it off when people said stuff like, "How are you the nicest person alive, Finn?" It was as if Finn didn't realize his consistent kindness added up for people. It is his default setting.

Was.

It's so hard to think about him in the past tense.

In history class, we read about these monks who would hit themselves while praying and go into ecstatic trances, and I could never understand that, but maybe I do now.

It hurts, yet it feels so good to think about Finn.

I can't stop tearing at the wound, because the wound is all I have left of him.

My parents murmur pleasantries to the other adults around them. A sort of knowing look passes between them, a *well, here we are* attitude, as if escorting a child through the death of a peer was an expected milestone.

Everyone agrees Finn was such a good kid, and they will agree forever, and nothing can ever change that.

People say only the good die young, but someone once told me it wasn't true, that we only remember the good things about those who die young. I don't know who is correct. I just know that Finn was good. I hope that years from now, all these people will remember Finn was helpful and kind because he was always those things—not because they forgot when he wasn't.

The line moves forward. I see kids I never expected to see again after graduation. I see kids I haven't seen in years because they went to private high school after middle school. Sometimes we raise our hands in a small wave. Some make the mistake of greeting others with an automatic "What's up?" or "How's it going?" before realizing the answer is all around us.

I look for Sylvie, even though I don't expect to see her. My instincts tell me that Sylvie won't come to this event, that she's saving her mental strength for the funeral.

I look around for Alexis and wonder if she felt her duty was done by holding her own wake, if she's at home hosting another morbid party. Maybe she's with Sylvie? I haven't heard from her.

Someone whose voice is unfamiliar to me is talking about how Finn told him it would be his job to keep a lid on the locker room talk next year during track season and how cool that was and how inspired he felt by that. I can't see his face, but he sounds young. It sort of sounds like something Finn would say but also not. I'm not sure what to make of it.

A funeral home employee approaches us, her golden name tag glinting in the warm light.

"Are you Jack Murphy?"

"Yeah?" I'm weirdly frightened.

"Are these your parents? Please come with me." She motions us out of the line. "The family asked for you."

We're clearly expected to follow her. It's strange, like being tapped to go backstage. My parents flank me in a way that feels formal. My dad puts his hand briefly on my shoulder as we walk.

The woman says, "I've worked kids' funerals before. I've never seen a line like this."

She means this to be comforting, but I don't know what to say in reply. *Thank you? How many kids have died this year?*

Then we are at the doors to the other room, and there it is. There he is.

And there he isn't, because Finn is gone, and the coffin is closed.

The employee points to Angelina standing by the coffin.

She stands by his picture, his senior portrait, taken in celebration. By his familiar face and flop of blond hair. His smile.

"They're expecting you," she says.

There's an odd aura around us as we approach. I feel so young, like I'm being escorted into kindergarten, and I'm resentful and grateful all over again. My parents shoulder themselves on either side of me, and I can tell all their focus is on me. They don't speak, but it's strange: the closer we get to the horrible box, to the grinning photograph of my friend that sits on top, it's like I can feel my parents saying to me, *See, Jack? This is death.*

I feel so small. I'm too young for this to be happening. My best friend can't be dead.

"Jack," Angelina says and hugs me.

I'm confused before I know why I'm confused. It isn't until she holds me away from her to look at me, as if it's been years since she's seen me, that I register she's smiling.

"How are you?"

"Fine," I say, even though it's not true.

Angelina doesn't look fine either. Though she doesn't look how I expected. There're tears shining in her eyes, yet her eyes are bright in a different, happier way. Her mouth twitches.

"He made a mark on a lot of people," she says with such certainty while looking at me for confirmation.

"Yeah," I say.

"Parents and kids have been telling me stories, things I'd never heard before." Her face crumples, but then it's like she pulls herself up over the edge of the cliff after hanging by her fingernails. She smiles at me. "He really was a good kid." She hugs me again, and over her shoulder, Finn is inside a gray and silver box, dead.

I cry, and his mother holds me.

Electricity ran through Finn's body, stopping his heart and burning him from the inside out, and I cannot unknow these things. I cannot stop from imagining his face.

I feel it again, the collision with that brick wall of "this must not be."

His mother lets go of me, and I realize I've stopped crying.

It feels like our mourning is all she has left of Finn. Our grief is proof of his life.

"I don't think I'll ever have a friend like him again," I tell her.

Angelina shakes her head a little. "You'll have another friendship like that, Jack, and you should." She pats my shoulder. "Just promise me that you'll never forget him."

"I couldn't."

And there it is again, the pained joy on her face. She turns to my parents and thanks us for coming. I am a child once more letting myself be led back to the car and driven home, sitting in the silence of the back seat.

For the first time, I wonder if I can do it tomorrow.

Carry his coffin.

Carry his body.

Place it over a hole where it—he—Finn, will stay forever.

four

_____

I HAVE TO DO IT. It's the last thing I'll get to do for my friend ever again.

I wake to that thought and hold it close all morning.

I'm doing this for Finn, I think as I get out of bed.

I'm doing this for Finn, I think as I put on my dress socks and shiny black shoes, as I shrug on my suit coat.

I drive myself to the funeral home early, for Finn, in case there's anything I can do to help.

I park and enter the building. I head to the room he will be in.

She's there.

Autumn sits on a stool next to his coffin, resting her cheek on its lid like it's his shoulder. She was talking when I walked in, but she falls silent and raises her head.

"I'm sorry," I say. It feels like I've walked in on them naked together, but Autumn shrugs and rests her head back on his box.

A few moments later, she asks, "Do you want to talk to him alone?" Her voice is still hoarse and quiet.

"No. I'm here in case…"

Autumn has closed her eyes as if she has forgotten I'm here.

"Should I go?"

"Only if you want to." Her nonchalance chills me. "We're just being close one last time." She presses her cheek against the gray metal, and my stomach twists.

"Autumn," I say, but she doesn't answer me. She's being with him. I watch her, worried to leave her alone but not alone. Minutes pass. I think she forgets that I'm standing by the door. She begins to whisper again, and I hear her giggle once.

"I love you too," she tells him in his box, and I bolt from the room.

I sit on the stiff couch in the hall. An employee asks if I'm here for the Smith memorial, and I tell him I'm a pallbearer. He tells me what I already knew: I'm early, and I should keep waiting where I am.

Before people start arriving, Autumn creeps out of the room. She's wearing jeans and a T-shirt. She looks at me as she passes, like she isn't sure if she should say anything to me or not.

"Where are you going?" I ask.

"I'm letting Sylvie have the funeral," she says over her shoulder. "It only seems fair. My dad and I are going to the art museum instead. Finny wouldn't want Dad at his funeral anyway. I'll go by the graveyard later and make sure he's settled in."

And then she strolls out.

five

ALL THROUGH THE MEMORIAL, THE image of Autumn nuzzled against Finn's coffin, her face against the cold metal, haunts me. I hear her absence in the stories people tell, even as I laugh and grieve with them. Finn feels so alive with all these people here. It's Autumn who is the ghost.

Sylvie sits in the front row in between Angelina and a man who must be Finn's father. I can only see the back of his blond head and a bit of his profile. His shoulders are tense, but they do not shake. He seems to stare ahead, unwavering, at whoever is speaking about the son he barely knew.

People talk about Finn, and they cry. They talk about Finn, and they laugh. Everyone is united in missing Finn, but I don't understand how everyone can act like this is all so ordinary. As if Finn being dead is logical.

There aren't as many people at the funeral as at the wake, but it's more than I expected. Jamie Allen, Autumn's ex, is there with a girl

I'm pretty sure Autumn used to be pretty close with, though it looks like she's pretty close with Jamie now. Finn had told me about the situation with her friends. They keep looking around and whispering. Maybe they're looking for Autumn.

Then the funeral director gives us a signal. The guys from the team and I all stand. We're done talking about Finn. It's time to put him away.

Before the memorial started, the funeral director explained how we would lift the casket together, but it feels like being in a play unrehearsed. We get through it though. One guy behind me stumbles, and for a second, I wonder if Finn felt the tilt, but then I have to bite my lip to keep from crying when I remember that Finn couldn't. It's done. He's on my shoulder. Finn. Inside this box is Finn, was Finn, and his head is probably near my own. As we walk him to the hearse, I hear Autumn's voice, *We're just being close one last time*.

This will be Finn's last car ride. The doors close behind the coffin, and my parents ask me if I will be okay if they skip the graveyard service.

I tell them that it's okay, even though none of this is okay, because their being there wouldn't make it any easier.

I ride with Coach to the graveyard. He asks me if I want to talk. I say no.

We follow the hearse to Bellefontaine Cemetery. Past the gates, the hearse travels down a long path past the mausoleums, some the size of houses, some like sheds of stone. Finn was the only one in class to get the extra credit question on the American Literature final, *What icon of the Beat Generation is buried in St. Louis's own Bellefontaine Cemetery?* He shrugged when I asked him how he remembered, and we never imagined he'd soon have something in common with Burroughs.

We pull up to a newer, more open part of the cemetery. No grand mausoleums here, simply headstones standing tall, for now.

We line up as a team again and lift him with more grace than before. This time, I try to cherish the weight of him on my shoulder. I lean my cheek where I hope is close to his.

And then on a quiet count to three, we set Finn down forever.

There is crying again but no more laughing.

In the row of chairs by the grave, the man who was supposed to be Finn's father sits, leaning forward with his head in his hands, and does not look up even once. Sylvie, seated next to him again, sits ramrod straight, like her purpose is to be a wall between him and Angelina. Perhaps it is.

I knew the poem about an athlete dying young was coming. I hadn't known how different it would sound as Coach read it here, by Finn's grave.

His final resting place. His final everything.

They're about to do it.

There's a mechanical hum as his coffin is lowered down.

It's not really him, yet it is him, and they're putting him away forever. I want to beg someone to stop this, to let me keep him, please.

But it's done. Finn, my friend, is in a hole in the earth. For the rest of my life, no matter how long I live, I will always know exactly where he is, because he's never going to move again.

People are lining up to throw a handful of dirt in the hole before they leave him, but I can't do this last thing for him, so I stand there and watch.

As the grave begins to slowly fill with dirt, I think of Autumn coming later, after the rest of us have gone, to be with him.

six

—

I WATCH AS THE LINE of people who have waited to talk to Angelina slowly winds down. Alexis met my eyes before she left, but we never spoke. When Coach was leaving, I told him there was something I needed to do, that I'd get a ride home from someone else. I don't know what I'm waiting for though. I don't need to say anything to her or Autumn's mom, and my duties are finished. Finn is in his grave.

I take off my jacket and tie, unbutton my collar.

Compared to the August heat, the metal of his coffin had felt so cool against my cheek.

I wonder how Angelina does it, comforting these people, mostly kids from school but a few adults too. They are waiting to shake her hand or give her a hug or share some sentiment, and her child is not fully buried a few feet away.

Autumn's mother stands protectively by her. I figure if Angelina wasn't getting anything out of talking to these people, she'd take her friend home.

"Are you waiting to talk to her?" Sylvie asks.

I jump because I had no idea that she was nearby, much less standing behind me. I'd wandered away a bit, and Sylvie and I are on a small slope among some graves from the 1970s.

"No," I say. "I wasn't ready to go. Are you?"

"No," she says. There's a bruise near her temple and a scratch along her cheek. Otherwise, she is outwardly, physically unmarked from the crash. Her blond hair is pulled back and up in a way that I'm sure has a special name. Her trim black suit probably has a French name on the label.

"I thought about texting or something," I say by way of apology, but Sylvie shrugs.

"Nothing was your fault," she says.

"Still, I could have said something." I'm not sure if we're talking about the crash or Autumn.

"You don't have to pretend that we were more than friends of convenience, Jack. I'm tired of people pretending to care more about me than they do."

"Geez, Sylv," I say. It's not that I think she and I would have naturally gravitated toward each other, but in the past four years, I'd come to think of us as comrades of sorts.

"Sorry," she says, which is more than what I said to her, but I decide to call her out on what was truly shitty in what she said.

"Finn didn't pretend anything about his feelings for you," I say. "He lied about his feelings for Autumn, but he loved you."

"Just not enough?"

192

"I—" I'm regretting not letting this go. "I don't think it was about 'enough,' Sylv."

She laughs, startling me again. I look at her. She isn't smiling, and her eyes are closed.

"That's what he said."

"Yeah?" I'm distracted, because I'll never know his side of that conversation. "What did you say to that?"

She shakes her head. "I can't remember." She opens her eyes. "The good news is the doctors say it's dissociative amnesia, not retrograde amnesia, which means that my not remembering the minutes before or after the accident isn't brain damage. I'm protecting myself, according to them." She laughs the same cold laugh, and for a moment, she looks like Autumn did on the couch, but she takes a deep breath, and it clears.

I shouldn't ask her, but it's bothering me, how Alexis described the scene to me in detail...but Sylvie's memory isn't complete about that night.

"Alexis said that you saw him when you woke up and called 911."

Sylvie doesn't laugh this time.

"That's what they tell me, but I don't remember making the call." She shakes her head. "I remember telling a paramedic that I knew Finn was dead because of his face. But later at the hospital, when the police tried to get a statement from me, I couldn't remember waking up or his face. They did all the brain scans, and it's a regular concussion. Apparently, when I'm ready, I'll remember."

"Oh," I say. "Can you choose to never be ready?" I'm being sincere, but she laughs again, and this time, it's real.

"I'll have to ask my new therapist," she says.

"What happened to the guy Finn liked?"

She sighs. "Dr. Giles always hated Finn."

The idea of anyone hating Finn silences me.

In the distance, Angelina and Autumn's mom are walking to the limo together, their arms around each other's waists. Soon, Sylvie and I will be the only ones here: us, Finn, and all the other dead people like him.

"Maybe 'hate' is too strong of a word," Sylvie continues, "but Dr. Giles didn't trust Finn. Plus he said Finn seemed codependent. That was part of the reason he thought I should go away for the summer. To give me space to take care of myself." Sylvie shrugs. "Dr. Giles and I agreed that after all the progress I'd made dealing with…other things, perhaps it would be best for me to start fresh with someone who didn't have preconceived notions about Finn, since he's going to be the focus of my appointments for a long time."

"Huh," I say.

Sylvie looks down the slope. Together we watch the limo drive off.

What a betrayal it is that Alexis told me that stuff about Sylvie and some teacher from her old school. I'd only half been listening, and part of me had wondered why she was telling me all that, but mostly I had been thinking about Alexis's body and not about whether she was a good friend.

Sylvie starts walking down the hill, away from Finn's grave, into the older parts of the cemetery, and I follow.

"It's funny," I say, simply to say something. "I was thinking about how no one could hate Finn, and you say your doctor at least hypothetically disliked him."

"Oh, I hate Finn," Sylvie assures me. She smiles softly at my shock. "Don't get me wrong. I love him too. If I had the power to stop loving him, I would have long ago. So I love him, and I hate him."

"I guess." I want to defend Finn, but this time, I can't. "I guess that's fair."

Sylvie smiles again and shakes her head. She stops walking.

"Jack, if you really are my friend, can you do something for me?"

"I mean," I say, "if I really am your friend, can you stop questioning it like that?"

"That's fair," Sylvie says, and I'm not sure she notices I was joking. "If I stop questioning our friendship, will you stop falling for Alexis's bullshit?"

"I–I thought Alexis was your friend?"

"Yes," Sylvie says. "But she has a lot of growing up to do."

I know Sylvie well enough to know that there's no point in reminding her that Alexis is two weeks older than her. Besides, she's right; Alexis hasn't matured much in the past four years. It's such a simple thing, but it explains so much about Alexis, not to mention my relationship with her, that I'm too stunned to say more than, "Yeah."

"I mean," Sylvie continues, "you'd outgrown her before junior year had even started."

We're on a gravel path now, and I'm matching Sylvie's brisk pace. Apparently, we're taking a walk together.

"Yeah," I say again for the same reason.

This time, she must hear it in my tone, because she says, "Didn't you notice how all your fights were because you'd said something she didn't want to admit was true?"

"I'm going to be honest with you, Sylv," I say. "I never knew what any of my fights with Lexy were about."

"That's okay," she laughs. "Lexy never knew either, but she didn't know that she didn't know."

"It sounds like you outgrew her too," I say.

Sylvie shrugs and keeps striding forward.

I add, "I'm seeing a lot about Alexis clearly. She's not always been a good friend to you."

Sylvie looks at me differently than I think she has before.

"Noted," she says.

The gravel crunches under our feet.

I feel like I should say something profound, something I can quote from Finn that will make her pain less complicated. If this were a movie, there would be a convenient flashback to tell me what memory to share with Sylvie, but nothing comes to mind.

Suddenly we're not walking anymore. I had noticed Sylvie pausing, and I'd thought she was taking off her jacket. But she pulls out a computer printout of a map and studies it, brow furrowed.

"Are you looking for, uh, William Burroughs's grave?" I ask.

Sylvie looks at me blankly.

196

"The writer? He's buried here."

"No." Sylvie says. "He was a junkie who shot his wife." She folds the map and puts it into her jacket, which she is still wearing in this heat. "I was going to see Sara Teasdale's grave. She was a poet." She continues on at the same brisk pace as before.

"You never seemed like a poetry fan. Like, at all?"

We're walking on the path again, but she veers off to the right.

"I'm not," Sylvie says. "Generally I find poetry tedious. But I like Teasdale's poems. Unlike most poets, she knew how to get to the point. And since I was going to be here anyway..." She trails off as we leave the gravel for the grass.

Sylvie counts the headstones we pass under her breath as I follow behind. I think about a hundred years ago, when these graves were new, how they'd been important, how people had come here to weep and remember. I wonder if Finn's headstone will, one day, be nothing more to anyone than a marker to be counted to find someone else's final resting place.

"Here it is. Oh."

At first, I don't understand, and then I see it.

Sara Teasdale was born on August 8, 1884.

"I didn't know her birthday," Sylvie says.

"Just a coincidence," I say.

She shrugs and stares at the date.

"What's your favorite poem of hers?" I try.

She smiles in a way that lets me know that I haven't changed the topic how I'd hoped.

Sylvie closes her eyes before reciting.

"Now while my lips are living,
Their words must stay unsaid,
And will my soul remember
To speak when I am dead?

Yet if my soul remembered
You would not heed it, dear,
For now you must not listen,
And then you could not hear."

Sylvie doesn't open her eyes; she stands there. The heat has finally gotten to her, and her face has a pink and dewy glow that makes her look like she's been crying, even though I'm pretty sure she's hasn't been.

"Is that it?"

Sylvie opens her eyes and blinks at me.

"It seemed complete, but it was so short."

"I told you she knew how to get to the point," Sylvie says. Finally, she takes off her jacket. "I found her book on the English language shelf in a used bookstore in Paris. I read that poem and bought the book." She folds her jacket over her arm and sighs. "I read it cover to cover twice on the train to Berlin."

"You know," I'm not sure what I'm about to say, though it feels important. "Finn would love this. You planning to visit the grave of the one poet you thought wasn't bullshit after his funeral." I rush to say, "He wouldn't love that he was…you know, having a funeral." I can tell Sylvie's trying to follow along, so I continue. "But if he had to have a funeral, he would love that you were doing this afterward. Are doing it."

"Because it's the sort of thing Autumn would do?" She raises her chin and looks me in the eyes.

I shake my head. "She wouldn't have a map. Or she would lose the map or get lost even with the map." I wave Autumn's ghost away with my hands. "But, Sylv, my point was Finn would have loved you having that map in your jacket pocket all through his funeral. He would have loved you saying that, unlike other poets, this one knew how to get to the point. He loved you."

Sylvie is back to staring at the grave. "But not the way he loved her."

I can't argue with that. More than anyone, I can't argue with it, so I join her in staring at the date on the grave.

The wind picks up, giving some relief. There are so many old trees in this part of the cemetery, and the rustle of the leaves is so loud I can barely hear her say, "Where was she?"

"Autumn?"

Sylvie nods. "I thought about asking Angelina, but I could tell she knew that Finn and I were breaking up that night and why. It felt better not to ask."

"Autumn told me that she felt you should have the funeral." It hadn't made sense to me when Autumn said it, and I don't expect it to make sense to Sylvie, but she nods.

"I didn't expect that of her," she says.

We're quiet again. The wind is starting to feel like the beginning of an afternoon storm. We won't be able to stay much longer.

"Um, you didn't want to be alone with your poet or anything, did you?"

"My poet?" Sylvie cracks another sad smile. "She was the first poet to ever win a Pulitzer, so she's hardly 'mine.' But no and thank you for asking." She pauses. "You need a ride home, don't you?"

"Um, yeah?" I say. "Sorry. I didn't plan my day well."

"Most people don't," Sylvie says as she puts her jacket on again. She touches the poet's headstone with two fingers. "All right, let's go," she says to me.

Sylvie remembers the way back to Finn's grave without checking her map. By the time we return to the site, the rain is starting, and we hurry past him and to her car. It feels like a betrayal to leave him in the rain.

Inside her car, I open my mouth to ask Sylvie if she's sure she wants to drive in the rain, but before I can, she says, "In case you're going to offer to drive, the reason I drove separately from my parents is because I can't ride in a car driven by anyone else. I'll be fine. Put on your seat belt."

I look back as she drives us away from him, but I comfort myself remembering Autumn will come by later to see that Finn is settled in.

seven

A WEEK AFTER THE FUNERAL, I get a text from Charlie, my next oldest brother and therefore, by Murphy tradition, the one responsible for things like getting me off the kindergarten bus and teaching me to drive.

Mom says you're not running.

Translation: Are you okay?
I text back.

Been hot. Busy packing for the dorm.

Translation: I'm fine.
Charlie replies.

Mom also said you hadn't packed at all.

Translation: Bullshit.

I'll go running later today.

Translation: I'm fine.

Mom asked me to come home and help you pack.

Translation: Bullshit.

I'll get her off your back.

Translation: I'll get it together.

OK. Same. Go run.

Translation: I'll tell Mom you're fine but don't make a liar out of me.

So now I have to go for a run.

The reason I hadn't gone for a run yet was because I knew I was going to have to find a place. It's not like I only went running with Finn. We went running together a few times a month. Finn liked to go to different places to run, for scenery or whatever. I always thought it was stupid to drive somewhere to run, so he'd invite

Sylvie when he wanted to go running at a sculpture park or a nature reserve.

But sometimes, he'd call or text me and say he wanted to go running right that moment, and I wanted to be running already, and we would meet at the halfway point between our houses and just *go*.

We would run all over Ferguson. There isn't a street within running distance of my home that isn't painted in memories of trash-talking with Finn, pushing myself to go harder because of him, or giving myself a break because he said it was okay.

So that's why I was putting this off. Now I have to drive somewhere to go running, which is stupid. But here I am putting on my running clothes and getting into my car as if there isn't a perfectly good sidewalk outside. I went with Alexis to her cousin's birthday party last May at this gazebo in a park, and I'm pretty sure it had a path around a lake or something, so I drive in the direction I remember the park being in until, to my surprise, I find it.

So fine. I'll go running.

I'm not going to stretch any more than I normally would, though Finn was always saying I didn't stretch enough. Just because he's dead doesn't mean everything he ever said has to be right.

After a normal amount of stretching, I'm off and it's fine.

But obviously I'm thinking about Finn since it's the first run.

Because he won't run again.

I feel like Finn's death has rattled my brain. How many times am I going to remember that being dead means you're never going to do shit again?

I should have checked how many times around this lake makes a mile. The gravel spread over the dirt path is ground down and causing more slippage than absorbing impact. This will be a stamina run, not a speed run. And that's fine. I didn't check the time before I started, and I'll have no idea when I've hit my first mile.

"Let's run and not worry about why," Finn would say, and we would just *go*.

Fuck. Fuck. Fuck.

Why couldn't he have stayed in the car? What did he think he was going to do? Save Sylvie with his bare hands? I mean, fine, this one time, we were watching a TV show, and he was all like, "That's not how you do CPR."

I said I figured somebody had looked it up before filming, but Finn started going on about how she'd never break through his sternum in that position. I said they probably wouldn't have gotten the cleavage shot in the position he was describing. He glanced at the screen and said, "Oh right," in this disappointed tone, as if the show had failed him by choosing boobs over accurate first aid. Which was weird, because I knew for a fact that he liked that actress's boobs.

So maybe Finn could have done CPR on Sylvie if she had needed it.

I'm starting my second time around the lake. It doesn't feel like I've been running for even a quarter of a mile.

Still, Finn should have been more careful.

That's the other thing that pisses me off. He was an annoyingly safe driver. What the fuck happened? Being in his car when it was raining was torture. He was so paranoid about it.

204

Suddenly, I realize who I should be angry at.

Finn once made us wait forty minutes because Kyle wouldn't put on his seat belt. Admittedly, Kyle is a bigger asshole than normal when he's drunk, and it was funny seeing him lose it when Finn said, "I'll just text my mom that a jerk in my back seat wouldn't put on his seat belt. She won't be mad if we sit here all night. Let's do it."

But my point is why didn't Sylvie have on her seat belt?

Until now, the whole "and Sylvie went through the windshield but is fine" thing has kinda run through my brain without being examined.

For that to have happened, her seat belt had to be off, and Finn never drove an unbuckled passenger.

Sylvie says she can't remember the last few minutes before the accident.

For about six yards or so, I wonder if she murdered Finn, but all the pieces of the puzzle are too random to be orchestrated.

It was evening when he called me. He died around midnight.

Finn would have wanted to find some kind of resolution with Sylvie, and she wasn't going to let him off easy, so after hours of driving, he must've been distracted or tired enough to spin out and hit that median. But why was her seat belt off?

I stop midstep and almost trip but catch myself and pull out my phone. Before thinking about what I'm doing, I pull up Sylvie's name and type Why weren't you wearing a seat belt?

I go back to running and let that anger course through me.

205

Why.

Weren't.

You?

I let that question be my only thought, over and over again, until the words become meaningless. I keep running until there is no more anger, no more thinking, only my breathing, only telling myself to keep pushing. I keep running, and I keep running, and I just *go*.

I don't consciously choose to stop; I think my body must demand it, because I stop short in a way that Finn would remind me was bad for my circulation.

I check the time. I've been running for forty-five minutes, and I have four messages from Sylvie.

Forty minutes ago:

I told you. I can't remember.

Five minutes after that:

I'm sorry.

Eleven minutes ago:

Even if I can't remember, it's still my fault.

And a minute after that:

I'm sorry, Jack.

Translation: I'm an asshole.

I stare at her last message, still gulping air. A drop of my sweat drips on the screen and blurs her words. What would Finn say to her?

It was the rain's fault, I type and hit Send.

She doesn't reply.

eight

———

I PROBABLY SHOULD HAVE CALLED instead of showing up like this. Coach shifts from one foot to the other and glances at the team running around the track.

The team that I'm no longer on.

Something Finn and I have in common.

"Technically," Coach says, "you're not supposed to be on campus. Once you've graduated, it's like you're any other adult, and those students' parents have entrusted me to not allow some random adult access to their child."

I stand there, feeling very much not like an adult.

Coach glances at the team again.

I just want someone to yell at me to hustle so that my brain can shut up. I want to use all my effort to make my body do something it doesn't want to do so that I don't have to stop it from thinking about things that I don't want to think about.

"Here's what we're gonna do," Coach says. "I'll fudge the

paperwork so that it says you were cleared to be a volunteer this summer."

He's using his pregame voice with me, and I feel my spine straighten in response.

"But you need to show me that you understand I'm putting my neck out for you, Murphy. Do you know what I mean?"

"Yes, sir," I say as relief washes through me. This I know. This I understand. This isn't like recent dinners with Mom and Dad when they want to know what I'm thinking and feeling for the first time I can remember. This is Coach telling me to shape up or ship out. This I know.

I join the team on the track seamlessly.

"Oh. Hey, Murphy," Ricky says, but no one else speaks. Everyone is focused on their own pace.

I'm part of the crowd. We are one breathing, moving organism, circling the track, again and again.

I breathe in with Ricky and out with Jamal.

My mind is a blissful runner's blank.

When Coach blows the whistle, I could still run for longer, and my mind remembers that Finn isn't with us, and I can't go running without him, but then Coach shouts, "Box jumps!" and all I can think about is how much I hate box jumps.

I hate box jumps.

I really hate box jumps.

Really, really hate box jumps.

Oh, and high knees now? Fuck high knees.

Fuck Coach for saying that we're doing high knees for four minutes straight.

Four fucking minutes.

The only thing I hate more than high knees are shuttle runs.

Which are probably coming up next, now that I think about it.

How has it not been four minutes yet?

Finn and I used to argue about which was worse, shuttle runs or high knees.

Doesn't matter though, because we aren't doing shuttle runs. We're doing squats.

Fuck squats.

So it goes.

———————

It's at the end of the day, when Coach yells, "Showers!" that my brain short-circuits. The feeling I had in Alexis's basement returns, and I'm watching myself.

Finn is dead.

High school is over.

I stand and watch as the kids jog to the locker room. Coach turns and sees me and opens his mouth to yell at me before he remembers. I take a step forward.

"I, uh, think I'm going to head home to shower?" I can't believe that I'm allowed to say that.

Coach nods. "Do you think you'll be back tomorrow or next week?"

"No," I say. "I got what I needed today. Next week, I leave for school, and I'll have places to run there that don't…" I was similarly inarticulate when I showed up three hours ago, but he understands this time too.

"The only way out is through," he says, nodding. It's something Coach has said a lot over the years, but it's always been when one guy was surrounded and he needed to push his way out before the ball got stolen.

But it makes sense here and now too.

"Yeah," I say. "I think I just realized that."

He claps me on the back once, then makes a face and laughs at how wet my shirt is as he wipes his hand on his jeans.

"Go get that shower, Murphy," he says. "Go off to school. You'll find the way through."

It's not that I feel better as I drive away, but I feel more hopeful that what he said was true.

nine

———

A FEW DAYS LATER, I take a break from packing my room and see that I have a voicemail.

"Hey, Jack," Angelina says. "It's Finn's mom."

I can tell she wasn't saying that because she thought I wouldn't recognize her voice or know who she was, but because she wanted to say his name, claim him. I swallow the lump in my throat and try to focus on the point of her call. She's selling Finn's car, but the garage said there were personal effects that needed to be removed. Would I help?

I'm surprised. Finn kept his car so clean that it became a joke on the soccer team. I call her back and get the address of the garage where his car was towed after the accident. They say I can come by today if that works for me, and it's a task I want to get over with, so I head over.

———

The man leading me out to the lot seems to have no idea that tragedy has struck.

As he unlocks the gate, he turns to me and says, "Damage was minimal. You sure your mom wants to sell?"

I shrug.

I'm holding Finn's key chain, one of the last things he ever touched. I squeeze it and think about time travel again. It would be so easy to save Finn's life if it weren't for time and space.

"So, uh, if you're sure you don't want us to fix her up, empty her out, and we'll have you sign something for your mom in our office."

I don't bother correcting him before he walks away.

Finn's little red car.

Like being in his house, I should have expected this flood of memories.

There's the first time I saw this car: Finn, proud but embarrassed to be proud, driving me around the block once before dinner because my mom was only letting me go because she had a soft spot for Finn.

The late nights after a party, the early mornings before soccer practice.

Sometimes we bickered. Sometimes we laughed.

Mostly, we listened to music and didn't realize that we had a limited time together.

Maybe if I had known that it would be this hard, I wouldn't have come. But who would?

And then there's the hole in the windshield.

Looking at it makes me feel like I saw Sylvie fly through it.

How did she live?

I remind myself that one life wasn't exchanged for another. Had Sylvie died on impact, Finn would still have run to her, would still have been so anxious that he didn't see the downed power line in the puddle next to Sylvie.

I take a deep breath and do what I came to do.

There isn't much. I grab his stack of CDs and an umbrella from the front. From the trunk, I retrieve his jumper cables and first aid kit. There're taco and candy wrappers in the back seat, which is a surprise bordering on shock. It's only because of those wrappers that I look underneath the front seat.

Then I see the bag.

As I pull it out, even though I know it's not drugs, the thought still crosses my mind, given it was concealed and wrapped so carefully.

It quickly becomes obvious why he had hidden the bag.

He'd said that he was running an errand before getting Sylvie.

He'd said he was "all the way sure" that Autumn loved him.

It also explains why there was trash in Finn Smith's car.

Suddenly, I hate that girl so much. Autumn was the reason Finn was breaking up with Sylvie and driving in the rain. She was the reason he was distracted that night.

If he hadn't been cheating on Sylvie the night before, Finn probably would have told her that they needed to go home, that they could talk on the phone the following day. But his guilt—his guilt over what Autumn had gotten him to do—had kept him out all night, even though it was getting late, even though it was raining hard and he hated driving in the rain.

If you took Autumn out of the equation, Finn would still be alive.

With a paper sack full of the meager items left in Finn's little red car, I leave the garage and call Finn's mom. She asks if I can come by, so I drive to Finn's house.

She looks thinner and like she hasn't been sleeping well, but Angelina's smile is genuine. She opens the screen door for me, and I go into the foyer. I normally wouldn't have gone so long without seeing her. I can't remember the last time that a week went by without me being at Finn's house. Hugging Angelina feels natural, even though it was something we never did when he was alive.

"Thank you," she says. "I hope that wasn't too much to ask."

"No," I say. "I'm glad to help. There was an umbrella in the car that had French words printed on it. I thought that was probably Sylvie's, but I brought the rest of the stuff." I hand her the paper sack.

She looks inside it for a moment. "Would you listen to the CDs, Jack?"

I nod. "Thank you."

She hands me the stack of CDs and then takes out the first aid kit. She holds it tenderly in her hands. A shadow crosses her face. "If only," she whispers. And I understand.

If only this could have somehow saved him. If only his cautious nature had somehow saved him.

"At first," she says, still looking at it, "I thought I would be the sort of parent who turned their child's room into a museum, leaving every object exactly as he left it, right down to the jeans on the floor, you know?"

I don't know. It never occurred to me that there were enough parents out there with dead kids for there to be different types of them. It seems like a whole secret world of people I never considered. Before I can think on it much, Angelina continues.

"But I saw someone at a stoplight asking for change the other day, and he was wearing pants that were too short, and I thought, *He needs pants like Finny's*, and I knew what he would have wanted me to do. It's his stuff, so if that's what Finny would have wanted, it's what I should do." She looks up at me, and I nod.

"I could drop off stuff or..." I trail off as Angelina frowns.

"Autumn isn't ready to let go of a lot of things in Finny's room yet. When I told her about wanting to donate Finn's clothes... Well, she knows that I'm donating them by Christmas, and she's keeping the jeans that were on his floor." She shakes her head. "I'm sorry. The point of this was to say that I'll keep the first aid kit in my car, but do you need a pair of jumper cables?"

"Yeah, actually." Finn had mentioned once or twice that I should have some and a first aid kit, but he'd have settled for jumper cables at least.

"I'd like to think of you using them," Angelina says. "Not that I wish you car trouble, but like the CDs and his clothes, I want his things out there in the world, being used."

"Yeah, I get that," I say. "I hope Autumn lets you do want you want with his stuff."

216

Another shadow crosses her face.

"Autumn is having a hard time accepting the reality of the situation," she says. "It's not that she wouldn't let me. It's that…" Her voice trails off again, like she's watching a scene play out in her mind. Angelina bites her lip and shakes her head. "I'm sorry, Jack. Autumn will be fine in time. I think I worry even more about her now because I can't worry about him, you know?" For the first time since she opened the door, tears come to her eyes.

"She's coming to Springfield, right?"

Angelina shakes her head. "Maybe next year. Autumn needs more time," she repeats.

"Oh," I say.

"I'm so excited for you, Jack." Angelina's trying to change the tone of our conversation. "College will be good for you. It's a whole new world."

"Yeah." I try to match her upbeat tone.

"And next year, you'll be able to show Autumn the ropes, hmm?" She tries to smile.

"Of course," I say. "Um, tell her I said hi?"

"I will." Angelina reaches out like she's going to stroke my hair, then she rests her hand on my shoulder. "Thank you for being such a good friend to us all."

Perhaps I'm not as good as she thinks, because I don't tell her about the plastic bag under the seat that was meant for Autumn.

I don't take it next door to her. I don't throw it out either.

I put Finn's jumper cables in my trunk and leave his gift for

Autumn hidden under my driver's seat, the way it had been hidden in his car. I can't get rid of it. It tethers him to this world, but it's also a symbol of how chasing her had killed him in the end.

Autumn will be fine without it. Angelina said so.

ten

It isn't until I get Alexis's text saying we need to talk that it occurs to me we haven't broken up yet. Somehow, the fact that we never officially got back together doesn't change the fact that we need to officially un-together ourselves. So I agree to meet her at the coffee shop in Ferguson.

I didn't put much thought into it, but apparently Alexis did.

As soon as I see her waiting for me at a table in the center of the room, I can tell something is off. For one thing, Alexis is always late. Something about the way her collar is buttoned up and her legs are crossed under the table gives off Sylvie vibes, and not in a good way.

"Hey," I say as I slump in the seat across from her. I used to think that I was in love with her.

"Glad you could make it," Alexis says, and it feels like she's cosplaying as Sylvie, or rather the worst sides of Sylvie. The Sylvie that looked down on you for being okay with getting a C on a quiz.

"Yeah." Even though I know it's hopeless, I try to steer the conversation to more casual tones. "Thanks for inviting me. Good to clear the air before school, you know?"

"No, Jack, I don't know," Alexis says.

"Oh." We stare at each other, and then I glance at her coffee cup. Hoping for a reprieve from whatever interrogation this is, I ask, "Can I get you a refill while I get my mug?"

"Sure," Alexis says. What she doesn't say is, "That's the least you can do," but she somehow manages to convey it.

I pay for my own bottomless mug and fill it up. I can't help, as I head over to the self-serve carafes, but think about all the times we'd come here with Finn and Sylvie to study. Not much studying was ever done, and that always bothered Sylvie but not the rest of us.

On a whim, I fill her cup up with an extra-dark roast like Sylvie drinks. I add sugar and cream before bringing it to her, but Alexis still grimaces at the first sip. She doesn't complain though. She pushes the mug to the side of the table and looks back at me.

"Well," she says.

"Yeah?"

"You have been a really shitty boyfriend this summer," Alexis says to me.

"How is that possible? When I'm not your boyfriend?"

"We've been sleeping together all summer." She says it slowly and sadly, like she regrets expecting better from me.

"You're the one who said, 'This isn't a thing. We're just convenient to each other,' remember?"

She waves my words—or rather her words—away with one hand.

220

"Whether we were technically together or not, it doesn't matter," Alexis says. "You haven't been treating me right, so I'm here to say, once and for all, that I'm through with you. We're over."

From the pout on her face, she's already decided on her reply, and it doesn't matter what I say next. So I answer, "Yeah, I know. Because we broke up last March, and we haven't spoken in three weeks."

"And why is that, Jack?" Alexis asks. "Why haven't we spoken?"

"Are you serious?" I had been blowing on my coffee to cool it, but I freeze with the mug held under my mouth as I gape at her.

"Yes, I'm serious." She raises her chin.

"Because Finn died, Lexy." I'm so confused. I set my mug down with a clink. Some hot coffee spills onto my fingers, but I don't react.

"Exactly." She throws up her hands like I've proven her point.

"I don't understand. I've been grieving, Lexy."

"And you left me to grieve alone!"

I'm not sure if the coffee shop falls silent at her outburst or if I've momentarily gone deaf. Either way, there's a ringing in my ears that prevents me from hearing myself when I say, "How dare you."

Alexis must have a ringing in her ears too, because she cups her hand around her ear as she says, "Huh? Speak up."

"How dare you say that to me," I say as this strangely serene feeling fills me. It's suddenly all so clear.

So many times, I told myself that I'd finally seen the "real" Alexis, that I'd never fall for her antics again, but I always did. I understand now. I'd seen aspects of the real Alexis, but I've never seen them together as a whole. Now all those pieces have come together, and I can finally see the whole Alexis.

It's actually a very simple picture. She's a really insecure girl who defines herself entirely by the people she surrounds herself with. Her friends are a collection, a planetary system she has built to rotate around her.

"How dare I? Jack, you—"

"No, no," I say. "If I wanted to, I could have called you here and said, 'Hey, we were sleeping together all summer, and then my best friend died, and *you* didn't even check on *me*.' I could do that. You don't get to do that." I try not to have my tone sound like I'm talking to a child, but it's hard.

"He was my friend too," Alexis says. "Why can't you or Sylvie see that?"

And it happens again. What's unfolding is so clear that I laugh.

She's surprised enough to lose her focus, and in the pause, I share my humorous revelation.

"This isn't about us, is it, Lex? Sylvie broke up with you."

I try not to laugh again, because now it feels a little mean, but it's all so silly and obvious. Sylvie hurt her, so she's trying to reenact that with me instead of looking at herself and wondering why Sylvie made that choice.

Alexis is sputtering.

"Sylvie and I didn't break up! We both have a lot going on, and I'm going off to school, and she needs to find a new

222

shrink—poor thing!—and we both needed to take a step back from our friendship."

Alexis, who I used to think I was in love with, glares at me.

"Uh-huh." I take a gulp of coffee, which hasn't quite cooled and burns down my throat. "So my guess is that's what Sylv said to you, and then you pushed back, because of course you did, and that's when she said what you said to me, huh?"

"Said what to who?" Alexis sips the highland grog that I know she hates and tries to hide her grimace.

"You left her to grieve alone, Lexy. Damn."

Once again, I feel like all the pieces have come together and I can finally see what should have been obvious.

"The day after the accident, why were people coming to your house instead of you going to Sylvie's?" I ask.

"I went to the hospital when her parents called me. I was tired and wanted to go home! And our friends needed a place to grieve together, Jack. Sylvie isn't my only friend."

"There's a basement in every damn house in this city and you know it," I say. "Sylvie needed you. Damn, I wouldn't have minded—" My serenity and my voice crack at this point, but it can't be helped. "It would have been nice if you had said something to acknowledge that he was my best friend, Lex. Maybe my only real friend, I don't know. But the fact that you compare your grief to mine? Or Sylvie's?"

I shake my head. The whole conversation is a moot point.

I push back from the table to stand. I don't think Alexis believes

223

that I will leave without her permission, because she makes a scoffing sound at me.

I look at her one last time. She has a pretty face. For now.

"Sylvie said that you had a lot of growing up to do, but honestly, Lex? If you're this far behind at eighteen, I don't know if you're ever going to catch up. I hope you do, but…" I shrug. I give up and stand up.

"Jack, you are not seriously—"

I am, and there's nothing she can do about it.

eleven

APPARENTLY, THE FINAL THING I must do to prove to my parents that I'm going to be okay is go out with "my friends" before I leave for college. This doesn't seem like the time to point out that I am questioning whether I have friends outside of Finn. I'm starting to see how superficial my other relationships have been. It almost makes me wish I hadn't given Sylvie such a hard time about everything. I suppose it wouldn't help to reach out and tell her that she might have been right, that maybe I never knew what friendship was until it was taken from me.

But then Kyle texts me that there's a party in St. Charles tonight, and even though it's the first time anyone from our class has reached out to me since the funeral, part of me melts a little. Part of me wonders if it would feel normal. It's not like Finn was at every party with me. Half the time, Finn was off making sure Sylvie wasn't giving herself alcohol poisoning on a dare anyway.

The way my parents light up when I say there's a party across the river that a bunch of the team will be at and I figure I'll stop by and say some goodbyes? That almost makes it worth the effort. If I can fool my parents that I'm okay, maybe I'll be able to fool myself eventually.

———————

As I drive over the bridge, I think about how whenever we went to St. Charles, Finn would say something about the airport expansion and white flight, and I'd be like, "Yeah, people suck. What are you going to do about it?" If Sylvie was in the car, she would talk to him about it, and I'd zone out or make out with Alexis if she was there. It's not that what Finn was talking about didn't seem important, but I figured we were kids. What kind of impact could we make?

I guess I don't think that way anymore, but I also don't have anyone to explain that stuff to me.

I could ask Sylvie, but there's a chance she's not speaking to me given our last text exchange.

Once I arrive at the address, I recognize the house. I've been here before. It had been a small party where everyone else knew each other. Finn, Sylvie, Alexis, and I were only there because an upperclassman from the team knew the host and invited us along with him. For a small party, there was a surprising amount of alcohol. At some point, late in the night, a dude said that the cop who lived next door would be coming home from his shift soon, and wouldn't it be funny if one of the girls flashed him?

Despite the number of people, including the host, who pointed out the obvious reason this was a bad idea, Sylvie volunteered for the job. It didn't matter that most people at the house were sober enough to not let the superdrunk girl antagonize the cop, Sylvie and Finn once again argued about whether Finn was trying to control Sylvie by stopping her from doing something stupid. Worse still, they had their argument in the front seat of Finn's little red car while Alexis and I were squeezed in the back seat and she was mad at me about some mysterious thing.

Whenever they had this fight in front of me, I always wanted to point out that sober Sylvie agreed whatever it was had been a bad idea about 90 percent of the time. I also wanted to tell Finn that he should know better than to force Sylvie to see logic when she was drunk.

Fuck, Finn, just let her sleep it off, I would think. And sometimes I would think, *You can't argue her into being Autumn, dude*. But I never said either of those things, and I'm not sure now whether I should have.

So.

At least there won't be any happy memories plaguing me at this party.

This party is thankfully much bigger than the last one. I can tell from the cars outside. I wonder if the cop still lives next door because it's pretty crowded on the street and the people in the backyard are not keeping their voices down, even if it's only nine.

My goal is to have conversations with at least three people whose names my parents have heard me say before, and then I'm going home. Tomorrow, when my parents ask, I'll say it was great seeing this person and saying goodbye to that guy, and then I'll say I'm going to my room to pack, and I'll take a nap.

I hop up the front steps and open the door without knocking, because it's already that kind of party. I don't see anyone I know, but the kitchen is at the end of the hall with a line for a keg, and I figure that's a good place to start.

Right away, I notice Trevor Jones at the end of the line. Perfect.

"Hey," I say as I approach, careful to stand back so that it's obvious I'm not trying to cut in line for the keg. Maybe he's in his own head, but Trevor blanches for a moment.

"Hey, Murphy," he says.

"What's up?"

"Nothing," he says, like I'm a teacher or a cop. "You good?"

"I'm okay," I say. "Who all is here?"

"You know, the guys and stuff."

"Right," I say to this nonanswer. Did Trevor always hate me and I never noticed? "Ricky here?"

"Yeah? Probably?"

The line shifts forward.

"Well, I'll let you get your drink, and I'll go say hi to some other people."

"Cool!" He sounds way too relieved. He faces forward, and I wander off.

Everyone loved Finn. Even the people who Finn didn't really

like loved him because he treated everyone the same. Did people only like me because I was attached to Finn? Was having me around the cost of having Finn there too?

That doesn't feel right, at least not quite, and I'm not going to let Trevor acting weird ruin my night.

There's an alcove off the hallway where some girls are gathered, and I see one of them pointing to me and whispering to her friends. Chloe dated Seth from the team for over a year, and they broke up after Finn gave Chloe a ride home one night when Seth refused to leave the party. Nothing happened, obviously. It was an act of kindness, driving her home when her own boyfriend wouldn't. But it seemed to kill her feelings for Seth. Seth acted like he wanted to blame Finn, but he could never find a way to do it.

That's the kind of high school memory I want to live in tonight, so even though I have no idea what Chloe was saying about me to her friend, I head over. A few of the girls rush off, but one of her friends stays.

"Heeeeeeeeeeey!" both girls say simultaneously at the same high pitch.

"Hi?" In their short black dresses and matching silvery makeup, they're suddenly giving off vibes like horror movie twins.

"How are you?" Chloe asks, as her friend—Sara?—nods in tandem to her words.

"Nothing much," I say, which isn't the right response, but neither notices. The way they're looking at me is too intense.

"Yeah?" they say together, both nodding.

229

"Leaving for school later this week," I offer.

Thankfully, only Sara cocks her head to the side as they both give me pitying looks.

"Yeah," I say to the question that they aren't asking. "Looking forward to it though."

"Of course," Chloe says. "It'll be a fresh start for you."

Sara nods.

"I don't need a fresh start," I say. "It's not like I killed someone."

After the words are out of my mouth, I try to turn them into a joke with a laugh, but that makes it worse. Chloe's and her friend's faces go through a strobe light sequence of reactions before settling back to pity.

"A change of scenery then?" Chloe asks. Her friend, who I remember is actually named Steph, doesn't nod this time.

"We heard about the practice," Steph-not-Sara says.

"The what?"

They wince in unison, and I'm starting to think they practice their creepy twin act in the mirror.

"You know? How you showed up at soccer practice like that?" Chloe touches my arm in a way that I used to think meant a girl was flirting, but now I'm not so sure.

"Yeah, I—" I start, but I don't want to explain to them why I was there. They haven't earned that from me. "You know," I say, "you're probably right about me needing a change of scenery."

They nod enthusiastically.

"So, uh, I think I'll go say hi to some other people." I'm surprised how their faces fall, but I don't care. "Nice catching up," I say as I turn away.

There's a lot of shouting going on in the next room, which should at least be interesting.

It turns out that's where most of the team is, Ricky and Jamal and the rest. A couple of new upperclassmen who joined the team from JV are there. Everyone is focused on Bunny and the video game he's playing.

I have no idea what Bunny's actual name is, something like Robert or John probably, but his last name is Bunnell, and he has gone by Bunny for as long as I've known him. I don't know whether I admire him for it or not.

I stand at the edge of the crowd and wish I had a drink in my hand or at least a soda to sip.

"Come on, come on," Seth is saying over and over as Bunny tries to hit the boss on its vulnerable spot. The character does not hit the monster and is immolated.

"Noooooo!" Seth says over everyone else's groans.

"Is this personal for you, Seth?" I laugh.

Everyone turns to me. The millisecond of silence cuts like glass.

"Oh, hey, Murphy," Ricky says, sounding exactly like at practice. "Long time no see."

Someone in the group finds that funny. Someone else shushes them.

"Kyle told me about the party," I say. Kyle is a graduate, like me. "Have you seen him?"

"Uh, maybe?" Ricky's holding hands with Jasmine, who never would have looked at him if Finn hadn't died. Jasmine is staring at me the same way as Chloe and her friend. The guys from the team all seem nervous, glancing away and talking quietly to one another. The video game is forgotten, and the group that had been sitting on the floor is standing and stretching. A few leave the room.

"Hey, Murphy, didn't think you'd come," Kyle booms behind me. He's holding two cups of beer. He hands one to one of the girls sitting on the couch.

"I wasn't sure either. Thanks for inviting me." I'm trying to figure out why Ricky claimed to not know that Kyle was here.

"You not playing anymore?" Kyle asks Jamal.

Jamal shrugs and restarts the level, but most of the room has cleared. There's Ricky, Jasmine, Kyle, and the girl he got the beer for, plus Jamal and Seth, all on the couch. There isn't room for me, so I stand.

I'm nearly certain that people liked me for me. Of course, everyone liked Finn more, but that's expected of the nicest guy ever. Ricky, Jamal, Seth, we were always cool. Not close, but we got along fine.

So I'm not sure what this is.

Jasmine leans forward. "So," she says, "how are you, Jack?" in a tone that is eerily familiar.

"I'm okay!" I respond with perhaps too much enthusiasm, "I'm looking forward to college, change of scenery and all that."

"That will be so good for you," she says, nodding. We've only spoken a couple of times before, but she seems to have solid opinions on what I need. "A fresh start."

I'm about to say, "It's not like I killed someone," this time on purpose, when I realize they're afraid they'll die too if they hang out with me. Death by association.

Ricky is studying the fingernails on his free hand as if he were the sort of dude to worry about a hangnail. Jamal is playing the game again, this time on autopilot, barely reacting to anything that happens. Even Seth is quiet.

"I guess," I say, and Jasmine nods again.

"You are so brave," she says.

Kyle, who's sitting on the other side of her, glances over at her and then at me.

"Hey, why isn't anyone calling me brave? I'm moving to California. Murphy is going to southern Missouri," he says.

The girl on the other side of Kyle, the girl he'd gotten the beer for, laughs and starts to answer, but Jasmine interrupts, leaning across Kyle.

"That's the guy whose best friend—"

And I'm done.

I think my dad calls it an Irish goodbye when you don't tell anyone you are leaving, and that's what I'm trying to do, but halfway to my car, I hear Kyle call my name. I turn, and he jogs up to me.

"Hey, um, sorry about that. I didn't think those dudes would be so weird."

"It wasn't just the guys," I say. "Maybe I'm off tonight."

"Yeah, I heard Chloe tried to flirt with you."

My mind races. So she was flirting, and somehow, it's already a story twenty minutes later?

"Look. Finn? He was a great guy, and he deserved better. Like, I keep thinking about that night, you know, when he wouldn't drive home until I put on my seat belt? Shit." He shrugs. "Like, what I'm trying to say is, everyone feels freaked. 'Cause if something like that could happen to Finn, it could happen to any of us."

"Yeah," I say. "It could."

Kyle winces. "No one wants to think about that. So..."

"Nobody wants the best friend of the dead kid harshing the vibe?" I venture.

"I'm not saying that." Kyle looks me in the eyes when he says it, but it doesn't make me believe him. He clears his throat. "I didn't want you to think no one liked you or something. Everybody knows you're cool, Jack. It's just..." He's already tried to say that he's not saying what he's definitely saying.

"It's okay, Kyle." Because it kind of is. I'm glad that no one hates me, but I'm also glad that the guys on the team aren't friends I should be concerned about losing. I clap Kyle on the shoulder. "Thanks for the invite. Good luck in Cali."

He looks relieved when I climb in my car.

The next morning, I tell my parents about catching up with Kyle

234

and the guys on the team, how it was nice to see everyone but how I'm starting to get more excited about college.

I think a fresh start will be good for me.

twelve

IT SEEMS IMPOSSIBLE, BUT IT'S time to leave for college.

I finished packing without Charlie having to come home. Before Mom could suggest it, I cleaned my car to rival Finn's, and I had room for all my stuff. The plan had been for me to drive myself. All my brothers went to Springfield too, and Dad helped move Joey, Chris, Dave, and James into their dorms, but Matt and Charlie knew the drill and took themselves down.

Suddenly, my parents wanted to come. I started to protest, and then I remembered the way Angelina looked when I gave her the first aid kit from Finn's trunk. So I agreed to let them come.

In the end, the drive was nice. Mom and Dad took turns riding with me and driving their own car during the five-hour trip. At first, during Mom's turn and then Dad's, the conversation felt a little forced. But with each of them, there was a thaw, and then we had fun. I guess I haven't had much one-on-one time with my parents. They're funnier when they aren't snipping at each other.

They both knew not to ask about Finn. They both knew his shadow will be following me all day. They know I'm as okay as I'm going to be, but only because I'm not having to talk about how he was supposed to be moving in with me.

"I swear, one of your bothers was assigned this floor," my mother says. She's carrying a box and holding the hallway door open with her back as my dad and I struggle with the suitcases. Other people come up behind us and walk through the door too, and my mother holds it for everyone. I'm about to tell her to move before she gets stuck there forever when I notice the handmade placards on the dorm doors. They seem to be themed by an assumption of what sports team the dudes are fans of, probably based on whether they live closer to Kansas City or St. Louis. Seems like a dangerous game for the RA to play. I'm already dreading whatever non-soccer team's colors will be surrounding my name. But more than that, I'm wondering if they know Finn's not coming.

Do I want to see Finn's name or not? I wonder. Would it be nice to see evidence that not that long ago, he had a future, or would it simply be a reminder that the future was taken from him so recently? I won't get a choice. Either his name will be there or not.

"Three-oh-seven, three-oh-eight," my mother says behind me. "There's three-oh—Oh!"

An older guy stands at what's supposed to be my door, removing the sign with Finn's misspelled name, *Phinaes*. He turns and sees us.

"Hey! I'm Josh, your resident advisor! You're—" He glances at the remaining name tag. "You're Jack!" He scans my face and

237

my parents. "There's been a reassignment! Not sure if you knew. Well, there's always a long waiting list for first semester, so they'll be giving us the name of your new roommate shortly. Had you connected with your first assignment?"

How much does he know? Maybe it isn't only high schoolers who think freak accidents are contagious.

"Yeah," I say. "I knew Finn. He's dead. This is my mom and dad."

These words seem to activate his RA training, and he launches into a speech about how happy he is to have me on his floor and all the good clean fun the dormitory will provide for its residents. I open the door and claim the bed and desk farthest from the hallway.

So much for college helping me move on.

It isn't long before Mom and Dad are able to extract themselves. It's a madhouse in the hallway, and Josh didn't seem anxious to get to know me in particular.

Mom starts putting sheets on the bed. Dad stands in the center of the room with the two suitcases he carried, awaiting instructions.

"Get the TV, George," Mom says without looking up.

"What TV?" I ask.

Dad hightails it out.

Mom pauses before smoothing the sheets. "I forgot to tell you. Mr. Smith came by a few days ago while you were out running. He'd bought a TV for Finn as a moving-in present. He thought you should have it." She picks up the pillow and an empty pillowcase before glancing at me for my reaction.

I don't know what to feel about this.

"He said something about wishing he could've known Finn better. I told him a few stories and how he was the most polite and helpful friend that any of you children had ever brought home. I knew he really wanted to talk to you. But he didn't ask me." Mom finishes fluffing the pillow. "And because he didn't ask, I let him leave the television set."

"I don't want to talk to him," I decide.

"I know, sweetie," she says.

Dad has returned lugging the TV. It is big enough to be almost alarming. A classic Finn's dad gesture.

"Why does he do things like that?" I asked Finn after he received a letter stating that a large savings bond had been taken out in his name. We'd finished a run, and he'd checked the mailbox as we headed inside. A drop of his sweat had dripped onto the paper.

"Proof of something," Finn said. "I haven't figured out what yet."

Inside, he tossed the letter on the dining room table where it was immediately lost among his mother's half-finished art projects. A bit over a year later, his dad invited him to Thanksgiving dinner at his house, and I was afraid that his heart would be broken, and I was right.

It's a tight fit, but Dad and I manage to balance the TV on the top of the dresser. It dominates the upper half of the wall like a black hole. I turn my back on it and start to set up my desk.

When no one else has arrived by the time Mom and Dad want to go to dinner, part of me hopes that the RA was wrong about there being a waiting list for campus housing.

Part of the reason that my parents are still married to each other is because they are creatures of habit, so there is no discussion of where

239

we will eat. We go to the same Chinese restaurant with the indoor fountain and six-foot-tall foo dogs that we eat at every time we've visited one of my brothers. Last time I was here, I was annoyed by my parents' inability to change things up, but right now, the familiarity feels comforting.

The meal with my parents is like the ride down, better than I expected, even with both of them there. We talk about the time Chris dared me to jump into the fountain and Matt asking for the waitress's number and being so surprised that she gave it to him that he was too scared to call.

They don't bicker at all. In fact, midway through the meal, I set a timer on my phone, and they break their previous record for not arguing by a full fourteen minutes, making it all the way out to the parking lot before disagreeing about who would drive back. I text the news to the younger half of my brothers, who think my timer is amusing, unlike the older three, who think it's disrespectful.

I tell Mom and Dad not to walk me back up to my room. They need to leave soon if they want to get home before midnight. Dad idles the car while Mom gets out to hug me. It's more of a squeeze than a hug, and I'm wondering if I should, for their sake, let them walk me up when Mom lets go and holds my shoulders. She looks me in the eyes and doesn't say anything, then nods to herself before stepping back and smiling at me.

"You're going to be fine."

"I know?" I'm pretty sure.

"Carole?" Dad says.

"All right," Mom says. She gets in the car. I wave again in case they're looking in the rearview mirror.

And then they're gone.

I'm an adult out in the world on my own.

I'm surprised that I feel as if something has shifted within me or perhaps in the air around me. I don't have to go back to my room. I could go somewhere on campus, or I could get into my car and drive away forever. Whatever I decide, there's no one to stop me. It's my choice what happens next.

I choose to go back to my room. I want to be alone.

It doesn't occur to me until I see the partially open door that I know I left locked that perhaps someone from the waiting list was assigned to Finn's open bed.

I remember reading the housing application with Finn, where it said it would honor as many mutual roommate requests as possible but that it was best to fill out their personality quiz just in case. I didn't, but if I had, I doubt it would have been taken into consideration in a last-minute reassignment from the waiting list.

There's already a new name on the door. I hope Brett likes the Chiefs.

As I push open the door, the three people in my room look up at me, startled.

"Hi," I say to them.

The guy sitting on Finn's bed looks surprised even as his mother steps forward to shake my hand. As I take it in mine, I see that she has tears in her eyes. I've interrupted something. His father has gone back to staring at his hands clasped in front of him.

"We're the Carters," she says. "And this is Brett!"

"Hi," I say. "Nice to meet you. I was going to grab my stuff and take a shower." It's early evening, but it's still hot as blazes out, and everyone was traveling and moving today, so my excuse to be antisocial is accepted.

"Well, if we don't see you again, have a good semester!" Mrs. Carter says. The tears in her eyes glitter. "Let us know if you ever need anything!"

"Thanks." I grab the basket of shower stuff that my mom forced me to pack up before we left for dinner. She told me that I would be glad later, though I don't think she could have foreseen this exact situation. Either way, I mentally thank her as I bolt out of there.

And here I thought my parents were getting emotional about me leaving home.

Suddenly, I'm grateful for my undemonstrative family. Which makes me miss them, especially my mom. Mentally, I thank her again, this time for not crying.

He's not dying, part of me had wanted to tell the Carters. Which would have been a dick move, so I'm glad I didn't, but it's how I feel. Angelina would give anything to be in that woman's position, yet she has the audacity to cry? It seems like such bullshit.

At least I'm thinking clearly enough to know that there's something off about my reaction, so I take that long shower as promised. I hear others coming and going, but a line never forms, so I don't give up my stall.

242

I hear two guys laughing together. Clearly, they've been friends for years.

I turn up the shower. The water pressure isn't great, but it blocks out the sound.

I give it enough time that Brett's parents would have to be seriously unreasonable to still be hanging around. My fingers and toes are wrinkled raisins by the time I get out.

It's not quiet on the floor of our hall, but it's the difference between going to a concert and going on a hike: the woods are full of noise and activity, but compared to a concert, it's silent. There's some laughter and conversation, some television noise. About half the doors are closed.

It's only nine o'clock, but I hope this Brett guy is asleep. When I get to the room, I decide he may as well be asleep, because he's reading the new student manual.

The stapled booklet was sitting on our bare mattresses when I arrived and is filled with campus phone numbers I could get online, rules about alcohol, and a couple of maps or something. Mine is sitting in the recycling bin, where any sane person would put such paper-wasting nonsense.

"Hey," I say.

"Hey." Brett doesn't look up.

Perfect.

I get into bed with my CD player and pull the top sheet over my head. I listen to Finn's best of Tom Petty album with headphones until the light filtering in through the sheet goes out.

I keep listening until I fall asleep.

243

thirteen

So what's college like?

It's hard to say.

At breakfasts, I wonder what Finn would have thought about the dining hall eggs that come from a cartoon or the soggy waffle machine. Walking around campus, I think about how Finn would like the trees here. Sometimes I look up and scan the crowds, expecting to see him. I don't know how to convince myself that it's not a mistake: Finn's not at college with me.

Of course, if Finn were alive, he wouldn't be at college with me. He'd really be at college with Autumn.

What a glorious nightmare that would be.

That's mostly what I think about on the walk between classes or while eating alone at the dining hall—just how annoying Finn and Autumn would be if they were here together.

After all these years of telling Finn that Autumn didn't return his feelings and he needed to get over her, I'd have had to let him talk about her constantly, at least for those last weeks of summer. By the time we made it to school, I would have been tired of it. Finn would have been making a conscious effort to not talk incessantly about the miracle of Autumn loving him, but I would have been rolling my eyes every time he'd catch himself from bringing her up. It would be mostly fine, and I'd be happy for him.

But I know that every time I would ask Finn if he wanted to go to the dining hall, he would text Autumn to see if she wanted to come. And we'd wait in the lobby for her, where he would resemble a puppy awaiting his master, perking up the moment he caught sight of her. At the dining hall, there would be their lingering looks across the table, their secret smiles.

I would have been happy for him, really, I swear. If the tension between Autumn and Finn was annoying before, I doubt it would have gotten better when they became a couple. That's the thing about sexual tension between two people: releasing it doesn't make less of it. It usually creates more.

Every flyer I see for a freshman mixer or campus activity, I imagine asking Finn if he wants to go and him telling me he'd see if Autumn wanted to come. Autumn would be the underlying impulse behind any decision Finn would make this week. And it would frustrate me to no end. Eventually we would fight about it.

For a few days, whenever I'm not in class, the fictional fight Finn and I would have had over Autumn if he were alive is my focus. Sometimes I imagine confronting him after he's missed plans with me or because I'm tired of vacating to the library so he and Autumn can hook up. Obviously, whatever is going on, Autumn tries to stick up for Finn, but he always tells her no, he needs to work it out with me, so she leaves, and wherever we are on campus or in the dorm, it's Finn and me and we're arguing.

Finn and I didn't fight a lot, but I know him well enough to predict his defenses. He would say that this relationship was still new, and "You know what having the chance to be with Autumn means to me."

In this dream world where Finn is still alive, I wouldn't have seen Autumn grieving. I would still be suspicious of her breaking his heart, so I would point out that I was the one who had always been there for him, not her. And if Autumn abandoned him again, was I just supposed to be there waiting for Finn?

It feels so good to be angry at this Finn, this living Finn who is neglecting me to hang out with his dream girl.

No matter what starts the fight or exactly how I decide that the dialogue goes down, it always ends the same way: with Finn apologizing and promising to make more time for me. I know that's how it would end, because I've always been a good friend to Finn, and he knows that. Knew that.

I tend to cry in the shower, same as at home.

Late at night, I can't distract myself by imagining how it would be if Finn were here. At night, I know that Finn is dead. Or do I? The thought still nags me, *but what if it wasn't really Finn?* What if someone about Finn's height and weight and wearing similar clothes stopped to help Sylvie, and *he* was the one who put his hand down in the puddle with the downed power line, and *he's* the one in the gray box in the grave with his face burned off, not Finn.

Maybe Finn hit his head, had amnesia, and wandered off. Except I know that's not true.

Other nights, I imagine Finn didn't hit his head. Maybe Finn thought he'd killed Sylvie and he was so grief stricken and guilt ridden that he ran away, and now he thinks he can never come back because everyone hates him. Maybe he's even scared the police think he killed Sylvie on purpose.

But Finn, the future doctor, ran to check Sylvie's breathing and pulse. Ran to help her, because of course, that's what Finn would do.

Even if I can make myself believe that we buried someone else in Finn's coffin by mistake, I cannot make myself believe that he would let any of us hurt like this.

So Finn still isn't here with me.

And there's not much else to say about college.

fourteen

AFTER MY FIRST WEEK OF class, I wake up on Saturday morning and decide that I need to figure out my running route. Everyone, from the RAs to profs to student advisors, keep saying that it's up to us to be independent, and no one's checking in on us. I know they're talking about homework and stuff, but I won't have Coach riding my ass anymore either, and I'm not going to be one of those jocks who goes to college and loses it all.

I was already the guy hanging out at high school after graduation.

For some reason, I only sleep until eight, but it's for the best since it's still pretty hot by midday.

Brett the boring, as I've taken to thinking of him, is still sleeping. For the past week, we've lived like an invisible line divides our floor after an argument we've never had. I'm not sure why he's as disinterested in getting to know me as I am him. He might have friends on another floor of the dormitory, because I've seen him in the common room every night doing whatever activity is being put on. He made a DIY stress ball; he went to movie night; he even went to the microwave cooking class. It's possible that Brett doesn't have any friends either and is attending those activities to make some. But during the day, he never seems to leave the room, and I've never seen him in the dining hall. The few times I've stopped by the room between classes, he's always been there, almost as if he doesn't have classes of his own.

I would be offended that he doesn't look up or greet me when I enter the room, except I don't want to go through those niceties either. I still say "Hey" sometimes, and I'm not sure if I'm doing it to be friendly or to be a dick, pointing out how rude he's being.

Brett keeps a picture of himself in a frame on his desk. It's one of those dopey baseball card pics, and he looks about fourteen or so. Must have been a stellar season.

So that first Saturday at college, I leave Brett, the middle school baseball star, sleeping on his side of the room and head to the dining hall. I scarf half a bagel and some juice and head out to scout my new route.

The track around the football field is the obvious choice, but it may not always be available, especially during football season. I head toward the quad, but it doesn't take long for me to rule it out. There're too many old trees in this part of campus, which means too many sidewalk squares being lifted by roots, creating tripping hazards. It wouldn't have bothered me much before, but best to avoid an absurd accident in college.

After one loop, I leave the shade of the old trees and move

into a newer part of the campus. The sidewalks here aren't simply smoother; they're wider and will make it easier to avoid someone walking.

Which I don't think I'm going to have to worry about today. All week, people have been handing me flyers for various official and unofficial welcome parties that took place last night. Brett woke me up when he stumbled home close to dawn. It seems likely he went rather than fell asleep watching TV in the common room.

Would Finn and I have gone out together last night?

Only if Autumn was coming too, and I have no idea what she would have wanted to do.

I'm halfway down a long straight path that might be a third of a mile. It ends in a plaza in front of the newest building and loops around from the other side for foot traffic. If the other side is as smooth as this side, this will definitely be my route.

Would Finn run with me, or would he be sleeping in Autumn's room?

I don't know the answer to that either. I can't really know what it would be like if Finn were here, no matter how certain I am that he and Autumn would be annoyingly attached at the hip.

My stride is long and even, and with each footfall, I recognize I need to try to stop thinking about what it would be like if Finn were here. I'm torturing myself, obsessing like this.

Part of me doesn't want to get better though.

What will I have left of Finn when the hurt is gone?

Second lap.

I'm not breathing deeply enough. I need to correct that before I get a stitch in my side.

I need to stop thinking about what it would be like if Finn were here with me.

It feels like I can almost touch that reality where he is alive and we're rooming together.

Breathe, Murphy!

It feels like, if I think hard enough, I'll cross over to that world.

Too late.

There's that pain in my side, just above the hip, the dreaded stitch.

I grit my teeth and keep running.

That's what you get for not breathing, Murphy.

I still know Finn so well. Someday I won't know him like this. I'm losing a bit of him each and every moment.

Time is changing me.

Nothing is changing Finn.

Keep breathing through the pain.

Will I someday dismiss the depth of our friendship as kid stuff? Will I someday remember Finn and realize it's been years since I thought of him?

Breathe.

No.

I could never go years without thinking about Finn. No matter how long I live, he's always going to be one of the best guys I've ever known.

Keep breathing. You got this.

It hurts to think that I'd go a day without thinking about him, but I surely won't hurt like this forever, which means I'll have to stop thinking about Finn.

Breathe.

Or I could find a way of thinking about Finn that doesn't hurt.

I don't know how to do that. Everything about Finn being gone is so wrong.

Keep breathing.

Then I remember the morning of the funeral, telling myself that I had to do it because I was doing it for Finn. Of Angelina, saying she'd like to think of his clothes and belongings being useful out in the world, of Finn wanting that.

It had almost felt good, thinking about Finn like that.

Breathe.

Finn would want me to have a good time in college, whatever that means.

What else would Finn want?

The stitch in my side is easing. I'm on my third lap. I've got a good rhythm going, and I need to maintain it. I try to stop my thoughts and focus on my body.

Keep breathing.

I don't know what it means, to have a good time in college. Some mythical combination of youthful hijinks and studiousness I suppose. Maybe it's different for everyone.

Except I won't figure out what it means for me if I keep thinking about Finn being here. Because he's not.

And that hurts.

But it's true.

Breathe.

So.

For Finn's sake.

Because he would want me to.

I need to let myself accept his death.

Breathe.

And that hurts.

But the truth hurts.

I'll just have to breathe through it.

fifteen

I'VE THROWN MYSELF INTO MY classes these past two weeks.

Finn would have wanted me to go to college, so I'm going to college, damn it.

In high school, I managed to squeak onto the honor roll every semester, and that was good enough for me. I didn't worry about moving up the rank or whatever. Sylvie was determined to be in the top ten, and Finn joined her in that goal while privately sharing his relief that she wasn't determined to be valedictorian.

In college, I've set myself a strict schedule. I'm up early (before Brett), and I eat a balanced-ass breakfast. I go to my classes and take thorough notes, and my mind never wanders from the lecture. After my last class, I head to the library. I type up my notes. I highlight my textbooks. I read ahead.

Between classes, it's more difficult not to think about Finn. I try to concentrate on the lectures I've heard, but when I can't do that, I read flyers as I walk. There're unending flyers posted on campus.

Flyers for parties, flyers for student films, flyers for political events. I've become knowledgeable about all that's happening on campus, even if I never attend anything.

Sometimes I see Brett the boring on campus at the Frisbee golf games or outdoor painting workshops, so I guess he's branched out from dorm activities. He has remained a mystery I do not want to solve, though it still bothers me that he feels the same about me, since he never gave me a chance.

At lunchtime, I put headphones in and zone out. Listening to Finn's CDs doesn't count as thinking about him. A couple of times, dudes have joined the table like they felt bad for me sitting alone, and I've motioned to my headphones and given them a thumbs-up, then ignored them until they leave. So far, that's worked.

One time, a girl sat down, and I did my routine. It wasn't until afterward that it occurred to me I wouldn't have wanted her to leave if I'd thought about it for a minute. Still, I couldn't imagine myself chasing a girl right now. How can I think about dating when Finn is dead?

It's best I motioned her away.

In the evenings, when I'm done at the library, that's when I go running. I take the same route from that first Saturday. The path is easy, and I push myself until I can't think.

Then I head back to the dorms, hit the showers while everyone else is at dinner, and go to the dining hall when it's mostly empty and I'm likely to be left in peace.

It's lights out after that, because I've got an early morning and a long day of not thinking about Finn.

So I've got the college part of college worked out.

I'm not sure about the rest of it.

It's like the girl who sat down at my table. How can I think about going to a party or joining the running club when Finn is dead?

I call my parents every other day. Charlie taught me that. "Day three is when they'll start to think you're dead," he told me.

My parents never ask about Finn, but Mom's "How've you been?" is worried. They seem to think a new friend will cheer me up.

She asks about that every time we talk. A few times, I've lied to my parents, told them that I've attended some of the student events from the flyers. That soothes them somewhat. They seem determined that Brett and I will eventually become buds, even though they've never met him, even though I've told them how he goes out of his way to ignore me. I suppose I'll have to make a friend soon, or next time Mom calls, she'll send Charlie to visit me.

Unfortunately, today would be a perfect day to make a friend.

I can't justify going to the library after class. I've turned in my first big papers, I'm caught up on reading, and there's no looming quiz or test.

I've accidentally set myself up to coast for a day or two.

Maybe I'll drive around and find a park to go running. Finn was into varying your terrain.

So after my last class, I head back to the dorm to change clothes and get in an extra-long run, location TBA, as Sylvie would say.

There's no reason not to call the 'rents as I walk, so I call their landline.

"Hello?" Dad always answers the phone like you're about to ask him for ransom money for someone he hates. It probably scares off telemarketers.

"Hey, Dad."

"Carole!" he bellows for Mom.

There's a click as she picks up. I know she's upstairs in her sewing room that used to be James's room, and Dad is in his workshop in the basement. I think they do this because it gives them an excuse to yell at each other even when they aren't angry.

"Jack?" Mom says. I'm probably the only reason they communicate these days.

"Hey, checking in."

"I'm glad you called," Mom says. She quizzes me on my laundry situation. Her words and Dad's grunts make it clear they are doubtful that I'm wearing clean underwear, but it's true. Doing laundry is easy. It's putting it away that sucks. Mostly I've been leaving my clean clothes in the basket and dropping the dirty in a pile on the floor until the basket is empty. Since she doesn't ask about putting it away, I don't share that part.

On our last phone call, she was worrying over my diet. It's funny because they were so hands-off when I was at home. Now that I'm out of their sight, they're certain I need them.

"Have you made any friends yet?" Mom finally asks.

"Met a guy from Taiwan last night. He seemed cool." I'd met him

257

in the elevator. He liked my Zelda shirt, and we'd talked for about twenty seconds before we got off and walked to opposite ends of the floor, but it still counts.

"Have you and Brett hung out yet?" Mom asks.

"No." I'm grateful the dormitory is in sight and I'll be able to hang up soon. "And I don't want to. I'm doing great, guys. You'll see when midterm grades are out."

"Grades aren't everything," Dad interjects.

I think Mom and I are both surprised into silence, though I recover first. "Who are you, and what have you done with my parents?" I ask.

"Well, grades are important, but your father has a point," Mom says. They must be really worried if Mom's agreeing with Dad.

"I'm doing good, seriously." I'm not sure if it's a lie or not. Maybe "good" isn't the right word for where I am, but keeping my head above water when I feel like I'm drowning is good, right?

It's like she knows I'm about to say I have to go. "You know you can call anytime?" Mom adds.

"Yeah, I know. I'm okay, okay? I should get off the phone. I'm about to go inside and get on the elevator."

We say our goodbyes, and after we hang up, I imagine they are calling Charlie to pack a bag and visit me.

As I get off the elevator, it occurs to me that Brett will probably be in our room and not expecting me. My schedule has been pretty exact these past weeks. If he's jerking off, he'd at least lock the door. And since the knob turns—

258

He's crying.

Brett tries to play it off like he's been reading the textbook on his lap, but the framed picture he'd been holding clatters as he sets it back on the desk.

I walk to my side of the room as if he isn't wiping his face. I put my bag on my desk, lie back on my bed, and stare at the ceiling. I listen and wait for Brett's breathing to return to normal.

After I minute, I say, "Do you wanna talk about it?"

I'm expecting him to say no. I'm expecting him to pretend he wasn't just crying.

Instead, he says, "I'm sorry if I've been so weird."

I glance over. He sits at his desk, in profile to me. He picks up the framed picture.

"The only person I've shared a room with before was Todd, my twin brother. He died when we were fourteen." He wipes at his eyes.

I am such a jerk.

Why didn't it occur to me that his parents had a reason for being so emotional about leaving him? Or consider that maybe there was a reasonable explanation for that Little League photo?

I wish I could apologize for the way I judged him and his parents, but first I'd have to explain my assholery.

"I'm so sorry," I say and leave it at that.

"It's the kinda thing that never really leaves you, you know?" Brett says.

"Yeah," I say.

Perhaps he can hear how I do know, because the rest of Brett's words come out in a rush.

"I've had four years to adjust, but whenever I hear you shift in your sleep or get up in the mornings, for a second, I think you're him. So I've been icing you out. You're this big reminder that he's not here with me."

"No, I get it." I think of telling him about Finn, but this isn't the time. "What was Todd like?" I glance over in case it was the wrong thing to say, but his face lights up and reminds me of Angelina at the wake.

Todd could have been an actor, Brett swears to me. He knows they were kids, but if I had seen Todd act, I would understand. Todd could turn on something inside him and become someone else. He did all the junior theater stuff in Kansas City. It didn't matter what the role was, Todd flipped that switch and became George Gibbs or Mercutio or the Tin Man, it didn't matter.

Todd also loved baseball and wanted to coach at any level he could.

"I asked Todd if he wanted to be an actor once," Brett says. "He shrugged. He said he only liked it. He loved baseball. And he wanted to be a dad, and being an actor could delay that." Brett pauses. "And I was like, we're fourteen. I thought it was a lot to ask about careers, and here he was talking about being a *dad*." He pauses again. "He would have been a good one though. A great coach too. He had a way of being happy for other people that was contagious. When the team won, he was happy for the whole team, and when they lost, he was happy for the teammates who had made good plays." He laughs. "There was a joke at school, 'You'd have to be a real asshole to hate Todd Carter.'"

It sounds like Todd and Finn would have gotten along well.

The way Todd died, Brett tells me, was stupid, and when he explains it, I have to agree. Todd was coming home from a practice with their dad, and their car was stopped at a red light. A drunk hit another car in the intersection, and that car was pushed into their family car, which caused an airbag malfunction that broke Todd's neck.

"Then he was..." Brett holds his hands open as his voice trails off.

"Gone," I finish for him, nodding. "Just like that."

Brett looks up at me expectantly.

"It's funny, but—I mean, it's not funny at all, but..." I fumble. "This room was open because my best friend died. Last month." My face feels hot. "It's not the same as a brother, especially not a twin, but I kinda get it."

Suddenly tears are in my eyes. Trying to be respectful of Brett's loss, I feel like I'm diminishing my friendship with Finn.

Before I can be embarrassed about crying, Brett is saying, "Last month? Dude, I'm surprised you didn't punch me on sight."

Which makes me laugh and cry a little more.

"What happened?"

Then I'm explaining how Finn's death was so unfair, how he was always so cautious.

How he was great at soccer, unfailingly kind.

How he'd loved this girl his whole life and had only just gotten to be with her.

How the funeral home was packed.

It's not like Brett and I instantly become friends.

But we talk about how we never used to believe that we would die.

About how easily bodies can break.

We talk for a long time. I skip running to go to the dining hall with him. The pizza is surprisingly good. Finn would have liked this pizza. I tell Brett that around a mouthful. And about how I don't want to forget.

"You won't," Brett says. He looks directly at me from across the table, his food forgotten. He's so certain. "You won't forget. You'll never forget," he says.

My throat is tight, and it's hard to swallow.

We're silent after that, and I'm starting to feel embarrassed. I barely know this guy, and I've almost cried in front of him twice in one day.

When we're done eating, we clear our trays and head out. We pause and look both ways before crossing the street toward our dorm. Halfway through the crosswalk, he starts talking.

"Someday," Brett says, "you'll think of Finn, and it won't hurt. It's not that the hurt ever goes away. You saw me today. But sometimes? Sometimes when I remember Todd, I'm just happy that I got to be his brother. Someday you'll have that with Finn. I know it."

"Thank you," I whisper, and we're quiet again.

It isn't until a few minutes later, as we're getting into the elevator, that he says, "So admit it. You thought I was an asshole with my JV baseball pic framed on my desk."

The panic must show on my face, because he laughs, which means it's okay for me to laugh too.

Like I said, we're not instantly friends, but it's enough of a start that Mom shouldn't send Charlie after me.

sixteen

AFTER FIVE WEEKS OF SCHOOL, I go back to Ferguson. It's the weekend before Finn's birthday, and it just feels right to be there.

When I get to town, I go out of my way to drive past his house. It looks like the grass hasn't been mowed since Finn died. There's been a drought, so it could be worse, but someone needs to do it before there's a citation or something. It's obvious that doing Finn's chore is more than anyone in his family can handle right now.

But I can handle it. I'll do it for Finn, not instead of him.

My parents are even happier to see me than I expected and nicer to each other than they've been in years. Perhaps time alone is good for them, or perhaps worrying about me brought them together.

"We should go to the art museum tomorrow," Mom suggests. Dad mumbles something about putting gas in the car first, which means he would be going too.

"I'm going to go by Finn's mom's house in the morning," I say. "Somebody needs to mow their grass." There's a pause, and I think they might protest, but my parents beam.

"That would be very kind of you," Mom says. Dad says something about watching the game afterward, and Mom says she'll make us a late lunch.

Under the table, I text my brothers that someone has kidnapped our parents and replaced them with actors who don't know that they're supposed to hate each other. As usual, only the younger three think this is funny.

———————————

I didn't call Angelina first. I simply loaded Dad's mower into the trunk of my car and drove over.

I've been better the past couple of weeks. I still cry in the shower sometimes, but not as much. It helps to have a roommate who I can talk to if I want and gets it when I don't.

I guess Brett is my friend, though I don't think he'll ever be a friend like Finn was to me.

Outside Finn's house, I unload the mower and start the engine. The familiar hum is a nice white noise. It is still hot but not unbearable. Down the street, a tulip tree is turning yellow.

I used to make fun of Finn for pointing out particularly colorful trees. Little did I know that because of him, appreciating seasonal foliage would become a lifelong habit of mine.

As I push the mower, I think about how the leaves above my head would soon be changing color and falling, and he won't see it. He won't see the new leaves in the spring.

I think about how Finn will never vote in an election, local or presidential. I'd never cared about politics, but Finn had been looking forward to voting for a president for the first time. It doesn't seem like such a bad thing to start caring about.

I think about a lot that morning. I go over promises I've made to myself and to Finn and then make a few more.

When I'm almost finished, I pause to wipe sweat from my face with my forearm. That's when I see her at the screen door.

I wave, but Autumn takes a step back.

I didn't see her on the porch, but there's a glass of ice water on the railing.

I'm almost finished with the front yard, so I wrap up the last bit, then make my way over. I drink until the ice clinks empty at the bottom. I knock on the doorframe and call her name softly. When there's no answer, I ring the bell.

"What?" she says when she finally answers.

I'm so surprised by her anger that I take a step back.

"Hi. Thanks?" I say, holding out the glass.

Autumn looks terrible, skeletal. She breathes deeply before answering, as if there is a massive weight strapped to her chest.

"I was pretending it was Finny mowing," she says, as if this should have been obvious to me. "And now you've ruined it."

"Oh," I say, because there is nothing else to say.

She snatches the glass from my hand. "It's fine." She laughs a laugh that is not a laugh. "It only helped a little bit." She closes the door behind her.

I think about knocking again, trying to have more of a conversation, or seeing if Angelina is home and telling her that I don't think Autumn is okay. But I don't. Even though I know Finn would have been worried about her.

I walk off the porch, pack up the mower, and go home. I watch the game with Dad, and Mom sticks around to eat tacos with us.

When Autumn crosses my mind again, I push away the thought the way I push away fantasies of Finn being alive. I don't have room in my head for her grief and my own.

I drive back to school the next day.

I don't do what Finn would have wanted me to do.

seventeen

DID YOU HEAR ABOUT AUTUMN?

I stare at the first text I've had from Sylvie since I'd texted her during my run a few weeks ago. I'm between classes, and I have a tight window to walk across campus, but I've stopped in my tracks on the sidewalk. Someone calls me an asshole as he bumps my shoulder, but I ignore him and type while the crowd moves around me.

Hear what?

Sylvie knew that Finn cheated on her, right? Was I wrong to assume that he would've told her? Is she only figuring this out now?

She tried to kill herself.

Another guy bumps into me in protest of my roadblock. "Excuse me," a girl says.

It's the first cool fall day. The sky is blue, and everyone is wearing light jackets. It's been almost a week since I mowed Finn's lawn.

I think about asking Sylvie if she's sure, but that would be a question for Alexis, not Sylvie. If Sylvie says it's true, it almost certainly is.

I don't need to ask why.

And it doesn't matter how.

She's alive, thank goodness.

Still, the need to find out more nags me. There's no more rush of folks to class, just casual walkers wandering the campus who sidestep me. No matter what, I'm going to be late. If I hurry, I might be able to slip in the back unnoticed. But class can wait.

Sylvie answers on the first ring.

"Hello, Jack," she says, as if I hadn't asked her why she wasn't wearing her seatbelt in our last exchange.

"Hi," I say. "What happened with Autumn?"

"She tried to kill herself. She survived, but she's in the hospital." She sighs. "Taylor told me. I don't even know how she found out. She thought I'd be happy."

"Gross," I say.

"Yeah."

"But Autumn's okay?"

"I doubt she's okay, Jack," Sylvie says. "But she is alive."

We're both silent for a moment. The wind picks up. I watch the leaves rustling. One lonely cloud wanders by.

"I should have said something," I say. "I saw Autumn last week, and I could tell she wasn't okay."

Sylvie snorts. "I don't know if I'm okay either," she says. "Are you okay?"

"I don't know," I answer. "But I knew Autumn wasn't." I take a deep breath. "Maybe we're on our way to being okay. When I saw Autumn, I could tell she wasn't on her way. I should have said something to Angelina or her mom."

I hear Sylvie breathing. I'm still watching the leaves in the wind. All the trees are starting to turn color.

"Why does it bother me so much?" Sylvie asks. "That she did that? Sure, I'm not a monster like Taylor thought, but why do I care so fucking much about whether Autumn Davis lives or dies?"

"Because Finn would want her to live."

"Yeah," Sylvie whispers. And then, "What if she tries it again? Statistically, there's a good chance of that."

"I'll tell her not to," I say, as if it's as simple as that, but hey, maybe it is? "I'll tell Autumn that Finn would want her to live." Something relaxes in my shoulders as I hear the words aloud. "I was just there, but I can go home again this weekend. Besides, my brothers and I have a bet about whether I can get my dad to go to the art museum."

"That's weird," Sylvie says. "But thank you. I'll be honest. If you didn't offer, I was going to guilt you into it. I don't think she'd want to see me."

"If I didn't offer, then I should have been guilted," I say. "I'm

270

telling you, Sylv, I really should have said something after I saw her last weekend."

Sylvie pauses and then says carefully, "There're always things that we could have done differently. What matters is what we do now."

It was the rain's fault.

"Yeah," I say. "You're right."

eighteen

I THOUGHT A MENTAL HOSPITAL would be a stately building at the end of a long driveway with a big green lawn, like in movies, but it's simply another wing at the hospital. It has its own front desk, waiting room with vinyl seats, and watercooler.

When I approach the desk and ask about Autumn, the nurse looks doubtful, like maybe he should send me away, but he says visiting hours start in forty minutes. The staff will give my name to Autumn.

"I'll let you know if she doesn't want to see you."

The nurse pauses to gauge my reaction. When I shrug, he seems satisfied and goes out a door behind the desk.

I sit down in one of the chairs to wait. Its possible Autumn won't want to see me. I suppose if I'd thrown a fit about it, it would be a sign I wasn't someone who should see a patient.

When the nurse returns, he says, "You're on her approved visitors list now, but you still have to wait another half hour." He eyes the bag in my hand. "Is that for her?"

"Yeah?"

"I'm going to have to go through it. And she can't have a plastic bag. I'll give you a paper one."

I pass him the bag and am grateful that I took out the condoms before coming. He roots around, looking for drugs or a knife, I guess. I think about the plastic bag being a danger to Autumn.

The nurse dumps the bag's contents into a paper sack and hands it to me. I smile and say thanks. This must be a tense place to work.

The half hour goes by quickly, because I'm trying to figure out what to say to Autumn. The waiting room fills with other visitors, but the room stays silent. Before I'm ready, the nurse tells us that we can follow him, and we're led to what looks like a school cafeteria.

The other visitors seem to know the drill, and everyone sits down at their own table. I pick one and look around the room. It even smells like a school cafeteria. There's a beep and a dull thud. A different set of doors opens.

Autumn emerges from the group of strangers. I watch her scan the tables before she sees me. Her blank expression doesn't change as she starts toward me.

"Hi." She slips into the chair across from me.

"Hey," I say. "Um, how are you?"

She looks like a store mannequin modeling baggy clothes.

"Even on a regular day, I've never known how to answer that question."

She doesn't look at me but up and over my shoulder, as if the answer is in the air.

"I think most people lie," I tell her.

Autumn doesn't smile, but her shoulders relax a bit, and she starts to look more like herself, so I continue.

"Everyone always says they're fine. Everyone can't be fine all the time. We all just pretend it's true."

"I guess I'm not good at pretending," she says.

"Maybe you used to be too good at pretending."

Autumn cocks her head to the side.

I try to untangle my thoughts. "Finn talked about you being depressed, and I could never see it. No one at school could. I thought he was—or you were—"

Am I seriously about to tell her that up until Finn died, I thought she was a fake?

"I'm pregnant," Autumn blurts out.

We stare at each other.

What?

"Sorry. I don't know why I said that. It's hard to think about anything else."

"And Finn—"

"Of course."

I burst out laughing, which is probably better than calling her fake, but still. She looks confused and perhaps even alarmed, so I try to explain.

"I cleaned out Finn's car for Angelina, and this was under the seat. He bought this stuff right before—" I clear my throat and push the bag across the table toward her. "I thought you should have this.

I probably should have given this to you then. Sorry." I pause. "It's more proof that he was coming back to you."

Autumn reaches out and touches the bag but doesn't open it.

"I laughed because, well, if you look at the receipt, he bought some—" I give up.

She opens the bag and touches the candy in a way that makes me think of his mother. She glances at me and takes out the receipt. She scans it and laughs too.

Then she blushes, and I look away. When I glance back, she's stroking the candy packets tenderly.

"That's a lot of candy," I say.

"There's only one place that sells these. Finny never liked that gas station. He only went there to get these for me. Maybe he was trying to avoid it for a while."

"Why didn't he like it?"

"I don't know." Autumn pauses, then picks up a packet and opens it.

"Maybe he thought it was unsafe for some reason?" I venture. "You know how safety conscious he was."

Autumn pauses with the candy dipstick in her hand. "I never thought of Finny that way, but I suppose you're right." I'm honestly stunned until she says, "I always thought of him as protective."

It makes sense, the way we're seeing the same trait through our different lenses.

"Have you told his mom yet?" I ask.

Autumn shakes her head. "You're the first person I told. I

found out a week ago. I'm still trying to wrap my head around it."
She's finally dipping the stick in her candy powder and stirring it
slowly.

"But you're going to make a go of it and all that?"

"Yeah, I want to have it. I don't know what I'd do if Finny were
alive though." She puts the candy stick in her mouth and gazes at
the table. She sort of laughs and shrugs.

She's pregnant. Autumn's going to have Finn's baby.

Finn's baby.

"Well, if you are going to be around St. Louis still, when I'm
home, maybe I can help or visit. Finn's baby."

Autumn smiles. The mannequin look is gone. "You were important to Finny. I'm going to need—"

She looks away.

I try to anticipate her answer. *Diapers? Rides?*

"I'm going to need people to tell stories about Finn, and I'm
going to need a copy of every picture you have."

I'm thinking about all the people crying at Finn's funeral. Of his
mom saying that it was proof of the mark he'd made.

"Yeah." In my mind, I start to make a list of people to ask about
pictures. Everyone I'd seen at the wake, at Alexis's party. The time
to ask people for stories is now. While the details are fresh. While
the grief is still fresh. "There're some people I can call too," I say.
"And down the line, if you need diapers or..."

"I don't know what I'll need," Autumn says. "Parents always
seem to need...everything..."

She's gazing over my shoulder again, like a list of baby items is floating in the air behind me.

I wait for her to finish her thought. When she doesn't, I say, "What do you think your moms—I mean, your mom and Angelina will think?"

Autumn shakes her head, and she looks down at the table between us. "They're going to be happy. But they're going to be worried about me."

"I can see that," I say.

"Ten minutes!" The nurse shouts from across the room, making us both jump.

We both laugh and fall into silence. She's looking more alive than at the start of my visit.

"So, uh—" I'm not sure if I should say this, but something is telling me that Finn would want her to know. "Sylvie wanted me to tell you something."

Autumn looks uncomfortable. She bites her lip, and I hurry my words so she doesn't think I came here to yell at her for Sylvie.

"She's glad you're okay. Or going to be okay."

Autumn's face turns from uneasy to skeptical.

"She wanted me to come see you," I insist. "She wants you to get better."

Autumn gives me a withering look. If I were lying or exaggerating, I would squirm under her glare. But I'm not.

"I don't think you get it." I'm angry, because she *should* get it. "Just like you need my memories of Finn? The part of him that

277

loved you is still alive as long as you are, Autumn. You almost took another part of Finn away from all of us. So yeah, Sylvie gives enough of a shit to ask me to make sure you're not determined to take yourself and all your memories of Finn to an early grave. And now that you're pregnant—" I stop. I'm practically yelling at a pregnant suicidal woman.

"I'm not going to do it again," she whispers. Her voice quavers.

"Oh shit," I say. "I didn't mean—"

"It's okay. I'm mad at me too."

"I shouldn't make you cry though," I say. I glance nervously over at the nurse, but he hasn't noticed. Yet.

Autumn surprises me by laughing instead of crying.

"Are you sure Sylvie will still want me alive when she finds out I'm having Finny's baby?"

"I mean, I don't think she's going to throw you a baby shower or anything, but she isn't a monster. So yeah, when Sylvie eventually finds out, she's going to want you to be healthy, happy." I shrug. "Just know that you have a lot of people who care for you. And everyone, fucking everyone, who loved Finn wants you to be okay too, okay? Even if something happens to this baby. Stay alive."

"Okay," she whispers.

"Time!" the nurse booms.

"Promise?"

"Promise."

When she hugs me goodbye, it doesn't feel like goodbye. It feels like hugging Finn. I know now that she's going to be part of my life for a long time.

———————————

It isn't until I'm driving home that it dawns on me: I've been thinking about Finn, and for the first time since Alexis's call that morning, it doesn't hurt.

I'm so, so grateful that Finn was once alive and that I got to love him. That he got to love and be loved.

And be loved still.

autumn

one

———

NOT WANTING TO BE DEAD isn't quite the same as wanting to be alive. There's a gray space in between where one knows the desire to keep breathing should lie but is coolly absent. This is the space I occupy.

There is a piece of Finny inside me to keep alive, so the rest, like breathing, must be endured.

Ever since I was released from the hospital six days ago, I've gotten out of bed, showered, and eaten three square meals that I sometimes don't throw up. Every day! I thought this was enough.

After nearly a month in the hospital, I thought that once I was back at home, I could coast on not actively trying to kill myself. But no. Apparently, gestating a future human does not prove my will to live.

Which is why I'm at this awful, garish baby boutique.

I can tell Aunt Angelina thinks this place is awful too, but we can't back out now. She and Mom came to me this morning and told me that showering and getting dressed were all well and good, but they were worried I wasn't showing much enthusiasm about the future.

"The baby still doesn't feel that real to me," I protested. "I'll probably get more excited later."

"We weren't even talking about the baby," Mom said. She was standing in the middle of my room with her hands clasped in front of her, looking oddly childlike for a pending grandmother. Angelina was leaning against my dresser in a manner that reminded me of him so much that I can't even articulate it.

"You need to show enthusiasm for something, kiddo," Aunt Angelina said. "You haven't touched a book since you got home."

"Is this because I didn't want to hand out candy to trick-or-treaters last night?" I was sitting on my bed (not *in* my bed!). I'd gagged down my prenatal vitamin. Perhaps they wanted me to be enthused about that.

Mom sat down next to me. "This is a lot, for all of us. We need to try to focus on the good. If it doesn't feel real yet, let's make it feel real."

So I mustered a smile and said, "Okay."

And now here we are, in a baby store of my mother's choosing.

When we arrived, a saleswoman eyed the three of us: Aunt Angelina in her hippie clothes, me in my faded T-shirt and ripped jeans, and Mom in her Chanel suit and expensive handbag. Rather than trying to figure out which one of us was pregnant, she focused on Mom, a smart move on her part. Still, we were all handed a glossy booklet, like the store is an event we are attending.

Apparently there're different kinds of babies one can have. There're the modern babies who are surrounded by smooth Danish surfaces and only wear beige, gray, or white; the funny babies who wear bright shirts with ironic slogans and have pacifiers that look like vampire fangs or mustaches; and the hippie babies with their wooden toys who only eat or wear natural fibers, also in beige, gray, or white.

Perhaps there're other types of babies, but this store seems to only cater to those three.

"We're just having fun today," Mom chirps. "Picking up a few things to get us excited."

The saleslady reads the room. We're not in the mood for her full pitch, and she returns to hanging Christmas decorations that it should be too early to put up.

Mom confidently leads Aunt Angelina and I to the newborn section and begins to page through the tiny hangers, so I mimic her.

There's no way babies are actually this small. I've seen babies before, and they've never been this little.

I remember holding Angie's daughter at the hospital. Had she been this size? I close my eyes and try to remember the feel of her, the weight, not heavy but so solid, and I turned to Finn and I—

Oh God.

Everything stops. There's no boutique. There's no onesie in my hand. I'm sitting on that hospital bed with him, and he loves me, but I don't know it.

How could I not know it? It's so stupidly obvious now, and I want to scream at us, but I can't. We say the things we said that day, and even though every word was "I love you," it also wasn't. And I can't change that. I can't change that. I can't, I can't, I can't, I can't... Oh God.

"They really are that small," Aunt Angelina says, and I'm back in the store. Finny is dead. He was always dead. It was only briefly in my mind that he was alive again.

I look down at the onesie with blue polka dots I am holding.

"I was just thinking that a newborn couldn't really be this size."

"They grow fast," my mother says. "You don't need too many newborn outfits. A few weeks later, they're a whole different baby."

There's a pause. Mom, Angelina, and I are assessing each other. If Finny was alive, this is when The Mothers would begin to reminisce about the two of us as babies.

Is it safe? We are asking each other, ourselves. Mostly, they are asking me, but Mom and Aunt Angelina have their moments too.

"You'll still need more than you think," Aunt Angelina says, moving the conversation forward. "It's amazing how many outfit changes babies need."

Babies. Not Finny as a baby.

Mom takes the polka-dot onesie from me and adds it to the pile in her arms. "They always throw up on the cute ones," she says.

The Mothers are now unsure about the outing. Mom glances at Aunt Angelina, her concern for her bleeding through her normal poise. But I'm not paying attention anymore.

When Mom mentions throwing up, I start thinking about how I haven't vomited in a while, which makes my body say, "Wait, yes.

That's a good idea." Before I can worry about Angelina, I'm needing to find someplace to expel my eggs and sausage.

I can already taste it as I exit the boutique and rush for the trash bin in the main mall.

I thought I was done with this. It had been two days since I'd thrown up.

Twelve hours since I've cried.

I barely make it, spewing chunks in an arch as I lean over the trash can.

Finny would be proud of me for that one, I think as I heave again.

"You're getting really good at aiming your vomit, Autumn."

I can hear his voice, really hear him say it.

No. I don't truly think it's him, though there was a time when I entertained the idea. I've accepted this new reality without Finny, yet I can't stop myself from thinking about him. And when I do? There he is.

My Finny.

"Autumn."

I gasp for air between heaves. My stomach muscles ache in new mysterious ways, even when I'm not vomiting.

"Autumn?"

"I'm okay!"

"I have a water bottle in my bag," Aunt Angelina says.

Water sounds amazing, and I hope my body lets me have some soon. I take a shuddering breath but don't move from the trash can.

"Where's Mom?"

"Buying the onesie you were holding. Plus another hundred or so other bits of overpriced fabric. Don't worry, kiddo. I'll take you to the resale shops and load you up on baby clothes that you don't have to be fussy about."

I stand up straight and take another breath, assessing my body. I feel like the captain of a ship amid a squall, telling the old gal to stay steady and ride the waves.

Aunt Angelina hands me the bottle and smiles.

Thank goodness she doesn't look too much like Finny. Her smile is different, her hair is darker, her chin sharper. I see him in her, but it could be much worse.

Like the way she carries herself, with a constant stoicism.

"Better?" she asks.

"What if I never stop throwing up? I read some women do that."

She shrugs. "Then you will throw up for another six months and it will suck."

"I don't think I could do it." I swish the water around in my mouth.

"You could and you would, because you'd have to, but you probably won't," Aunt Angelina says. "Being a mother is all about losing control and then surviving it."

I spit into the trash can and take a sip of water, but my throat still feels raw.

"That makes motherhood sound really terrible."

Aunt Angelina pulls me into a hug. "It's worth it," she says.

I feel sick to my stomach in a way that has nothing to do with the baby. I squeeze her tighter.

"I'm sorry. I shouldn't have said that," I whisper.

"It's still worth it, Autumn, even if they die."

My stomach drops again, but she releases me from the hug and smiles sadly at me.

A security guard approaches and asks if we need help or an ambulance. He's not thrilled about my use of the trash can and points out a restroom on the other side of the courtyard, as if that would have helped. Mom comes out with her shopping bags. The guard eyes my middle before getting on his walkie-talkie and asking for cleaning services.

Mom describes every outfit she has purchased in great detail so that by the time we're in the car, I almost don't need to go through the bags. But I do so that I can thank her for each one as we drive home. Our chatter covers the hole in our day's adventure, the lack of excitement they'd hoped to inspire.

Everything having to do with this baby reinforces the fact that Finny's not here.

For all of us.

Yet we want this. I want this.

He would want this.

But that doesn't make doing this without him any easier.

So this is where I live, in a place where every shade of joy must be painted over in the black of Finny's death, muted to the gray of willfully existing.

two

————

"THIS IS AWESOME," ANGIE SAYS, glancing up from Guinevere to smile at me. Her face is luminous and shadowed with exhaustion.

I hadn't planned to tell her so immediately. We've hardly spoken in months, but the moment I saw her round face and short figure, my heart leapt, and a feeling of safety came over me.

I suppose it has been a while since I was with a friend.

The tiny basement apartment is cluttered with the lives of three humans and their shoes. I'm perched on the edge of the second-hand plaid couch, which is covered in unfolded laundry. Angie is on the floor changing Guinevere into a "First Christmas" onesie, even though it's the first week of November. She snaps the last button and looks up at me.

"It is awesome that you're pregnant, right?" She sits back on her heels.

"It's good." I sound like I'm talking about a meal at a restaurant that wasn't quite what I expected. "It's scary," I add, and I still sound like I'm talking about mayonnaise.

"It's terrifying!" Angie sings as she tickles Guinevere's chin. She rolls the baby onto her stomach in a square of sunshine cast through the small window. "And it doesn't stop. Sorry."

"What doesn't stop?"

"Motherhood never stops being scary."

She laughs. I don't.

Angie stretches her arms above her blond head and groans. She yawns and blinks at me.

"Stand up and let me look at you," she says.

I oblige, and she nods sagely.

"I can tell," she says. "I totally see it."

"No, I can barely feel it, Ang." The button on my jeans is undone, but my zipper zips.

"I see it," she says. "When are you due?"

"May Day," I reply, and then, "May first. Not the distress call."

Angie smiles and yawns again. "Yes, I can see Auntie Aut's bump, can you, Guinnie?" She lies down on the floor with a groan. "Sorry, Autumn. I am just so tired."

"It's okay. I'm tired too." I sit back on the couch and watch her coax a smile from her child. The Mothers were thrilled when I said I had reached out to Angie and needed a ride to her place. It's nice seeing her. It's weird seeing her as a mother.

There's this confidence about Angie that startles me. I'd first noticed it at the hospital last summer, but it's more pronounced now.

291

When she answered the door, she was holding the baby on her hip, and after hugging me and inviting me inside, Angie said, "Sorry. I felt her head, and I need to change her into something warmer," so she had.

"Is that a trick or hack or something?" I ask her. "What you said a minute ago about feeling her head?"

"No, her head just didn't feel warm enough."

"What's warm enough?"

"How she normally feels." She yawns again. "Sorry. She sleeps through the night most of the time. But when she doesn't..."

I wait, but she says nothing more. I gaze around the room, at the crib and queen-size bed. It felt like a lot more space when I visited a year ago, when we were all still in high school.

"Isn't it weird," Angie says, "to think about the last time you were here?" She stares up at the ceiling.

"So much has changed since then," we say at the same time, then laugh.

"I know I sent a text," Angie says, "but I want to say in person I'm sorry about Finn."

"It's his baby," I say.

Angie laughs so loud she covers her mouth. I'm startled enough that the pain of thinking about Finny is stunted.

"Yeah, of course it is," she says and giggles. "I mean, who else?" She sits up and looks at me.

I raise my eyebrows. "Some people would have guessed Jamie."

Angie shakes her head. "You were never going to do it with Jamie. Anyone could see that."

"I would have," I say. "If he hadn't cheated on me."

"Nope." Angie's voice has a finality like her certainty while talking about her daughter. "It wasn't there with you guys."

I can't disagree, but I don't like her seeing something in me that I didn't know about myself. If it was obvious to her that our relationship wasn't meant to last, how dense was I to have missed it?

"How did you know it was Finny's though?" I ask. "We haven't seen each other in months. I could have met someone new."

"No way."

"I don't see why that's an impossibility," though I don't know why I'm protesting.

Angie gets off the floor and comes to sit next to me on the couch.

"It was obvious at the hospital after Guinnie was born that something had already happened with you guys," she says, but I shake my head.

"We were only friends then."

Angie rolls her eyes so hard that it looks like it hurts.

"You guys were never just friends, Autumn, and you know it." She studies my face. "You know that everyone knew, right?"

"I didn't know that there was anything to know," I say in a daze.

"You didn't know that Finn Smith was into you?" She says it like I'm telling her I don't know my middle name.

"You really didn't know?" he asked me that last night.

"I thought you never talked about it because you were embarrassed," Angie says.

"Embarrassed by what?"

293

"Well, for years, I thought you were embarrassed because he was like a brother to you or whatever? But then I started noticing how you both did the animal thing with each other."

"The what?"

"Like, have you ever seen an animal see another animal?"

"Have I ever seen an—"

Angie puts both hands up to stop me. "You remember my dog, Bowie, at my parents' house? Whenever I walked him and he saw another dog, he would go real still, and the other dog would too. It was like you could see the million thoughts going on in their brains. And then suddenly, they'd either want to fight or play. Whenever you and Finn Smith would see each other, at school or the mall or whatever, you guys would freeze for a split second. And then you would be moving and talking again, but it was like part of you was still frozen, waiting for the other person to do something."

Flashes of memories assault me, a montage without music. *Finny. My Finny.* I cannot speak. Angie doesn't seem to expect anything from me though.

"After a while, I was like, okay, she's going to break up with Jamie and be with Finn," Angie says. "But you never did. I thought maybe your moms didn't want you dating or something."

"No," I whisper. "I just didn't know it was an option."

"That's really sad," Angie says gently. "But obviously, you had some time together." She motions with her eyes towards my midsection.

"A day. Or rather a half a night and then a day."

294

"Oh, Autumn." The weight of him, smell of him, of Finn—

"Shit," Angie says.

"I don't know if I can talk about it anymore," I tell her.

She nods, then reaches over and hugs me. I relax into it. Like seeing her, I hadn't realized how much I needed it until it happened.

When Angie pulls back, she looks over at her baby. "I–I–It's been kinda lonely, Autumn."

"Yeah?"

"Yeah."

Guinevere is pushing herself up on her elbows. We both watch her.

"What about Dave?" I can't call him "Preppy Dave" now that he's a dad. It doesn't seem right.

"When he's not at work, he's at school, and when he's home, I need him to look after the baby so I can have a minute to myself, because somehow—even though I'm so lonely—I'm also never alone." She looks from her daughter to me. "Shit, I'm scaring you, aren't I?"

"It's not that I wasn't scared before," I say, "but I'd kinda thought that you had it made. The perfect teen mom situation."

"I don't think such a thing exists," Angie says. "The whole nature of the job is..." She looks up at the ceiling. "It's a lot, Autumn. It's worth it, but it's a lot. You'll understand."

Everyone keeps telling me this. No one will elaborate. I don't bother asking her what she means. I look at the baby practicing push-ups on the floor, and I count the months. She's five months old. A year from now, I'll have a baby a month younger than that.

I'd think that was impossible if it wasn't for how much has already changed in a year.

"Have you been keeping up with everybody?" I ask.

Angie doesn't answer at first. I glance over, and her eyes are closed, and for a moment, I think she's dozed off while sitting up, then she speaks.

"At first, they all emailed or called from school once a week, and I was like, 'Cool. That seems reasonable.' But then it stopped." She pauses again. Her eyes are still closed. "And I tell myself, 'I'm busy too. We're all going through stuff. Doing new stuff.' And I know that we'll hang out when they're home for Christmas, but I guess I already know it won't be the same. Because I'm not the same. And they won't be the same, but at least they'll be the same kind of not the same." She takes a deep breath and opens her eyes.

I nod at her. Everything she has said makes sense, but I'm not sure what to say about it.

"I hope this doesn't come off as 'misery loves company,'" Angie says, "but I'm glad that I'm going to have a friend who knows what it's like to be a mom."

It has come off that way, but I know that if I voice it, Angie will only assure me that motherhood is worth it, that I'll understand later.

Angie yawns again, rubs her face, and glances over at her daughter. The baby has fallen asleep on the play mat, and Angie brightens. She puts a finger to her lips.

"Should I leave?" I whisper.

"No, and you can talk in a normal voice as long as you're quiet. She's a deep sleeper. I'm lucky."

"Okay."

"So kinda like with the Finn thing," Angie says as she picks at the upholstery. "I know I said it in my email back in July, but I had no idea about Jamie and Sasha."

"I believe you," I say. I have no reason not to, and I want it to be true.

"When they told me they were a couple, I was really pissed. I tried to tell them how shitty it was, but they kept saying 'We know! We know!' and talking about how terrible they felt about it."

"They should have felt terrible," I say.

"That's what I said!" We both look at the baby who gives a little snore. "That's what I said," Angie says in a stage whisper. "That they should feel bad. It was a couple of weeks before Guinevere was due, so it was easy to avoid them. But then at the hospital— well, you said you didn't want to talk about that stuff anymore." She glances at me. "When I saw you at the hospital, you seemed great, and then I went home with the baby, and, well…" Angie bites her lip.

"What?"

"I feel bad that I let us go this long without talking," she says. "I should have called you first."

"It's okay." I haven't told her about my hospital stay, but something tells me she knows. I'm not ready to talk about that yet.

"So when you were hearing from everyone," I say in my best casual voice, "how were they doing?"

Angie tells me that Brooke and Noah had a harder time with their planned breakup than expected, but last Angie heard, they were both glad they went through with it. We laugh about Noah joining a frat. Brooke had a big date for Halloween, but Angie never heard how it went.

"Sasha told me that you never answered her or Jamie's emails or texts or anything," Angie says. "So I don't know if you want to know how they're doing?"

"Oh." I shrug. "I kinda want to hear. Not wanting to hear from them isn't the same as not wanting to hear about them. When I say that I don't forgive them, I mean I don't want them in my life anymore, not that I wish them ill."

"Last I heard, they were fine, still together." She adds, "But that's easy in a new place where you only know each other."

I prod deep for any hurt, and there is none.

Except for the memories of the time after they cheated, that final spring in high school.

If I had known.

If I had only known.

Things would have been different.

That place still hurts.

That place can't forgive.

For a long time, I imagined a scenario where I found out Jamie had cheated on me with Sasha, and we broke up and Finny and I got together, and the whole trajectory of our lives would have been different. I can't even predict where we would be now if we had known we were in love last spring.

"Autumn?" Angie asks. "Are you okay?"

"Sorry," I say. "I was in my head."

"You looked sad."

"I was wishing I had known they slept together when it happened instead of weeks later, because maybe Finn and I..." I shrug once more. "It's pointless to think about, but it's hard not to."

Angie nods. "I know that feeling." She looks at Guinevere asleep on the floor. The sun has moved, and the room is darker. "I'm glad to have you here, Autumn. Please don't—"

And then I know that she knows I was in the hospital, because she struggles to find the right thing to say.

"—go anywhere?" she finishes.

"I won't," I say. "For a little while, I thought being dead might be better, but that was before the baby."

Angie keeps staring at her daughter. "You'll need more than that," she murmurs.

"What?"

"I—sorry." She looks back at me. "It's better to be alive, Autumn. Please don't forget that again, okay?"

"I won't," I say, and then to distract her, I add, "You should tell me your birth story again."

"I don't want to scare you," she says but then launches into the tale.

When Mom picks me up forty minutes later, I know a lot about episiotomies. I wish I didn't know what one was, to be honest, but now that I do, it seems important to be well informed. I'm going to need to make a trip to the library.

"How was it?" Mom asks as I buckle my seatbelt.

"Good" I say. "It was nice to see her and Guinevere."

"Were you able to catch up?"

"Sort of. So much has happened. It was almost more than we could talk about." I pause. "She seems different. Not in a bad way, but it's like—" I struggle to find the words and am not fully happy with the ones I find. "It's like she's confident and resigned at the same time."

My mother surprises me by nodding. "It sounds like she's adjusting."

When the car stops at an intersection, I catch her looking at me.

"Did it make it feel more real?" she asks. "Seeing the baby?"

"A little," I say. "In an overwhelming way."

She nods. There's nothing to say or do to make this situation less overwhelming. I'm surprised then that Mom continues.

"You know, Autumn, if Finny were alive, I would tell you to think about what you wanted more than what he wanted. And I should tell you to do that now too." She takes a deep breath, and I'm glad we're pulling into the driveway in case she starts crying.

"Do you not want me to have it?" I ask.

She puts the car in park. "I want you to have this baby more

300

than anything," she says. "But you must want it, Autumn. You have to want it more than anything. Especially as a single mother." She takes off her seat belt and turns to me. "Angelina and I will give you all the support in the world, I can't overstate that. But you still have to want this and want it for yourself. Not for me, not for Angelina or for Finny, but for you."

I don't know what to say. I'm not sure how to answer her question or if she's really asking me a question.

"I want to have Finny's baby for me," I finally say. I look at my hands in my lap and pick at my thumbnail. "But I probably wouldn't want to if he were alive," I admit. "And I don't know how to love this child without Finn."

My mother sits back in her seat and faces the windshield like me. She sighs.

"All we can do is live in the reality we're in. Maybe you would have still had the baby if Finny were alive, maybe not. But he's not alive, and..." She pauses. "If you think having this baby is the right thing for you, then you should know that I'm not worried about you loving this baby. That will come."

"But what if I can't?" My voice sounds hoarse. "What if something is broken inside me?" I wrap my arms around my middle. "The baby deserves a mother who can love it properly." I close my eyes and grit my teeth. Finny's baby deserves better than me.

"The first step to being a good mother is questioning whether you can be a good mother. And it's okay if you're feeling broken, Autumn, because becoming a parent breaks you in a new way. It's

301

the most joyful and heartbreaking thing you'll ever do." She shakes her head. "Losing Finny was a tragedy, but you're strong, Autumn, even if you can't see it now, and you'll be a good parent."

"I think I'd be a better parent if Finny were here."

"But we'll never know," my mother says. "Especially since you think you wouldn't decide to be a parent if he were here."

I shrug and look away from her. Briefly I see Finny and I as college students trying to decide what we're going to do with the pregnancy. She's right; I don't know what we would have decided together. I'm not used to having deep conversations with my mother.

"Would you marry Dad again if you had the chance to do it over?" I ask. It's been on my mind since before everything that happened.

Mom sighs. "I wouldn't change having you, that's all I know. If it was just about your father? If I was to time travel back to age nineteen when I got engaged? I wouldn't want to have a different child with him or do things over again with him a different way. Time travel isn't real, so it's not a problem to solve." She reaches for my hand, her foray into tangential speculations done. "Look at me."

Her tone is urgent, and I turn to meet her eyes.

"When this child is alive and breathing in front of you," my mother says, "I promise you will love it. And you won't care about what you would have done under different circumstances. Children have a way of making you live in the present."

Her face is solemn, familiar, and tired. Losing Finny hurt her too, and then she almost lost me, yet she's carried Angelina and I through these last few weeks without complaint.

302

"I suppose that's another thing I won't understand until it happens?"

"Parenthood has a lot of those," she says.

"I want this," I say. "Thank you for asking."

"All right," she says. "Let's go." She means into the house, but it feels like so much more.

three

IT'S STUNNING HOW LITTLE DR. Singh's office has changed over the years. I wish other things in the world were as static as the pictures and diplomas on his walls, the piles of patient charts on his desk.

The only thing that has changed is the green plant on the top of his bookcase, which has continued to birth new leaves, one after another, in a long chain that almost reaches the floor.

Dr. Singh was very pleased when he weighed me this time.

"You are looking very healthy," he says. "When I saw you in the hospital, it was—" He throws up his hands. Apparently there aren't words. "But now? You have some color. You have some weight on you. How are you feeling?"

"I think I'm done with the nausea," I say. "So that's good."

"That is good, that is good," Dr. Singh says. "And how is the new therapist? I'm sorry Dr. Kleiger didn't work out."

I can't help making a face. "I didn't like the new lady either. I don't want to go back. She didn't feel right."

Dr. Singh frowns. "It can be hard to find the right therapist. But you are in dire need, hmm? You were suicidal not that long ago, and with a baby coming? Did you know that the brain changes more during the months of pregnancy than it does during all the years of adolescence? It's amazing! But—" He shakes his head. "It is a lot. So *I* am here to make sure that the new medication that's safe for you and the baby is working, but you need someone to talk to every week, Autumn. You have so much work to do."

"I know," I say. "But I also have so much to do to prepare. We only started talking about where and how the baby will sleep, and I'm so tired all the time."

"You must try again with someone else," Dr. Singh insists. "My office will call with another recommendation, hmm?"

I nod, and he smiles. I can't help but smile back.

"While we are here, you can tell me, how are you feeling, in your head, not your body?"

I tell him the truth. "I don't know. I want to have this baby, but it's like the hurt of missing Finny cancels out the joy. I feel blank. I don't know how to be myself in this new reality."

Dr. Singh sighs and rubs his face. "That is not as much of an improvement as I would have hoped, and it speaks to your need to find a regular therapist. Tell me again why Dr. Kleiger did not suit you?"

"I felt like a bug he was studying," I say. "The way he peered at me."

"And Dr. Remus?"

"I was a book she was reading."

"And how do you feel about our conversations?"

"Like you're a paramedic and I have a wound that you're treating," I explain.

He loses his smile, but not exactly in a sad way. He sighs again and takes off his glasses to inspect them, then puts them back on.

"I am extremely busy, Autumn," he says. "But I am certified as a therapist as well. I could see you every other week, hmm?"

"Really?"

"You would have to go to the group therapy sessions I run at the hospital on the other weeks."

I can't help it; I make a face.

"What is so bad about that?"

I look away from him and down at my hands. "When I was in the hospital... Dr. Singh, I'm sad. Depressed. Back at the hospital, I had group therapy sessions. There was one woman who talked about seeing demons. She said that even when the meds were working, she would see them, but as long as she remembered they weren't real, it was fine. But then one of the demons said something to her, so that's how she knew it was time for a med adjustment. I mean..." I've failed to articulate what I want to say, because part of me knows that I shouldn't be thinking it.

When I lift my gaze, Dr. Singh looks absolutely exhausted.

"Autumn, you tried to end your life because you believed your life was not worth living without your lover, yes?"

I nod.

He sighs again and holds out his left hand. "So here you are, a

306

bright young person full of possibility, and you saw nothing worth living for and thought you were better off dead. Now over here"—he holds his right hand like a balancing scale—"we have another young person. When she looks at the world, she sees demons sometimes." He moves both hands up and down like he's weighing us against each other. "To me, you are more or less the same. You are both seeing something that is objectively not true. But then at least she knows that her demons aren't real." He folds his hands on his desk. "So, eh? But that is how I see it as a doctor. You both have chemical imbalances in your brain that make you see the world incorrectly."

"Finny really is dead. I'm not imagining that."

"No," Dr. Singh says. "But thinking that you are better off also dead? I know you cannot see it now, but it is objectively true that you are capable of living a happy life full of love—with or without this baby. You are so young. What a waste it would have been..."

He isn't looking at me. He is looking over my shoulder, like his brain has short-circuited, and I recognize the feeling.

"Dr. Singh?"

He shakes his head. "And finally, Autumn, the group I want you to go to is for my patients with PTSD. It's on Tuesdays, so you just missed it, but I'll see you next week, and the week after that, I'll see you here. Hmm?"

I agree. It can't be worse than my in-patient stay at the hospital or trying another therapist who doesn't listen to me like a person.

four

THIS KIWI SMOOTHIE IS THE ambrosia of the gods. I was unaware that anything could taste this good.

Angie asked me a question, but I don't want to stop drinking to answer her yet. Finally I take my lips off the straw with a gasp.

"It's not only soldiers. Anyone can have PTSD," I say.

We're at a smoothie-coffee shop that recently opened in the next town. Angie suggested we go out somewhere because she's sick of being at home. She dropped Dave off at community college this morning so that she could pick me up and we could get lunch together. Guinevere is in her carrier on the chair next to Angie. She's studying the rainbow teether in her hands like it is a Rubik's cube, her blond hair sticking up wildly, making her look like a tiny Einstein. During the ride here, I'd come clean to Angie about my hospital stay, even though she'd already heard about it as I'd suspected.

"So you'll be in a group with all sorts of grown-ups?" Angie asks. She picks up her sandwich and takes a bite.

"We are grown-ups," I remind her before returning to my smoothie.

"Yeah, but how are you going to relate to someone in group therapy who's, like, thirtysomething?"

I chew on my straw. "I don't know. I figure Dr. Singh must have a reason."

Guinevere squawks and shakes her teether with a tiny clack-clack. There's a satisfaction to her sound that tells me that she's solved her riddle, and I'm pleased for her. Angie smiles at her and touches her small foot.

"Oh my gosh, Autumn," she says. "I thought the baby was dead this morning!"

"What?"

"Yeah, she slept in a little, so when it was time to take Dave to school, I went to the crib, and she was so still, I really thought that she wasn't breathing. When I picked her up, she didn't stir for a second, so for this horrible moment, I really, really thought she was gone." She laughs. "But then she woke up and was so grumpy with me! She must have been having a good dream."

"Why would she be dead though?" I'm confused by her story.

"Sometimes babies just die," Angie says. "I'm serious. Usually, it's in the first couple of months, but sometimes"—she shrugs and winces simultaneously—"infants stop breathing, and no one knows why."

"No one knows why?" I repeat, my brain trying to process. I thought when it came to babies, doctors knew everything there was to know. "How can they not know?"

"There're theories," Angie says, "and stuff you can do to lower the risk. It's rare. It's unlikely to happen to Guinnie or your baby. It just scared me this morning when she was sleeping so deeply."

I go back to drinking my smoothie. I also have a sandwich, but I don't care about the sandwich, at least not right now. Angie is cooing at her daughter, who she had believed to be dead. I wonder if she always carries that fear. It's probably not at the forefront of her mind. She probably always expects her daughter to be alive, yet that knowledge, that you could be one of the mothers whose baby never wakes up...I don't think that ever leaves you. I don't think it will leave me now that I know it.

Angie tickles her daughter's socked feet. "What were you dreaming about that was so nice?" Her cell phone rings, and she smiles before answering. "Hey babe." Her smile melts, and she bites her lip. "Well, I have to take Autumn home after lunch, and then it will be time for Guinevere's nap. I—maybe—" She looks over at me and puts her phone to her shoulder. "Autumn, after we're done eating, do you mind if we pick up Dave? Both of his afternoon classes were taught by the same guy, and he's sick."

"It's fine. Not a big deal at all." This smoothie is the only thing on my schedule today.

"Okay, but after that, I'll have to put Guinnie down for her nap before I can take you home. I can't mess up her schedule. What, Dave?" She puts the phone back to her ear. "Oh. Or Dave can take you home."

"It's all fine." I'm almost done with my smoothie, and I'm going to ask for a box for my sandwich and another smoothie before we go. Guinevere gurgles thoughtfully, turning her teether over in her hands again.

"Okay," Angie says into the phone. "Yeah, we'll be there in an hour. Because we have to finish eating and then drive all the way out there! Webster Groves? What does it matter? Because I thought I was dropping Autumn back and going home to put Guinnie down and then would have two hours before picking you up! Oh my gosh, I'll see you in an hour." Angie rolls her eyes at me. "He's annoyed that he has to wait."

"It's not like you knew this would happen," I offer.

"Yeah, but he's in a bad mood a lot of the time."

"Why?" I slurp the last of the smoothie.

She shrugs and looks at the baby. "I mean, we're both tired. Even when she sleeps through the night, we're tired. And he's going to school and working sixteen hours at the burger place on the weekends. I don't know. I feel like I have more to complain about than him since nobody spits up on him at school or work, but I see why everything is hard for him too."

"He does get thrown up on at home sometimes," I point out. "You were telling me that story about his favorite shirt."

"Yeah, that's true," Angie says.

"Are you guys okay?" I ask. "Like, relationship-wise?"

"Yeah? I think so? I don't know. There's always so much other stuff to talk about. And even after the episiotomy healed, I really didn't want to have sex. I think we've had sex twice since Guinevere was born." She shrugs.

311

"How does Dave feel about that?"

"I don't know. I probably should ask him, but I feel kinda guilty about it," Angie says.

"Why would you feel guilty? Doesn't everybody know that happens after people have babies?"

"Yeah," Angie says, "but we had been joking the whole pregnancy about how there was no way that would ever happen to us because we were like, well, rabbits. Now here we are. Honestly, he's probably upset but trying to be nice by not bringing it up, but I don't bring it up because I'm just too tired."

I can't let her leave it unsaid. What if something happens to Dave?

"You should tell him that you care," I say. "That you've noticed him not complaining and that it means a lot to you. 'Cause how much worse would it be if he was complaining?"

"Yeah, maybe," Angie says.

"Definitely, tell him," I say. "I mean it."

Angie cocks her head to the side and starts to say something, but then her face goes pale. Her mouth drops open.

"What?" I look over my shoulder at Sylvie Whitehouse waiting in line at the counter. She's studying the menu. "Did she see me?" I ask.

"Definitely," Angie says. "Do you wanna go?"

"I wanted another smoothie." I'm so sad about it that I want to cry and really might. This smoothie was the best thing to happen to me in a long time. I wanted to have another, and now I can't, because

I obviously can't wait in line behind the girl whose boyfriend I slept with right before he died.

Angie's face hardens. She glances at her baby and looks back at me.

"Wait here with Guinnie." She leaves our booth and walks to the counter and gets in line behind Sylvie. They both stare straight ahead, but by the set of Sylvie's shoulders, she knows Angie is behind her.

"Meh?" Guinevere asks, and it truly is a question. I can hear it. "Meh? Meh?"

"It's okay."

Her gaze had been wandering around the room, but it latches on to me. "Meh," she tells me.

"She'll be right back," I say, and the baby bursts into loud sobs. I launch out of my seat and around the table. "Shh," I soothe, though it comes out too high-pitched. "It's okay." I fiddle with the straps on the seat, trying to unbind her from the carrier's rigorous safety features. "I'm here," I say, as if that is comforting.

Once she is free, the baby stops crying, but seemingly only out of confusion. "Beba?" She waits for me to do something, but I don't know what to do, so I continue to hold her from under her armpits out in front of me. "Meh?" she tries again and whimpers.

I start to swing her back and forth in a tick-tock motion. A series of emotions passes over her face: surprise, pleasure, and then annoyance. I think she likes what I'm doing but is annoyed that I'm distracting her from her mission.

"Baby swing, baby swing," I sing to her for some reason, and that makes her laugh. Out of the corner of my eye, I see Sylvie waiting for her drink. I've honestly tried not to think about how much Finny and I hurt her. She and I were never friends, yet what happened is too similar to what Jamie and Sasha did to me for me to be comfortable thinking about it.

Guinevere regards me distrustfully, like she knows people would say I stole another girl's boyfriend.

"Life is really complicated, Guinnie," I tell her, still swinging her back and forth. She isn't very heavy, but my arms are getting tired. Still, I keep rocking in fear she cries again. "Baby swing," I sing again, but this time, she is less impressed.

"Looks like you're a natural."

Angie's reappeared with my smoothie in a to-go cup and a box for my sandwich.

"Thank you, Angie." I feel like crying again, and I realize, for the first time, it might be a pregnancy thing.

"I saw the look on your face, and I remembered that feeling," Angie says. "I wasn't going to let you leave without one."

I stand up and trade the child for the to-go cup and take a big drink.

"Thanks," I say again.

"It's not a big deal," Angie says. She straps the baby back into her carrier. "She said something to me."

"Sylvie?"

"Yeah." She looks up at me. "She said to tell you that she's glad you're feeling better and congratulations."

I feel my mouth open, but no words come out.

314

Angie finishes strapping in her daughter and looks at me. "How does she know?" she asks me.

"Jack probably told her," I say. "You remember Jack Murphy, Finny's friend? He came to see me in the hospital." I haven't seen Jack since that visit, but he texts me every three days or so. He's checking in on me, which would annoy me, but I know he's doing it for Finny. Usually, he asks how I'm holding up and sometimes he sends a knock-knock joke. My answer to how I'm doing, like the quality of his jokes, varies widely.

"Yeah, I remember Jack," Angie says. "Are you ready, by the way? I didn't know you were close with him."

"We're not," I say, standing up to leave with her. "He came to see me for Finny's sake, I guess."

"Huh," Angie says. "And he told Sylvie, and Sylvie doesn't hate you?"

"I don't know. Did it sound like she hated me? Was she being sarcastic?"

Angie pauses. "I don't think so. She sounded solemn. I don't think she's thrilled, but she genuinely sounded glad that you're better." She shoulders the diaper bag, and we head to the parking lot.

"I guess it's good for both our sakes if she doesn't hate me," I offer, and Angie only nods, because like so many things in my life right now, there's nothing to say.

At least I have this smoothie.

five

——

I FOUND AN ARTICLE ONLINE that was titled "What You *Really* Need for Baby," and they had already earned my trust by dropping "the" or "your."

It said that you need

1. A place for baby to sleep safely
2. A place to change diapers and the supplies to do it
3. A way to carry baby
4. Clothes
5. A swing
6. Toys and books

And even though I knew that each item was full of its own subcategories, I decided to trust its deceptive simplicity and showed the list to my mother. This empowered Mom to show me her much, much longer list.

In the end, we compromised by agreeing to let Aunt Angelina choose the store we're going to today. That's why we are here, standing outside a resale shop.

My mother feels betrayed by her lifelong best friend.

"I thought you would at least pick one of the big cheesy department stores," she says to Angelina, who is aghast.

"Why would we put more money in the pockets of those corporate shills?"

"This place looks fine, Mom. Let's go in," I say.

She sighs and moves her handbag to the other shoulder, so I turn and head to the door.

Inside, a blue-haired woman behind a glass counter shouts a bit too loudly, "If you need anything, just ask!" She's either crocheting or knitting, but she's too stooped over for me to see clearly. There's something witch-like about her, the way she hunches over her textile crafting as if it were a cauldron.

There's a row of changing tables on the left, and I head to my number two agenda item. Once there, I am unsure what I need in a changing table. Obviously, I don't need anything fancy, but what is fancy? I'll need more than the pinewood one with two shelves, but what about the one that is also a playpen and a bassinet? Should a baby be playing and sleeping where its poop gets cleaned?

My mother and Aunt Angelina are still talking near the

entrance. Aunt Angelina points to a rack of clothing, and Mom remains stony-faced as she walks over and begins to inspect the wares.

"This is Ralph Lauren," she exclaims loudly enough for the old lady behind the counter to look over at her questioningly.

Mom drapes whatever it is over her arm and begins to peruse happily. I'm glad the store has met her standards. I return to the changing table conundrum.

"Those are really useful," Aunt Angelina says.

"Which one?" To my surprise, she indicates the one with the bassinet next to the changer.

"The first two months, they spend so much time sleeping and pooing, and you spend all your days napping on the couch or watching TV next to one of those." She walks around it and looks at it like she's kicking tires at a car dealership. "It has a pouch for wipes there," she points out.

"You and Mom always—" I start, then realize I shouldn't.

Aunt Angelina's shoulders tense. "Your mother and I what?" she asks gently.

"You always made it sound so idyllic, Finny and I in a playpen together while you talked."

"That was later. I didn't have the house until you were almost five months old, and those first three months, your mother and I hardly saw each other."

"Really? But you still lived so close? And you weren't working."

"And neither of you were sleeping!" She laughs. "Even if I hadn't been a single mother, I still wouldn't have had the energy to pack up Finny and his diaper bag and drive over. We talked on the phone, but we were both trying to survive. The early stages of motherhood can be very lonely."

"That's how Angie made it sound." I flip the price tag over on the poopsleepplay. The price does not seem resale.

Angelina whistles. "No matter what, having a baby is not cheap."

Mom appears, carrying armfuls of clothing. "Oh, this is perfect for downstairs, Autumn." She flips the price tag over and nods. "And we'll need another table for changes in your room, a crib, a dresser..." She begins to wander among the furniture, talking to herself.

I watch her, and a sinking feeling starts in my stomach.

"Feeling sick, kiddo?" Aunt Angelina asks me.

"No," I say. "I just...I'm not going to school, so Mom's not getting child support from Dad anymore and..."

Angelina looks startled. "You know that she isn't paying for any of this, don't you?"

"What?" I ask.

"Your mom told me that she was going to tell you," Angelina says. Her face is stony. "She swore she had this whole speech planned about how some people aren't meant to be parents, but later in life, they regret—"

"Oh, right," I say, even though I was given no such speech. "Still, I'm going to owe you both so much, all the emotional support and knowledge. I'm really out of my depth..."

I've spoken to my father on the phone twice since getting out of the hospital. The last phone call, he told me that he'd been assigned a business trip in Japan that would last six months but maybe more, depending on the markets.

"I'll probably be home just before or after you to make me a grandfather—if you're still determined to do that?" There was a hopeful note that I'd get an abortion or at least arrange an adoption.

"It's happening, whether you're here or in Japan," I said.

"Well, I've talked to your mother, and you're all sorted financially, so there's not much more to say."

I figured that was his way of telling me that if I was so determined, he might as well pay for it.

I suppose his symbolic monetary support should mean more, but it's The Mothers' support that's giving me the courage to do this, to find out what people mean when they say it is all going to be worth it.

I'm about to cry, and Angelina pulls me into a hug.

"Oh yes," she says into my hair. "Money can be paid back, but all this wisdom and love we're showering you with? You're going to be in debt to us forever. You're going to have to let us babysit this grandbaby three, four nights a week to make it up to us."

I laugh and she releases me. My mother has returned with the saleswoman trailing behind her.

"Is everything okay?" Mom asks.

"Hormones and daughterly gratitude got to Autumn," Aunt Angelina says.

"Aw." Mom puts a hand on my back. "Well, I have some good

news. This place delivers!" She says it like it is some sort of miracle.

Luckily, the saleswoman either can't hear my mother's shock, or she doesn't care. "Mondays through Thursdays, between eight a.m. and two p.m.," she recites and adds, "You'll have to wait until after the weekend."

"What day is it?" I ask.

The saleswoman laughs reassuringly at me. "The brain gets tired from pregnancy, dear," she says.

"Saturday," Mom says. She knows that my lack of awareness has more to do with the monotony of my days than my pregnancy, but it's nice for us to pretend otherwise for a moment.

So with Dad's money and The Mothers' wisdom and love, I begin to build my nest.

six

THIS LOOKS LIKE AN AA meeting.

Not that I've ever been to an Alcoholics Anonymous meeting, but this scene fits the depictions of books and movies. We're in a room in the hospital basement, which makes it both a little too cold and too humid, creating a creeping chill that makes me hug my elbows. We're sitting in a circle of folding chairs. By "we," I mean myself and twelve other people, all older than me, except for one girl who's around my age. She arrived late, in pajama pants and reeking of cigarettes. Her shouted apology as she grabbed another folding chair sounded cursory and insincere.

I'm trying to focus on the woman who's speaking; she's describing how much she misses her work as a public defender in the juvenile system, though the job gave her PTSD. I kept thinking that she was going to describe being attacked or something, but it seems the system did it to her, the unrelenting waves of children who'd never been given a chance passing through her office, then being funneled on.

I'm trying to listen to her talk about the times the job had given her joy, when she'd won motions to clear someone's record or keep someone out of the adult system. The girl my age sits directly across from me and fidgets in her seat, playing with her dirty-blond hair and smacking her gum. I watch her face as her bored gaze wanders around the circle. I avert my eyes before she reaches me.

"And I worry about the kids," the lawyer is saying. "The kids I defended before and the kids I'm not defending now that I do contract law." Her voice quavers. "Is anyone listening to them? Do they have anyone who cares about their stories?"

I look back at the new girl to see if she's listening, but she's staring straight me, and she doesn't look away. She cocks her head in what seems to be a greeting, but I turn and refocus on the lawyer, who has quietly started crying.

"But I can't go back. I can't face it. I tried for ten years, and it broke me, but sometimes I wish I could go back."

From the other side of the circle, Dr Singh says, "It's hard when the source of our trauma is also a place where we once had joy or a sense of identity. Does anyone have thoughts on what Marcia or someone like her should do with those feelings, hmm?"

"You should be focusing on the kids you did help," the blond girl says loudly. "Like, when I was in juvie, I wish I'd had a lawyer who had given a shit. Maybe I'd be in a better place now if you'd been my lawyer."

"Remember language, Brittaney," Dr Singh says, his accent making her name three syllables.

"But like you said," Marcia says, "maybe you would be in a better place if I'd been your lawyer. I'm not putting kids in a better place anymore."

Brittaney shrugs and smacks her gum. "You did what you could for as long as you could, and you can't anymore, so what else can you do?" She shrugs again, as if the matter is settled.

"What about the loss of identity that Marcia spoke about? Did that resonate with anyone else?" Dr. Singh asks.

A former soldier named Carlos begins to speak, and the next half hour is more productive. We have another forty-five minutes to go when Dr. Singh says we should take a bathroom break and stretch our legs.

The moment he says "bathroom," I need it urgently, and I sprint out of my chair into the hallway, where the restroom is easy to find, thankfully.

When I come out of the stall, she's waiting for me.

"You're pregnant, right?" Brittaney says before I've reached the sinks.

"Yes," I say, then I turn on the faucet.

"I knew it!" Brittaney crows. "I can always tell. Sometimes I know and the girl doesn't even know it. I'm like that. You're what, four months?" She spits her gum into the trash can.

"Three." I'm a little over three, but I don't owe her my medical information. I begin to rinse the soap from my hands.

"Girl! You having twins then? I'm kidding! You're not that big. You're so tiny that you're showing early. Not that most people could even tell, but whatever. When I'm pregnant, I don't show until I'm almost seven months gone."

"How many times have you been pregnant?" I can't help asking. Our eyes meet in the mirror.

"Three. But I miscarried once, and I just got the three-year-old with me now." She looks away from my gaze and shrugs, similarly to when she'd been talking about the lawyer's PTSD.

"I'm sorry," I say. I'm as shocked by the statement as I am by the way it has been relayed, as if it is of little consequence.

"Oh, it was real early, and the baby daddy was an asshole, so..." She shrugs again.

I'm drying my hands and praying that she won't ask me about my "baby daddy" when she says, "So you're what, eighteen?"

"Nineteen." I toss the brown paper towel into the trash can and turn back to her.

"I just turned twenty-one," she says proudly. "It's nice to see someone here besides the old fogies."

"Yeah," I say as I head to the door. I don't need a friend here, and I don't imagine we have anything in common.

Brittaney chatters at me about all the pregnancies she's successfully predicted in the past the whole way back to the room and our folding chairs. Before sitting down, she assures me that she'll be able to tell me the sex of my baby if I give her a few more weeks.

"Cool," I say and am relieved that Dr. Singh is calling the room to order. I manage to not meet her eyes for the rest of the group therapy session, and afterward I quickly leave and find Mom in the waiting room, ready to escort me to the car. The same chill I'd felt in the basement greets me outside. My jacket is too tight around my middle. I'm going to have to let Mom buy me a maternity coat before much longer.

"How was it?" she asks. "Do you think it will be helpful?"

"I don't know," I say.

seven

"Oh, this would have been nice to have." Angie eyes the poopsleep-play, which is standing next to the couch in my mother's immaculately decorated living room. She sits down next to it and nods. "You'll barely have to move. Change the diaper, put the baby back down…"

"I'll read to it too," I say. "And play? You're supposed to do that even in the early weeks, right?"

I've been doing my research. I conquered my fear of judgmental looks from the staff that had watched me grow up checking out stacks of books each visit and made my way to the library. In addition to a book on French parenting and another on baby development, my bravery was rewarded by excitement from the librarians and flyers about story time and pre-K reading clubs.

"Yeah, you will," Angie says. "Mostly you'll…rest." She says "rest" like a gentle euphemism for something more grim. "Guinnie is starting to get really fun to play with though." She laughs in an odd way. "It's so weird not to have her with me."

"It was nice of Dave to offer to spend the afternoon with her so we could hang." I sit next to her on the couch and groan a little bit. For being so small, my bump now stops me from closing my jeans, and I'm running out of dresses and baggy shirts. My mother wants me to go maternity clothes shopping with her. She hasn't mentioned bringing Aunt Angelina with us.

"Dave owed me," Angie says, and I raise my eyebrows. "We had a big fight because he had the fucking gall to tell me that all I ever talk about is the baby."

"Ooh." I know how this comment would have stung. I've started to realize how difficult it will be to be a mother and a writer. Just one of those feels impossible some days.

"Autumn, the way I burst into tears..." She grimaces. "We ended up better for it. We understand what each other's going through more, you know? But he still owed me."

I'm quiet because I don't know. When Jamie and I fought, even if we both apologized for the things we said, nothing was ever resolved, and we certainly never ended up understanding each other better for it.

It wouldn't have been like that with Finny when we eventually found something to fight about if he'd lived. I know we had learned our lesson about making feelings known.

"Hey, I promise this whole hangout won't be baby related, but can I show you upstairs?"

"Yeah," Angie says as she stands. "Did you get a crib?"

I lead the way to the stairs. "I haven't decided what sort of, uh, sleeping method I believe in."

"What do you mean? You put them on their backs to sleep. That's the only thing. People argue about everything having to do with parenting."

We reach the top of the stairs, and I open the door to my room. "Yeah, I'm learning that."

It isn't about having a modern baby or a hippie baby; I have to choose whether I'm a Montessori mom, an attachment parent, or one of the many other theories or combinations I could ascribe to in my pursuit of a more perfect child. It's like suddenly being asked to choose a religion when it never occurred to me there may be a God.

"I was told we had to let her cry it out. We live in one room with the baby, so that didn't happen. No matter what you chose or do, someone is going to tell you that you are wrong, as if it were their business."

"Well, of course. I'm already an unfit mother because I got pregnant as a teenager in the first place, right?" I snort. "Here, this is what I wanted to show you."

At the resale shop, Mom found a dresser to double as a changing table that matches the wood tones already in my room. She was so pleased that I said yes, even though it felt, at the time, like it was all happening too fast.

But now, having it feels like proof, proof that Finny's baby is real.

"I have all the drawers sorted." I open the second from the top. "Look at this one," I say, and we paw through together, unfolding each onesie to exclaim over it and therefore undoing all the meticulous work I had done.

The feeling remains. I've proved something to myself or Angie. This is real.

Really real.

Sometimes it's hard to believe.

Usually, it's hard to believe, actually, and the rare times that it does feel real, it's the most terrifying thing I've ever experienced. And then I wish Finny was with me to make me less afraid, and the grief takes over.

Without my asking, Angie helps me fold everything again. She suggests a different drawer for pajamas that makes sense. I try to ignore the part about how I won't want to have to root around in a lower drawer "while covered in something or other."

"I promise that was the last mom thing we talk about today," I tell her as I close the last drawer. "We should watch a movie."

"I don't want you to feel like you can't talk about mom stuff with me," Angie sighs. "It's an impossible balance. On one hand, Guinevere is everything to me, and on the other, I'm still me."

"Yeah," I say. "I think I get that." Hoping that she understands my line of thinking, I add, "I finished my novel over the summer."

"Autumn, that's amazing," Angie says as we descend the stairs.

"That is not the word for it," I say. We stop together at the bottom of the stairs. "I mean, everyone knows someone who's written a novel."

"I don't!" Angie says.

I try to suppress my smile and fail.

"I mean, I didn't until now!"

"It's great that I finished it," I say. "Hopefully it will be amazing someday." I'd tried to begin edits last week, but I had to stop to cry, and I haven't been able to look at it again.

When I'd first written it, my novel felt like a place to put all the secret feelings I carried for Finny. But now that I know I could have told him, that I didn't have to hide in my writing, it makes the manuscript impossible to read.

"Can I read it?" Angie asks. We're heading back to the living room couch.

"Um—" I try to think as we sit down.

"Has anyone read it?"

"I thought you'd recorded my devotion in perfect detail and then dropped it in my lap without considering my feelings."

I freeze, but since I was about to sit down, I sort of fall on the couch. I close my eyes.

"And I still loved it as a story."

"Autumn?"

I open my eyes. Angie is leaning toward me, frowning in that concerned way I'm used to from The Mothers.

I take a deep breath. "Finny read it. That was part of our last day together."

"I bet he said it was incredible."

"You're a good writer, Autumn. You've always been good."

If only he could tell me that I'll be a good mother.

I know I'm a good writer. Now I want to be both a good writer and a good mother.

"Autumn? You okay?"

"Sorry, I was thinking..." I trail off.

"It's fine, Autumn. We've been friends long enough for me to know you get weird sometimes."

"That's offensive, Angie. I'm always weird, and you know it," I tease, trying to shift the mood. "So how are other things with Dave?"

Angie sighs. "I took your advice. I told him I appreciated his not making a big deal about the sex thing. It meant a lot to him, and we had this great conversation about how I want to get back to having sex regularly, which actually turned into us fooling around a bit."

"That sounds good—"

"For a couple of days, things were so much better. Then yesterday he hit me with the 'all you talk about is the baby' comment—"

"But you said that it led to a good conversation too?"

"It did!" Angie leans back against the couch. "But I can't shake it. I hate that he even thought it."

"I'm sure he didn't mean to hurt your feelings," I say.

"I know he didn't." Angie scrunches up her face. "It's just—I'm glad you have your writing, Autumn. It's good to have a life and a purpose outside being a mother." She sighs and rests her head on the back of the couch.

"What do you mean? Do you not have that?" It hadn't occurred to me that being a writer, spending time on myself, could help me as a mother. I curl my feet under me, adjusting for the strange new ache that I've been feeling in my hips.

"I guess I thought that Dave or our love and the life we were building together would be enough. I knew it would be hard, but I thought that while we were working and saving money for the future together, we'd be more *together*? Maybe doing better than we are now?"

"Do you mean financially or in your relationship? It sounds like you aren't doing too badly."

"Financially, we're always trying to save, and whenever we make a little progress, something happens. Last month, it was the car, and two months ago, we had the bill from taking Guinnie to urgent care for her ear infection. There's always something."

"But you're saving money and working things out as they come up," I remind her. It feels so strange to be talking about such adult problems with her.

"Yeah," Angie agrees. "Yeah, we are. There's still always something."

There's a beat of silence, and I find myself saying, "Do you have any regrets?"

"I don't. I'm exactly where I want to be. It's just so much harder than I thought, at least for now."

"Eventually you'll be able to move out of Dave's parents' basement," I say.

"And eventually Guinevere will be potty trained or starting kindergarten. But that doesn't feel real. It's not that I don't believe that Dave and I can't beat the odds," Angie says, meeting my eyes again. "But some days, it is a lot more conscious choice than belief."

"I think that's the difference between the people who get out of the basements and those who don't," I say. "You're choosing to believe."

Angie shrugs, but she's listening to what I'm saying, so maybe it's helping.

"Maybe you're right. I hope you are." She laughs. "Listen to me. Complaining because choosing to do the hard thing turned out to be hard."

I'm in the position that she and The Mothers have found themselves in when they're talking to me. There's nothing more to say to make it better, because it is hard, and it's going to be hard for a while.

"Just because something seems impossible doesn't mean it's not worth trying," I say, because it's something I've said to myself before.

"I need to find something to make me feel like I'm still me outside being a mom," Angie says. "It's not like I can watch horror movies with Guinevere asleep in the same room."

"Well, we can watch one together," I suggest. "And afterward, we can go to the library, and I'll help you find some horror novels to read when you're home alone with the baby."

"Yeah, okay."

This time, I can tell that I've definitely helped, and I'm glad. Because she released me from a worry that I hadn't fully articulated; that it was selfish of me to keep my dream of publication when I'm about to become a mother.

Angie winks at me. "Oh, you just want a ride to the library."

"I actually haven't been reading much for myself lately," I confess. "Only a few parenting books." Angie mimes being physically bowled over by my words.

"Who are you, and what have you done with Autumn Rose Davis?" She jumps off the couch and grabs my hand. "That's it, we're going to the library right now. Movie later. You need this more than I do."

"I won't say no to that." I let her help me off the couch. Everyone knows voracious reading is the best way to improve your writing, well except for actually writing. So until I can hold myself together enough to edit the novel inspired by Finny, I need to be reading.

"We're going to be okay," Angie says to me.

Today, I choose to believe it.

eight

GOING TO THE LIBRARY WITH Angie to get books made me feel like myself again, and a few days later, I was able to edit the whole first chapter of my novel. Inspired by my own bravery, I approached Mom cautiously about shopping for maternity clothes. She was so enthused that she was unable to keep it from Aunt Angelina. So now it's a trip for all three of us. Or, I guess, four.

"You need me to stop you from buying half the store," she proclaims from the passenger's seat.

"What would it matter if I did?" Mom retorts. "We want Autumn to be comfortable and confident during this phase of her life. It's good to be prepared to dress for any situation that may arise."

Most of the time, when people argue, they aren't actually arguing about what they're arguing about. The real disagreement flits between their words like a persistent dragonfly. I'm not sure what The Mothers are really arguing about; they've always had different ideas about consumerism. That isn't anything new. But there's an undercurrent to this discussion that is eluding me.

"I mostly need jeans," I say from the back seat. "I think most of my T-shirts and sweaters will still work." I again become aware of the heaviness of my middle, the sense that something is there that wasn't before.

"A dress, pajamas, and some lounge wear too. Maybe a swimsuit?" Mom suggests.

"She's due May first," Aunt Angelina says. "She will not need a maternity swimsuit. That's where I draw the line."

Perhaps they are arguing because Mom will be using the little gold credit card that I've seen her use for all the other baby-related purchases, the card Dad must have given her in place of him being any kind of real support to me. Angelina probably thinks that letting Dad pay for things is like letting him buy his dereliction of duty.

"Maybe I'll go to the indoor pool at the Y this winter?" I say because I'm not sure whose side I'm on. It doesn't matter what we buy or don't buy with his money; Dad's always seen his involvement in my life as a sort of gift he bestows on me. He'll congratulate himself on his generosity no matter what we do with the little gold card.

"Why not a ski suit?" Angelina asks, throwing up her hands. "At least it would be seasonally appropriate!"

"I don't think they make maternity ski suits, but we can check," Mom muses. " Though it may not be the best time for Autumn to take up a winter sport."

It's obvious now, which one of us is pregnant, and the saleslady addresses me directly.

"Looking for anything in particular today?"

"Jeans." All the clothes here look like they're for, well, *moms*. Like, real moms who got pregnant on purpose. I feel like an imposter with my messy hair and my baggy Pixies T-shirt covering my unbuttoned jeans.

"Right this way," she says.

I'm not sure if I'm imagining the tightness in her smile. I've been bracing myself for the disapproval this pregnancy will bring me, for being so young, for not having an engagement ring. So far, it's not so bad, but maybe that will change when I'm large enough for strangers to want to touch my belly and give me unsolicited advice, like Angie says they will.

The saleslady leads us to a shelf of pants and points out the changing rooms, but my focus is on the heavy place in my middle that is now fluttering.

I don't know if it's the baby moving—it could be—but it also doesn't feel that different from anything I've felt in my body before. It's disappointing that I can't tell the difference between Finny's baby and gas.

My mother has already gathered a pile of pants to try on, not just jeans but khakis and linen palazzo pants. Perhaps I should have sided more with Aunt Angelina.

But I follow her to the dressing room because I need clothes.

I sit facing away from the mirror to pull off my pants. My reflection is disconcerting these days.

As I've slept and cried and dragged myself through the past few months, my body has carried on with its new work as if everything was going according to plan. Without asking my opinion, my nipples have become large and dark and my breasts dense and heavy.

And then there is the round swelling, starting at my pelvic bone and sweeping up gently toward my navel.

I should feel affection for it, shouldn't I?

I pull up the jeans and examine the elastic at the waist, stretch it out to see how big of a belly it could accommodate, and let it snap back.

This doesn't feel like my body. It doesn't feel like a baby moving. It's hard for me to imagine that this weight, this fluttering, is going to become a child. It seems like I'll blow up like a balloon, then I'll deflate, and someone will hand me a baby. Somehow, even though I understand the biology, even though I look at the pictures online, I still can't believe that this is how humans get made, how every human was made. I always imagined that it would feel more magical. If this experience were a novel I was writing, it would be more sci-fi than fantasy or romance.

I always imagined I'd be certain I was ready when I had a child.

I always imagined I'd have a husband, a plan.

"It's you and me now, right?"

I bite my cheek to stop his voice.

Mom raps gently on the door. "Autumn, how's it going?"

339

"These jeans are weird," I say.

"Your body is going to feel strange for a while, kiddo!" Angelina chimes in.

"Do they fit?" Mom asks.

"I guess so?"

I come out and she tugs on the waistband like she did when I was a kid and nods. I try on and accept and reject a few other pairs of pants. A couple of the blouses are okay. Finally, Mom wants me to try on a cocktail dress.

"Every woman needs a little black dress," Mom insists.

I look to Angelina for support, but she grimaces.

"You never know what might come up, kiddo. It's not a bad idea to have a dress just in case."

I'm about to say, "Like for another funeral?" when I feel Finny in me.

"Come on, Autumn," he scolds, and I deserve it. As punishment, I make myself take the hanger from her and go back into the changing room.

As I strip off my T-shirt, I pause, looking in the mirror.

It's bigger than it was yesterday, the mound between my hips. I study myself to be certain, because surely things couldn't change that fast?

But it's somehow true.

More sci-fi than fantasy.

I put my hands on my stomach and wonder how I didn't notice it when I put on the jeans. Should I have? Am I already not paying enough attention? I look away from the strange body in the mirror and pull the black dress over my head. It's a stretchy knit that hugs all my curves, the new ones too.

When I look back in the mirror, I'm surprised by how nice it looks. I feel like a woman in this dress, not a girl. I look like someone who can handle what's coming. The bump seems smaller, more reasonable under the cover of black.

And I feel pretty for the first time in a long time.

I wish Finny could see me.

"You're so beautiful."

"Autumn?"

"It's nice," I tell Mom. "We should get it."

On the drive home, the tension between The Mothers is gone. We bought an amount of clothes that everyone felt was reasonable.

I have jeans to wear with my vintage tees, a couple of blouses and a pair of khakis in case I want to look a little nicer, and then there's the dress. The dress looks like something I should wear for an important meeting, perhaps with a publisher for my book or, equally probable, a rendezvous with someone from the CIA.

I have the dress as a talisman more than anything, proof that I am an adult woman, more or less.

Even if I don't have Finny to tell me I look beautiful, I can tell myself for him.

nine

————

"It's not uncommon for a pregnant woman to feel disconnected from her body, nor is it uncommon for a first-time mother to find it hard to believe that there will be a baby. This is not indicative that you will be a poor mother," Dr. Singh says.

"Shouldn't I love it more or something?" I ask.

He raises his hand in a gesture of ambivalence. "Eh?" he says. "Are you taking your prenatal vitamins?"

"Yes."

"You've been to all your obstetrician appointments, yes? Getting gentle exercise, yes?"

"I take walks a few times a week." I don't understand why this therapy appointment is suddenly about my physical health.

"Then it sounds to me like you are loving this fetus as much as you can," Dr. Singh says. "Love is an action, and all the actions you are taking speak of love."

It's my turn to shrug.

"I wanted to talk to you about your plans outside motherhood," he says. "You will still be a person with dreams. You said you wanted to write a novel, yes?"

"I wrote one."

"You're writing a novel?"

"No." I laugh for the first time in days. "I wrote one. I finished it. Well, I'm still editing it." I still cry while I edit, which slows me down, but I don't have to stop anymore because of the crying, so that's an improvement. And I'm reading books that aren't about babies when I'm not editing. I may not be going to college this year or the next, but that's no reason I can't give myself my own literature course.

"But the story is complete?" Dr. Singh raises his bushy eyebrows in a way I've never seen before.

"Yeah."

"That is very good. Very good." He adjusts his glasses. "Do you know how many people start novels they never finish?"

"Probably a lot? Lots of people finish them too."

"My son is thirty-two and has been working on his since college," Dr Singh says. "I think you should be proud of yourself."

"Finny was proud of me," I say.

"I can't wait to read it."

Dr. Singh shifts in his seat. "I was hoping that at next week's group therapy session, you'll share with the others why you are there. I understood why you didn't contribute last week, but I do hope it is a space that you can feel comfortable."

"Yeah, maybe," I say. "That Brittaney girl was kinda annoying."

Dr. Singh surprises me by laughing. "Oh, ha! Brittaney is what my generation calls a spitfire. She is someone I've known a long time, or rather I once knew her parents in a professional—Well, her story is not mine to tell, but she is someone you could learn from, Autumn."

I can't help what my face does at that idea.

Dr. Singh suddenly looks old. He presses his lips together before speaking. "Autumn, she is a survivor." His voice lands heavy on the last word.

"Of what?" I ask.

"Everything," Dr. Singh says.

ten

"EVERYTHING LOOKS GOOD," THE DOCTOR says as she scans my chart. "If you could try again to pee for us before you go…"

"Sorry," I say. "It's like all I do is pee, and then I can't when I'm supposed to."

"Happens all the time," she says. "Just try again because it is the best way to predict preeclampsia. Do you have any questions before the organ scan?"

"The what?"

"The ultrasound."

"Uh, no." The room is cold, and I'm anxious to put my new maternity jeans back on.

"That's scheduled for next week, right? No, week after next." She pauses, makes a note, and looks up at me and smiles. "Let's see about peeing again, okay?"

In the restroom, crouched over the toilet with a cup between my legs, I think about what Dr. Singh said about love being an action and how my actions say I'm doing the best I can to love myself and the baby I don't quite believe in. I wonder if trying to urinate for the preeclampsia test counts as an act of love, which makes me giggle, and then I finally pee.

When the nurse takes the cup from me, I ask, "So they'll make sure the baby has all its organs and stuff week after next?"

"Yup. I'm sure it'll be fine."

I say, "I'm not worried. I was just surprised when the doctor called it an 'organ scan.' I mean, it makes sense, but I never thought of it that way." I'm babbling and not exactly sure what I'm talking about. The poor nurse smiles tightly at me and says something about needing to get this—with a nod to the urine—into the back.

I check at reception to see if they need anything more from me, but Mom has already made my next appointment and paid the copay with the little gold card, so we're on our way.

"Everything good?" Mom asks. "You were in there awhile."

"I couldn't pee."

"But all you do is pee, Autumn."

"That's what I said!" I lean my head against the window. There's a fluttering in my middle that could be Finny's baby, or it could be yesterday's lunch. I still can't tell.

Organ scan.

They'll scan for the organs and make sure they're all there, all in the right places, all in the right sizes and shapes, because sometimes they aren't.

Sometimes the kidneys aren't there, or the brain isn't the right size, or the heart isn't the right shape.

Sometimes babies die in their sleep for no reason, and with a gasp of breath, I realize that someday this baby will die.

Hopefully, this baby will live for a hundred years, but someday it will die, just like Finny. Just like I will.

The best I can do is hope that I will die before the baby.

The absurdity of it all.

"Are you okay?" Mom asks.

"Thinking about the ultrasound," I say. "I hope everything is okay."

"It probably will be," she says, but nothing more, because she knows that for eighteen years, Angelina believed that Finny would outlive her. She knows that sometimes babies die in their sleep.

And neither of us is foolish enough to believe that lightning doesn't strike twice.

eleven

"MAYBE I SHOULD START TAKING you to all my resale shops," Aunt Angelina tells Mom. We're on our way back to Vintage Mother Goose to buy a crib.

"Angelina, I will turn this car around and head straight to Pottery Barn, I swear to God," Mom replies.

"No, no, I'll behave."

I've chosen how the baby will sleep: in a mini crib in my room for at least a year. I won't let it cry it out, but I'll try to wait for the baby to settle themselves like the book about French parenting I'm reading suggested.

Now there're only a million other decisions about this baby that I'll have to make in the next few months.

But it's a start.

The Mothers have been trying to let me figure out this stuff on my own, letting me decide what kind of mother I want to be, not telling me how it must be done like Angie's family. Aunt Angelina co-slept with Finny in her bed until he was two, while Mom kept me down the hall with the baby monitor on the lowest setting so that I really had to scream to wake her. Neither method is recommended these days, and neither of them has tried to convince me otherwise.

So when I said that I had decided to get a small crib for my room for the first year or so, there was no questioning my decision. Angelina called and confirmed that the mini crib we'd considered last time we were at Vintage Mother Goose was still available, but Mom insists that we look at it one last time before purchasing it.

The same elderly woman is sitting behind the counter when we arrive.

"Back again, dears?" she says without a pause in her knitting, proving my suspicions that she is a witch.

Mom, the expert shopper in all situations, leads the way to the furniture corner where the little crib sits. "It doesn't quite match the rest of the wood in your room," she muses. "It would almost be better if it was totally different. This will look like we tried to match it and failed. I'm certain I could find one online in a better color."

"This is perfect," I say. "Last I heard, none of the interior design magazines were doing spreads on teen mom's nurseries, so I don't think we're missing any opportunities." I rest my hands on the adjustable bar possessively.

"All right then, sweetie. If it were me, I'd find the coordination soothing when in the trenches."

"In the trenches? Why do people always talk about motherhood like it's going to war?"

Mom and Aunt Angelina look at each other and shrug.

"What are we thinking then?" the saleswoman asks, approaching us.

Mom begins to set up the purchase and delivery. I stare down at the crib and try to convince myself that someday there will be not only a mattress inside it but an infant.

"Are you thinking what I'm thinking?" Aunt Angelina asks.

"That we should let Mom order a bespoke crib mattress made of organic llama hair or something?"

"Exactly. She's respected your wishes not to turn your dad's office into a Victorian nursery full of chintz and should be rewarded."

I turn from the crib to face her. "Since it's Dad's money, I'll have to let her do something to his office eventually."

Angelina stiffens. "What did you say?"

"Since it's Dad's money—"

"It's not your father's money, Autumn. Is that what your mother told you?"

"No, I just assumed," I say.

Angelina looks stricken. This must have something to do with Finny that I don't understand. She looks past me to where I can hear the saleslady and my mother talking behind me. Her mouth tightens.

350

"Your mother didn't tell you about the arrangement with Finny's father?"

Everything tilts in my mind.

"The what? With *him*?" I ask.

"Autumn," she whispers, "I'm sorry, but I'm going to kill your mother."

"Mom?" I shout as I twist around. She and the saleslady simultaneously turn from each other to me. "What is this arrangement that Aunt Angelina is talking about? With Finny's...Finn—"

I can't bring myself to call that man a father to Finny.

"Let me finish arranging the delivery, and we'll talk about it later," Mom sings out to me, using a customer service voice.

I'm not buying what she's selling.

"What's this arrangement?" I ask Angelina. She's tried so hard to give me support along with respectful space. Through all these months, I've remained in awe of her composure, but she looks like she's about to lose it.

She trusted her best friend to tell the mother of their grandchild this delicate bit of information, this involvement of the man who abandoned her child.

"I don't know the details, but apparently, in exchange for whatever access you are willing to give him, updates or pictures, Finn's father gave access to Finny's trust fund." Her voice has started to rise, and she catches herself and swallows, then takes a breath.

I'm still trying to understand why she said the words "trust fund" and "Finny" so close together, so we both clearly need a moment.

"Well, that's done!" my mother exclaims from behind me.

I don't turn to look at her. I can't stop staring at the hurt on Aunt Angelina's face.

"Is it, Mom?" I say.

We agreed to wait until we were at home to talk.

"Yes, I want to be able to see your face when we talk about this," I told my mother when she suggested waiting until after the drive home. The drive was quiet and as frosty as the late autumn chill outside.

At home, seated around the kitchen table, finally looking at her face, I say, "We already know that you thought what you were doing was best for everyone."

"And that's not an excuse," my mother agrees. "I should have told you."

"So why didn't you?" Angelina presses. "We agreed this was Autumn's decision."

"How does he even know that I'm pregnant?"

"That part's my fault, kiddo," Aunt Angelina admits. "He reached out to me right after you went to the hospital. He has this project about Finny he wanted help with, and it had all been such a whirlwind of emotions from losing Finny to thinking we might lose you to finding out about the pregnancy, and I don't know. I told him."

"And he made Mom an offer too good to refuse?" I ask them both. I feel like a piece of me has been sold.

"I meant to tell you," Mom says. "But then I didn't, and it seemed easier to wait until..."

"What? Until that man demanded access to my child that he'd already paid for?"

"Until you were able to think about it more rationally and less emotionally," Mom explains, but I can hear she knows how pathetic it sounds.

"Look, I told you before, Claire," Angelina says. "If Autumn wanted access to that money, she'd have a good legal case, and we could have sued John instead of letting him hold the strings."

"Yes, I remember, Angelina," Mom says. "But I th—"

"Okay, what money is this?" I say. "Let's start there!"

"Every time John felt guilty for abandoning his son, he put some money in an account he'd secretly opened with Phineas's name on it, or sometimes for an especially plagued conscience, he'd buy another government savings bond. It wasn't until after Finny died that John realized how much his guilt had added up."

"How much had it added up?"

"Enough that if you were to sue on behalf of Finny's heir, after we've settled out of court and paid the lawyers, there'd still be enough to raise this baby to age eighteen and send both you and the baby to college." Aunt Angelina continues, "It's an open-and-shut case, Autumn. He has access to the account, but the name on it is Phineas Smith, the father of your baby."

"And if we don't sue and tell him never to contact me?"

"He keeps the money," my mom says. "And we would have to use the money from your college fund to raise this baby."

"I would sell the house," Angelina adds. "I was thinking about it anyway since I've been staying here most nights." She glances angrily at my mother, and I suppose that won't be the case tonight. "We'd find a way to make it work."

"But it would be so much harder for everyone, Autumn, including your child," Mom says. "I don't have to tell you that being a teen mother puts a lot of obstacles in your way. This money could alleviate, or even obliterate, those obstacles."

"But you promised that we would let *her* choose," Angelina says, shaking her head. This is a betrayal between the two of them that goes deeper than my part in it. The Mothers have always been a team, and this disconnect is unprecedented. If Finny were here, we'd be sharing meaningful glances across the table about this historic conflict.

"I'm sorry," Mom says again. "I know that saying it doesn't change anything. But I'll keep saying it."

"And if we don't sue, and we keep using that little gold card?"

"I told him that you weren't ready to discuss the particulars." Mom begins to blush as the depth of her lies starts to sink in. "But he wants to be part of the baby's life in whatever capacity you'll give him, Autumn." She gives Aunt Angelina and I look that is more pleading than when she was advocating for herself. "The man has so many regrets."

"He should," I say. "And so should you."

Mom nods. She either mouths or whispers that she's sorry, but it's too quiet to hear.

twelve

MARCIA, THE FORMER JUVENILE PUBLIC defender, brought a box of coffee to share with everyone at group therapy today. It smells amazing. I never liked coffee before, and I want to get some too, but everyone can see that I'm pregnant now. I'm not sure if they'll judge me.

It's not that pregnant women can't have caffeine; it's that you're not supposed to have over a certain amount. The doctor said I could have a large cup of coffee every day and it would be okay. Until now, I didn't really care to have any.

Everyone acts like the rule is no caffeine when you're pregnant, and I'm already feeling self-conscious enough in this room full of people mostly in their thirties.

But the coffee smells so good.

"Are we ready to begin?" Dr. Singh asks us. Everyone is murmuring assent when I jump up.

"I'm just gonna…" I mumble over my shoulder as I rush to the table. My mouth actually waters as I pour the cup and stir in a bit of milk. I hurry back to the circle, careful not to spill a precious drop.

One of the older women leans over as I sit down.

"Do you think you sh—"

"Oh my God, Wanda! Mind your own fucking business," Brittaney groans. She rolls her eyes in my direction, and I give her a weak smile of thanks.

Dr. Singh doesn't remind Brittaney about her language, which I think means he agrees that Wanda should mind her own business. He starts the session talking about how trauma causes physical changes to the brain. I can't help but think about how Finny would find it interesting, all this talk about inflexible neuropathways.

"Your novel came from your brain, Autumn, word by word, and I wish I could understand how your brain is able to do that." His hands on the steering wheel, his face illuminated in the dashboard light. Just being near him made me feel more alive.

Brittaney chimes in, "Sometimes it's like I hear my ex-boy-friend's voice, saying, 'You killed my baby. You killed our fucking daughter,' over and over, exactly the way he said it. And it feels like I physically can't stop myself from thinking about that moment. My brain gets caught in a loop."

Part of me thinks I had to have misheard her. I've covered my mouth with my hand, and as I lower it, I look around the room, but no one seems to think that Brittaney has said anything particularly shocking. A few people are nodding. Someone else talks about being unable to stop analyzing the moment before their assault.

I drink my coffee and listen and wonder why I am here.

But then I remember; I can hear my boyfriend's voice in my head too.

This time, I'm not surprised when Brittaney is waiting for me when I come out of the bathroom stall.

"You're having a girl," she announces without preamble. "I thought you should know." She's leaning against the counter so she's practically sitting on it, her toes barely grazing the ground.

"Cool," I say as I head to the sink.

"I know you don't believe me," she says, "but I'm always right. When's the ultrasound where you find out?"

"Next week." I begin to wash my hands. This seems to be our routine.

"Are you excited?"

I look up. Our eyes meet in the mirror.

"No," I admit to her.

"Why not? You have someone to go with you? Where's the daddy?"

"He's dead," I say, because I figure if we're going to talk, I might as well match her speed. I turn from the mirror and grab a paper towel to dry my hands. "My mom will go with me. But I'm scared that there'll be something wrong with the baby."

"Oh, girl, it'll be fine!" She shrugs. "And if it's not, it's outta your hands. Sometimes shit is." She sighs.

I hesitate before asking, "You had a baby die?"

"Brain cancer," Brittaney says. "It was fast. They found it on her one-year checkup, and she was gone before she was two."

"I'm so sorry."

"It is what it is," she says, and for the first time, I can see that her nonchalance is her armor. I feel guilty for not seeing it before.

"If it was cancer," I say, "why would your ex-boyfriend say it was your fault that she died?"

For the first time ever, Brittaney looks uncomfortable with our conversation.

"Like I said before, I don't start showing until the third trimester, and I'd only gotten my period a couple of times before I got pregnant, so it was easy for me to be in denial for a while. By the time I knew for sure I was pregnant, I was six months gone, and I was thirteen. I'd been smoking cigarettes since I was eleven, so it was hard for me to give up." She looks at my face. "I tried. I really did. But finally my doctor told me that at a certain point, my being so stressed out was more harmful to the baby than a cigarette. I was really stressed too, you know? The foster mom I had that year was a bitch. Her nephew was my baby daddy, and since he was nineteen, she was worried she was gonna get in trouble with my social worker. It was a whole thing."

"He was nineteen? And you were only thirteen?"

"He was the one buying our cigarettes anyway!" She holds her hands up in exasperation. "I asked the cancer doctor, and she said those cigarettes would have only increased the chances by one percent, that it was mostly genetics that gave my baby that kinda cancer, not me having one cigarette a day." Brittaney gives her trademark shrug. "I was able to quit smoking last time I was pregnant. I was your age, and things were a little better for me. I'd just bought my house and stuff."

"You own a house?" She should probably be insulted by my surprise, but she doesn't seem to notice.

"Okay, so you won't believe this, but before my parents lost their shit to drugs, they were *doctors*." She chuckles and leans forward to whisper, like she's telling me a dirty joke. "Can you imagine going to medical school, getting married, having a kid in preschool, and *then* getting hooked on fucking dope? Couple of losers, those two." She laughs and rolls her eyes so hard this time that it looks like it hurts. "But the one thing they couldn't sell for drugs—and trust me, they sold everything for drugs, even me—was their life insurance policies. I got to collect on those when I turned eighteen, and I bought my house, free and clear. Neighborhood's a bit rough, but the school's okay, and I can save money on gas most days walking to my job."

"Girls?" Wanda sticks her head inside the restroom. "We're waiting on you. Is everything all right?"

"Yeah, yeah, tell Singh we're coming," Brittaney says. "She's a total suck-up," she whispers to me.

I nod.

She is a survivor, Dr. Singh had said.

I don't share anything during group therapy, even though Dr.

360

Singh gives me several significant looks. I don't know what he expects from me. The others are talking about being unable to save children or getting shot at or raped.

Perhaps when Dr. Singh said I could learn something from Brittaney, he meant I could learn that I didn't really have anything to be traumatized about.

But then, even though our circumstances are so different, the things the others say about their traumas sound like the things I feel about Finny's death, like we carry an indelible mark on us.

I don't speak, but I listen.

When the session is over, I have a text message from Mom. Her car has a flat, and Angelina is coming to change it for her, but they'll be late picking me up. I stop short in the lobby. I should have brought my book about French parenting to read in case of something like this.

"You okay?" Brittaney asks. She's already holding her cigarettes and lighter in one hand, and we aren't even outside.

"Yeah, my ride is late," I say.

"Oh shit, where you live?"

"Ferguson."

"My favorite foster mom lived in Ferguson! I live in North County too. I can drop you off."

"No, no—"

"Girl, people bring their unvaccinated, snot-nosed kids through this lobby all day long. You'll catch a new kind of measles that gives

361

your baby superpowers or something. Don't worry. I don't smoke in my car. I'll have this done by the time I reach the parking garage. Wait right here."

Before I can protest again, she heads outside and lights up to smoke as she walks, ignoring the landscaped pathways and crossing flower beds, stepping over the bushes surrounding the building as she makes her way to the garage.

A car pulls up a few minutes later with a muffler that rattles, and I know it's hers. She waves me in, and I open the door and sit down next to her.

"I'll keep the window open a minute until the cigarette smell gets out of my clothes."

"No, you don't have to," I say as it occurs to me that maybe she needs to go overboard to protect my child for her sake, because of what she went through. "But thank you."

Brittaney makes the wide turn on the roundabout to leave the hospital's campus. "So I called my old foster mama in Ferguson, and I'm gonna go see her after I drop you off!"

"Oh, that's nice," I say. "When did you live with her?"

"That was while Dione was sick."

I feel an ache at the way she says the name.

"She took care of me afterward. She was the one who got me to fill out all the paperwork to get the money from my parents' insurance, 'cause at first I was like, I want nothing to do with anything that has their name on it, you know?"

"Yeah, I kinda do," I say.

"Oh?" she glances as me as she rolls up the window manually.

"I recently found out that my, uh, baby's daddy's father put a bunch of money in his name before he died, so like, legally, the money should be the baby's. To get it, I'd either have to deal with him or sue him, and part of me doesn't want to do anything about it."

"But it's not your money," Brittany says, still smacking her gum. "It's your kid's money, right? So you gotta think about that."

"I know," I say.

"You have to think about the future, even when it feels like there won't be a future. That's what Sherry, my foster mama, said to me. You got dreams and shit, Autumn?"

I can't help my smile.

"Yeah, I got dreams and shit. I want to be a writer," I say. "I mean, I am a writer. I wrote a novel, and I've started editing it, and when I finish, I'm going to look for an agent, then a publisher."

"No shit? Look at you, girl. Fucking proud of you. But writing doesn't pay out, does it?"

"No, probably not."

"Man, I was so glad I had that money when I found out I was pregnant with CiCi—my daughter's name is Cierra, but nobody calls her that but me when I'm mad—but babies are expensive. Have you read *The Hip Mama Survival Guide*?"

"Uh, no?"

"Okay, so that's, like, required reading for you, okay? What's her fucking name... mermaid politician? Ariel Gore, that's it! Read it. You need it."

"Okay," I say. "Thanks." I wasn't expecting a book recommendation from her, and it's a pleasant surprise.

"I'll be getting off the highway soon. What street are you on?"

I give her directions to my house ("No way! I used to get drunk at the creek by your house!"), and we settle into a surprisingly comfortable silence.

I look out the window at the splendor of the season I was named for.

"You should try not to stress about the ultrasound," Brittaney offers.

"Most of the time, this baby doesn't even feel real," I admit to the fall colors outside the window. "But when it does, then it hurts, because I can't think about this baby without thinking about Finny and how he died and how someday, somehow this baby will di—"

I realize what I'm saying and start to apologize, but Brittaney is nodding.

"Being scared for the kid is a big part of the job."

"How do you live with it?" I'm asking about so many things.

"I don't know," Brittaney says. "I guess the reason I don't break down scared that something will happen to CiCi is because if I did, who would be her mama? Like, maybe she deserves better than me, but I'm the only mother she's got. I guess if me and my girlfriend get married someday, she'd have two mamas, but you know what I mean. Right now, CiCi needs me to make sure that she's clean and fed and knows she's loved, so I can't lose my shit."

"Clean, fed, loved," I repeat. A puzzle piece feels like it's falling into place for me.

"Yeah, those three things are, like, ninety percent of the job. They're also the only things you'll be able to control. The world's gonna fuck with your kid no matter what. All you can do is teach 'em to brush their teeth and love themselves."

"That's the first thing about parenting that anyone has said that actually makes me feel like I can do this," I say.

My home is in sight, and as Brittaney pulls up, I'm reciting "clean, fed, loved" to myself. This is the list that I needed, the measuring stick of minimum standards. As long as Finny's child is clean, fed, and loved, then I'm doing an okay job.

Sure, as children grow, they're mostly cleaning and feeding themselves, and the loved part becomes complicated as they start to break away, but by then there will be a foundation to our relationship, and knowing who they are as a person will help guide me.

For now, when I'm envisioning this baby, all I have to tell myself is that I will be dedicated to keeping them clean, fed, and loved.

"So one last thing?" Brittaney says as she stops the car. "About the ultrasound?"

"Yeah?"

"If there is something wrong with your baby, then your baby is lucky to have you for their mama, because you'll love it anyway and do whatever you can for her. Your kid is lucky to have a mama who cares, so no matter what, they're already ahead of the game."

"Thanks," I say. "I'll think about that. And thanks for the ride and talking with me. I appreciate that."

"Oh, no biggie," she says.

I get out of the car and start to shut the door but turn back when she shouts from the car window.

"And hey, Autumn?"

"What?"

"I'm right about it being a girl. You'll see."

thirteen

THE MAN WHO WAS SUPPOSED to be Finny's father has written me back. He's agreed to my terms.

I have an occasion to wear that black dress after all, especially since the restaurant he suggests sounds like a place my father would like, the sort of place where it's easy to feel like the waitstaff is dressed better than you.

I think about pinning up my hair, but I decide that's too formal and go with a ponytail. I keep my makeup understated.

I want to look like an adult.

I don't want to look like I'm trying to look like an adult.

For perhaps the first time ever, I wish that I was able to drive myself somewhere. Mom is dropping me off, perhaps as penance.

She and Angelina seem like Angie and Dave; they're having conversations that are necessary and good, but the relationship takes effort right now.

I've actually found it a bit easier to forgive Mom. Maybe there's too much going on in my brain for me to be able to sustain anger, but somehow, I've managed to shrug off her subterfuge by telling myself that she and I are both trying to do what's best for our children while muddling through a complicated situation.

"I'm going to the botanical garden," Mom tells me as she slows down to drop me off outside the restaurant. Mom doesn't parallel park in the city. "But I'm not going to stay in the Climatron, so I can be back in a flash to pick you up if you need me. Honey, are you sure—"

"I'm doing this alone," I say. "Because this is my decision."

"Right."

I open the car door. "Thanks," I say before I get out. Before opening the door, I square my shoulders and raise my chin to make myself look more confident than I feel.

It's dark on the other side of the restaurant door, as if the patrons wished their lunches were taking place at night. The lighting fixtures are artfully set to a dimness that evokes candlelight without the fire risk. I hold Mom's little clutch I borrowed confidently in front of my baby bump as I stride up to the hostess.

I look directly into her expertly done eye makeup and say, "There's a reservation for two, Smith?"

"Yes," she says without looking down at her list. "Your party is already here." It's obvious that she was told to look out for a pregnant girl pretending to be a grown-up, but I smile and thank her before following her deeper into the pretend evening of this place.

At the last minute, there had been a shoe emergency, which is luckily the sort of thing for which my mother lives. Apparently, along with everything else that pregnancy can do to you, like changing the color or texture of your hair, giving you allergies you never had before, or even losing your teeth, pregnancy can change your shoe size.

So it's in Mom's unfamiliar heels that I'm following this woman to meet Aunt Angelina's former lover, which is an easier way to think about him than as Finny's father.

The thought withers within me as I approach the table, because that is Finny's father sitting there.

That's Finny sitting there, Finny at age fifty or so, with gray streaks in his blond hair, with deep smile lines from decades of flashing his crooked grin. And there it is, that familiar smile that I know better than my own, greeting me.

He stands, and I know his height before I see it. I know the length of his legs. I recognize the head tilt as he says, "Autumn, hello."

"Hi." I'm trying not to stare at the ghost before me, but the hostess has pulled out the chair, and everyone is waiting for me to sit. To compensate, I sit too quickly as she tries to push in the chair for me, and I end up four inches too far from the table. I adjust myself as she assures John that a waitress will be by shortly.

"It's good to see you again," he says when we're alone.

"Again?"

"Yes," he says, his uncanny features still mesmerizing me. "When you and Phineas were seven or, no, nine? It was after my father died.

369

I had a short visit with Phineas, and when Angelina came to pick him up, you were with her."

"I don't remember that," I say. I will myself to look away.

Sometime later, I'll have to figure out what to do with this knowledge, the knowledge of how Finny would have looked as he aged, the way that the boyish charm of his face would have stayed even as markers of maturity occurred. I allow myself to feel just enough of the hurt to keep myself sharp.

"It's strange that I don't remember it," I say, raising my chin, "considering how rare it was for Finny to see you at all."

John Smith nods and takes a breath. He adjusts his posture as he takes my verbal blow, and I try not to be haunted by the width of his shoulders as he shrugs.

"And that's why we're here. So thank you for this."

I'm about to thank him in return, reflexively, when I catch myself and simply say, "You're welcome."

"Yes, well," he says, and the befuddled, eager-to-please look on his face, which is almost Finny's face, is almost breaking me. "I'm incapable of expressing how much I regret not knowing and appreciating Phineas when I had the chance."

The waitress is suddenly there, and I'm agreeing to lemon in my water and being handed a menu that looks like a wedding invitation. John already has what looks like a dirty martini, but it appears untouched. Condensation is beginning to form under the chill of what's probably incredibly expensive vodka.

"So what is it, John?" I say after we've ordered strange-sounding appetizer salads and the waitress has faded into the shadows. "Why did you stay away for most of his life?"

"I was trying not to be a terrible father." He laughs bitterly. "I understand that I failed at that, spectacularly, but at the time, I thought if I wasn't there, then I couldn't mess him up." John lifts the martini to his lips and takes a sip, then stares into the liquid. "The few times I got the courage to ask to see him, Phineas always seemed so happy. Not happy to see me, just happy, thriving. He'd tell me about you and playing soccer and the things he was learning in school that excited him, and I'd tell myself, 'See, he's doesn't need you.'"

"You had to have known, on some level—"

"Yes, of course," he says. He sets the martini glass down and looks me in the eye, urging me to believe his sincerity. "I was a coward. Being a real father to Phineas would have meant going back and facing all the ways my own father had failed me. Have you ever had something like that in your past, where when you look back, your feelings are so obvious and your own thoughts were clearly lies to yourself?"

"Yes," I say, because I owe him honesty in return, even if he hasn't earned my trust yet.

John nods gratefully. "It all fell apart after my daughter was born," he explains. "Somehow, my ex-wife convinced me to have a child with her, and the moment I saw Stella in the NICU, I wished I could go back in time and see Phineas when he'd first come into the world."

"Why do you call him Phineas instead of Finn or Finny?" I ask.

371

There're so many other questions that his story has inspired, but this one keeps nagging me.

John blushes.

He blushes the way his son would, not turning red but pink in the cheeks in a way that highlights the delicate bones of his face, offsets the gold of his hair.

"As I've talked to people, I have come to learn that no one called him that," he says. "But Phineas was my grandfather's name."

"Angelina named him after your grandfather?" The idea is shocking enough to be suspicious.

"Not exactly," John says. "I never knew my grandfather, and my own father was an alcoholic. But all through my childhood, my good-for-nothing dad would tell me stories of his own amazing father, the fishing trips and poignant life advice he'd given. I told Angelina that I'd grown up with only the mythology of a father and that any good in me probably came from that man who I had never met."

"So she named her son after what good there was in you," I finish for him.

He nods. "Perhaps she thought her son was the only good that was going to come from me. I knew when I saw the name on the court papers that Angelina was being poetic, not malicious."

"And after your daughter was born, you couldn't lie to yourself anymore?" I don't want us to lose focus on his failings.

"No, I couldn't." He fiddles with the martini glass on the table but doesn't take another drink. "But he was almost fourteen, and

I thought that it was probably too late. I went into a depression. I bought him that car the year after that..."

We pause then, reflecting on that little red car, the car he had loved and that had been at the scene of his death. That little car where I had stared at his profile in the dashboard light and wanted so much to whisper those three words that would have changed our lives.

As you wish.

"Are you all right?" John asks.

My vision is blurry from unspilled tears. I take a steadying breath that sounds more like it's going to become a sob instead of calm me.

"For the record," I whisper, "he loved that stupid fucking car."

"At least I did one thing right," he says.

My laugh makes the tears spill but also stops more from forming. I touch my fingertips to my eyes for the sake of my mascara and look back at John. The gentle concern on his face almost melts my resolve to continue to hold him to the fire.

"I know there's still so much to talk about, but can I ask you how you're feeling? Is everything going okay with the..."

"Tomorrow is the big ultrasound," I say. "The one where they make sure the baby has everything it needs to be viable."

"Are you going to find out the sex?"

"I don't know. I haven't decided." I remember that information like this is supposed to be part of a financial agreement between us, and I try to get us back on track. "So in addition to the car, every time you felt guilty, you were putting money away in Finny's name?"

"Yes. I have documents here with me if you want to look over—"

"Last Thanksgiving, you had Finny over to meet your wife and daughter, but then you disappeared again. What happened with that?"

"He didn't tell you anything about it?" he asks.

"No. Somehow I'd known the hurt was too much for me to touch, and so I'd never asked."

This time, John takes a big gulp of his drink before he answers me.

"My ex-wife had always known about Phineas. I think she thought of him as an amusing anecdote from my playboy days. But when she saw us together, it became real to her."

I can only imagine the shock it would have been to see Finny and John standing together, to see a youthful version of her husband sitting at her table, next to her daughter who she'd thought of as an only child.

"What happened?"

"She was"—he takes another small sip from his glass and sets it back down on the tablecloth—"cold to him is I suppose the way to describe it. She went out of her way to word things so it was understood that she and Stella and I were the real family. And I did nothing, Autumn." His gaze is firm as he admits it. "I should have done or said something, at least to him alone. But the marriage was already half-dead, and I was envisioning losing my second child by trying to reconnect with my first, and I—"

The waitress appears with our salads. Mine is seaweed and shavings of cucumber, which looks like a pile of green spaghetti. John's salad is red somehow. I find myself ordering both steak and

374

lobster and wondering if the waitress will faint if I ask for a doggy bag at the end of the meal. Before she leaves, she asks John if he would like another martini. He hesitates and says no but to ask again after the entrées have arrived.

After she leaves, we look at each other. Our conversation was interrupted at a point where it does not need to be continued. We both know how he abandoned Finny again. We both know he didn't attend graduation or reach out all summer. We both know how the story ends.

"I don't want to feel like I'm selling my child to you," I finally say.

He closes his blue eyes and nods. "The more I think about it, the more I see how it was a desperate and manipulative move, Autumn. To dangle money that by rights should belong to your child anyway. That's why I brought the papers today. The money is yours and the baby's, even if you choose to never see me after this." He takes a briefcase from under the table and pulls out a manila envelope and sets it on the corner of the table.

"Thank you," I say. I'm still unsure whether I can trust him. Perhaps this is still a manipulation.

"Whatever you can give me," he says, "I'll take it. And if you never want me to know your child, I'll accept that. All I ask is that today, you stay for this lunch and tell me about my son."

"Tell you about Finny?"

He swallows, and his eyes are beginning to look wet.

"I've been meeting with different people who knew him. I've

been taking notes and even recording some of the conversations. I had lunch a couple of weeks ago with his soccer coach and a couple of his teammates." He reaches back into the briefcase and pulls out a much larger file that he opens and flips through. "I've met with teachers, some from all the way back to elementary school, who've given me insights into his character. There've even been classmates and parents who've started reaching out to me with stories, and then Sylvia Whitehouse and I—" He glances up at me.

"How is she?" I ask.

"Healing," he says. "I hope you know she hopes the same for you."

"I'm honestly surprised that she doesn't hate me," I say. "It seems like she should."

"She is incredibly mature beyond her years," John says. "She told me that she understood what I meant about looking back and knowing I was lying to myself about Phineas, because when she looked back, she always knew she was standing in the way of you two."

"If you see her again, tell her that we were standing in our own way. And I'm glad to know that she's healing."

He nods, and I can see that he's wondering whether he'll ever see me again.

"I'm going to need those stories that you're collecting," I tell him. "And Jack's been working to get all sorts of pictures from people. Maybe we could put them together as a book for the baby."

"Phineas always said that you were an amazing writer."

"Well, for authenticity, we should try to keep the original

voices as much as possible, but I can edit for clarity, maybe help with the timelines," I say. "I think your insight into how the mythology of a good father can help shape a child will be very helpful to this project."

When the waitress comes with our entrées, John doesn't order another martini. There isn't space at the table anyway with all the documents spread out. Together we build another inheritance for Phineas's child.

fourteen

"AUTUMN, YOUR LIPS ARE BLUE," Mom says to me. "You're going to alarm the technician when they arrive."

We're waiting for the ultrasound to begin. Mom has already grabbed a white towel and is running water on it.

"Claire, that's to wipe the gel off her afterward," Aunt Angelina says.

"You need to let me finish this first." I hold up the precious candy packet that Finny bought me those few long months ago.

At first, I had planned on hoarding them forever, running my hands through them like a miser with gold coins. But one day, the craving hit me. My body was demanding the colored sugar powder. My body needed it for the baby; that's what it was telling me. Perhaps it was the baby telling me it needed it. And even though I knew what Finny, the almost premed student, would have said (*The flaw in that theory is the lack of nutritional value, Autumn.*), I also knew that if he were alive, he would have been reading up on the topic, and he would have learned that what the mother eats can influence the flavor of the amniotic fluid in the womb. He would have to concede that maybe, on some level, my body was telling me to give the baby a treat.

Imagining that conversation made me cry, and as I wept and ate the candy powder, I went through and counted the rest of the packets. To affect the fluid, I'd probably need to eat a whole strip of the packets at a time, and I had enough to do that once a week.

That's why it's important that I finish this last blue packet before the technician comes; it's my way of sharing Finny's gift with our baby.

Mom advances with the wet cloth, and I flinch away from her.

"Mom—"

"Hello! Hello!" A woman in scrubs bustles into the room.

"She doesn't have heart failure. She was eating candy," Mom says.

Angelina sighs and rubs her forehead.

"I'm done now!" I say, because I am and because I realize how childlike I look in this situation. I grab the cloth from Mom's hand and wipe my mouth.

"We'll need to get another towel for you later," the technician says as she sits down with a grunt.

"Sorry," I say. "I have these cravings."

"It's fine. There are more towels in the cupboard. My name is Jackie, and I'll be the technician doing the main scan, and then your doctor will come and meet with you, go over any images if need be. Is this your first time?"

"Oh, I mean, of course?" I say, blushing.

"Oh honey. I've seen a few your age with their third on the way. Why don't you go ahead and lie back—there you go. And pull your shirt up—perfect." She turns to look at the screen in front of her and presses keys on the machine. "The way I see it, it doesn't matter how old you are when you have your kids or how many you have, just as long as you can take care of them. Okay, to confirm a few things, you are Davis, Autumn R., born on nine-two-eight..."

After a few more questions and the cold spurt of bluish clear gel on my ever-expanding belly, Jackie looks at me and gives me a smile that is genuinely excited for me.

"Are you ready to see your baby?" she asks.

Mom and Aunt Angelina squeal harmoniously in the corner as I whisper, "I'm ready."

The wand presses firmly into my bump. There's a swirl of black and white on the screen, and then—

"There it is," Jackie says. "Posing for the camera already. I should get this shot before they move. That's the keepsake right there." She mumbles to herself, and I hear the clack of the keyboard. I even hear The Mothers crying over my shoulder, but in another way, it's all very distant.

Finny, I tell him. *That's our baby.* I swallow the lump in my throat as if I were actually saying the words to him. *We really did make a baby.*

The leg—their leg, our baby's leg—kicks, and I feel the flutter, the one I've been so unsure about all these weeks.

I've been feeling our baby move, Finny.

"I've saved that one to print. It's time for me to start doing my job. I'm going to move over here and start taking some measurements of the head and brain…"

She alternates between ignoring me as she works and explaining what she's doing. A few times, she points out the clearer images for me to see, like the gentle curve of the spine and the feet tucked together with all ten toes.

The Mothers are still crying a bit, but it's mostly happy whispering now. I told them that I both wanted and didn't want them here, because it's always a moment you think you're going to share with the father of your baby, but I also didn't want to face it alone.

This situation is working. They're here, and I feel supported, but I'm free to let myself feel how much I wish Finny was the one supporting me today.

"So did you tell me whether you wanted to know the sex and I forgot?" Jackie asks. "Or did I forget to ask you?"

"You didn't ask," I say. "But I still haven't decided if I want to know."

There has been a lingering controversy about this. Angelina believes in bonding with the child without considering their probable gender identity; Mom believes in planning for future photo shoots.

I don't know what Finny would want.

He would tell me that whatever made me feel the most confident about becoming a mother would be the right thing for us, but when he said it, I would be able to tell that he was hoping I would choose one or the other.

I don't know which it is.

It's not that I would choose what I thought he wanted, but knowing what he would have wanted would have been something I considered, and I hate not knowing.

"You should probably look away now if you don't want to know," Jackie says, and I don't actually have to look away at first, because tears are blurring my eyes.

I close them to stop them from spilling and ask, "Can you write it down for me? I'll decide later."

"Sure can," Jackie says. "Do you want me to give the envelope to you or one of your family members?"

"I'll take—" Mom starts to say as Angelina says, "I can hide—"

"Give it to me," I tell Jackie. "Aunt Angelina, you're not as good at hiding things as you think, and, Mom, we all know you would open it. I'm surprised you looked away when Jackie said to."

"Angelina made me cover my eyes," Mom grumbles.

"You mean I covered your eyes for you, Claire," she says, but it's their normal banter. The differences in their temperament have always been the linchpin of their friendship.

"So far, everything looks good. The baby has genitals that will remain TBA for now. But don't be surprised when your doctor adjusts your due date after looking at my measurements," Jackie adds, "probably a few days later than the previous estimation."

Panic starts to creep in me.

"But I know, um, very specifically the exact, uh, date of the event of this baby's conception. So if the baby looks too small—"

She turns to face me. "The baby isn't too small. The baby is a fine size. But actual conception can take place a few minutes after the event, as you called it, or several days later. Based on the size of your baby, I'd say that conception happened more than two days after your event."

"Oh," I say. There's a stillness in the room as I hear The Mothers take in this information with me.

"The next ten minutes might be pretty boring," Jackie says. "I'm going to be going through your baby's abdomen and making sure all the organs are there and growing nicely. It won't look like much on the screen."

"Okay." I'm already gazing out and away, thinking about the time of conception being so different than I thought.

I had thought that this baby was what remained of our love story, but that isn't the case at all. There was a bit of Finny still in me when he died, and it wasn't until after he was gone, sometime as I was weeping and screaming, some moment when my soul was crying out for his, that Finny's child started to form within me.

This baby isn't what's left over from our love story. This baby is our story's continuation.

I feel that flutter within me and look back at the screen to see if I see movement, but what I see is a heart.

I'm surprised that I can recognize it, and perhaps I'm wrong, but it looks like the shape of a human heart in that way that isn't much like the valentine. I turn my head to Jackie to tell her I can recognize this one when I see her slight frown.

It's not a big frown. She isn't hugely distressed, but it's a frown of concentration, the sort a mechanic makes when someone is describing the sound an engine is making.

Behind me, I hear The Mothers discussing whether not knowing the gender means Mom gets to buy from the more expensive stores.

"They have better options in neutral," she says.

"Is everything all right?" I ask Jackie, loud enough to be certain that The Mothers can hear. They fall silent.

"Yes," Jackie says, still with her frown. "But I'm going to need to take extra pictures of your baby's heart, and she's moving around. I think that candy you were eating is hitting her now—"

"Why do you need to take extra pictures of the heart?" I ask.

Jackie stares at the machine before looking over at me. She opens her mouth.

"Did you say 'she'?" Mom asks.

Jackie's eyes widen as she glances from Mom to me.

"It's okay," I say. "You can answer both questions. Mine first though."

"Your doctor has to be the one to explain it to you," Jackie says. "I'm not qualified to go into the specifics with you, but I can tell you that she is probably going to be fine. And yes, it's a girl. And she's absolutely perfect, except for one little thing that will probably be just fine. Okay, Autumn?"

"Okay," I say and nod to prove I'm all right, that she can get back to taking the pictures she needs to.

"Mom, Aunt An—" I start to say, but they're already by my side. Mom takes my hand, and Angelina puts her hand on my shoulder, and we cry a bit and smile together some, because Finny and I are having a daughter, and she's probably going to be fine.

Probably.

fifteen

FINNY WOULD HAVE LOVED THIS view. Perhaps calling it a view is a bit much. It's just the street we grew up on, but the sunlight makes it look vibrant in a way that isn't guaranteed every year, and this year, Finny isn't here to see it.

I breathe through the ache.

I have to get used to the sight of things that Finny would wish he could see, because I'll hopefully, probably, be seeing our daughter for the rest of my life.

There is a small hole in her heart.

Sometimes, these holes close on their own before the baby is born.

Sometimes, the hole gets smaller but doesn't close all the way until the baby's first birthday or so, but it's closed enough that it's not a problem.

And sometimes it is a problem.

Sometimes, babies go to sleep and don't wake up.

Sometimes, toddlers need surgery to save their tiny hearts.

It's too soon to know with Finny and my baby what path this will take. The doctor told me that she's treated women whose fetuses had bigger holes in their hearts than the one in my daughter's, whose babies are now in high school or college.

For the time being, I'll have extra ultrasounds to monitor the hole's size as she grows so that we can plan for whatever it is that she needs. Angie is going to come with me to the next appointment. I'm thinking about asking Brittaney if she wants to come with me to the one after that.

I won't be able to take these walks much longer, not because I'm getting so big or anything, though I feel huge, but because of the chill in the air.

It's Thanksgiving, and it isn't always this cold in St. Louis. Often the roses are still blooming after the leaves have turned, but not this year. This year, the roses completed their lives' work, bloomed in the time they were given, and accepted their fate.

I pulled a few dead blossoms from my mother's bushes, tearing them apart and scattering them, talking to the baby quietly as I walked.

I'm taking a break from editing my novel, not because I need to cry, but because I need to think. I feel like Izzy and Aden might need to have more disagreements in order for the reader to feel their love is real. I've taken to discussing plot points with the baby, who is, at this moment in time, a very good listener.

"I mean, I am inserting this fight they're having about the dance," I explain to her, "except it doesn't feel natural, little beloved." I call her by the pet name that came to me one morning when I woke up after a good dream I couldn't remember.

As for coming up with a real name, that I'm stuck on. I doubt it's going to come to me in a dream. Mom is anxiously gritting her teeth in impatience. There are so many engraved and embossed, personalized and monogrammed items she's desperate to buy. It's a good thing that I'm in charge of the gold card now.

Aunt Angelina is even less help when it comes to names and tells me that she likes every name I float by her, even the ridiculous ones. She likes to tell me the story about how she came up with a long list of names that she liked and that after the baby was born, she read the list to him. She felt that he responded most to being named Phineas and called Finny by family. Sometimes she says he wiggled, sometimes she says he cooed, sometimes it's both, but she's adamant that he chose his name.

I haven't revealed that I know how she got that name for the list, but I will talk about it with her eventually. Right now, I'm relieved that she's fine with the situation I've negotiated with John, the updates and occasional visits that I've planned. She and I have both agreed that we'll be there in case he breaks her heart too.

For the time being, I called John to let him know that the baby is a girl, and I told him about her heart. He babbled a bit about being able to afford the best doctors, and I was surprised by my confidence when I told him that everything was probably going to be just fine.

"She already has so many people watching out for her," I told him. "If she has a congenital heart defect, then she's lucky to have good doctors and people who love her."

Down the block, I see Jack's car pulling into my driveway. Lately it's been easier for me and Angelina and Mom to talk to each other about what we need when grieving for Finny, and we all agreed that facing the empty seat at the table was stopping us from discussing Thanksgiving. When Jack showed up to rake our leaves, we asked if he would have two Thanksgiving dinners, but he told us that his house would be overflowing with his brothers and their wives and kids, and he would be happy to spend as much of the day with our family as we wanted. He seemed excited to have an excuse to escape what sounded like a madhouse.

It's hard to explain why seeing Jack's face will help, but it will, and I'm looking forward to telling him that the baby is a girl. I'll have to explain about the hole in her heart and how it's probably going to be fine, probably, but I'm getting good at that, I think.

I spoke to Jack on the phone yesterday, but I want to tell him those things in person. Besides, the context of the call wasn't right.

"So...uh," he said. "I hope telling you this isn't too weird, but I think you should know before I come to Thanksgiving tomorrow in case it's a problem for you. Something is happening with Sylvie and me."

"Something is happening?"

"Well, I had this umbrella of hers, and when I went to return it, something happened," Jack said. "I think it's going to keep happening too. I know it's a really weird situation, but I wanted you to know…in case it was a problem?"

"It's really not," I said. "She said, like, one or two rude things to me in high school. So what? It was my fault Finny and I weren't together, not hers. I'm happy for you, Jack, and I think Finny would be too."

"Really?" he said. "Because I also wondered if it was wrong in some way?"

I didn't see anything wrong. I thought it made a sort of sense. I told him that my only concern was that if they became serious, would it be awkward for him to continue to be in the baby's life? He said that he would talk about it with Sylvie before they became serious. That the baby was important to him too. I felt myself smile. He was taking the possibility of them becoming serious, well, seriously.

I was sort of impressed by Sylvie's and Jack's maturity. So I've written back to Jamie and Sasha. I told them that they can stop writing and texting to ask for my forgiveness. They have it. I've learned that life and hearts are complicated. Even though they have my forgiveness, I explained that I need them to not contact me again. It's time for me to focus on the future, and because of what happened between us, between them, I need our relationships to be a thing of the past, part of our childhoods, where we made mistakes and survived.

For now, for the beginning of my adult life, I'm surrounding myself with people who carry pieces of Finny with them, like I do. Like Jack does, and Mom and Angelina, and even John. And people who give me good advice and care for me, like Angie and Brittaney.

Jack has seen me approaching and is waiting at the top of the hill. He raises his hand in greeting, and so do I.

I know that there will be days when it feels like there won't be a future.

But for today, I can feel how Finny is still with me.

selected drafting pages
from laura nowlin's

if only i had told her

[Lety]
comparison

More Sylvie

How is Sylvie+
doing?)

Don't have
to explain what
they loved
about Finny

Pen to end w/Author
page

within me Chicago

Reflection of IHKIBWM

Adsent Dad

Letter to Finny. Forgiven

what is Autumn's grieving Plan?

Even after gone w/a gone piece of us were traveling to

so un, and Yet so easier Never kno

organ
scan
body brain

TV watchin
W/o Finny

Gone
Sulpicia

Back to 1st
page

what would
he think of
her new body?

Angie talk others
at college

The candy

Angelina
conversation
on grief

Reflection
on the
Mothers

reflecting on
exercising

Drive to Plow?

Jackson
gets umbrellatos

St Louis
Autum Rose
not dying so
blowing hits flowing
so no more crying

choosing
motherhood

like choosing

knowing Finny loved
her- hurts more

choosing Finny loved

choosing

love anyway

Bits of
Finny
/everywhere

writing
career?
still

Need More Finny's
voice

Candy!

Jack
leaves?

continue
turning page

writing
story
in
mind.

a conversation
with the author

Q. What inspired you to write *If Only I Had Told Her*?

A. I would like to again apologize to every fan to whom I swore this book would absolutely never exist. I could never have imagined that years after my first novel about Finny and Autumn was published, an audiobook of the story would shatter my heart in a way that made the story new again. I would have never attempted to write this book unless I was 100 percent certain that I had Finny and Autumn alive inside me, and that never would have happened without the audiobook.

Q. Did you always know how this novel would end?

A. Despite all the requests from fans that I find some fantastical way to have Finny somehow survive the accident, I always knew how his section would end, down to the last line.

I had no plan or idea where I was going with Jack. I just knew that I'd eventually need him to get to the hospital with Autumn, though I thought that was going to take place in her section, not his.

I don't like it when novels feel like everything has been wrapped up too neatly, and I wanted there to still be a lot of questions about how everything turned out. In the end, the way to achieve that feeling was to reveal a lot more about Finny and Autumn's child than I had ever planned.

Q. Were there any surprises while writing this novel?

A. I thought, *I killed him once before. I can do it again!* I could, and I did.

It was living with the consequences of my actions that was hard. In *If He Had Been with Me*, I didn't have to sit with or even depict much of the pain that came with losing Finny. I knew I couldn't write coherently about Autumn's early grief, and I thought Jack's perspective would be easier. I was wrong though. Living in that space was harder than I expected.

Q. Do you have a favorite character from *If Only I Had Told Her*?

A. Phineas Smith, of course.

Q. You've shared what drew you to write *If Only I Had Told Her* earlier and in your author's note. How was that a different writing experience from *If He Had Been with Me*?

A. For the first hundred pages of *If Only I Had Told Her*, I kept my writing a secret. My agent, my husband, my parents, everyone thought I was hard at work on a completely different novel. I was honestly a bit shocked and embarrassed to be visiting these characters again, and I secretly worried that this was navel-gazing nonsense. I am proud of the end result though, and I feel that this book was always meant to be.

Q. What was it like to write from three different points of view in *If Only I Had Told Her*? Did knowing Finn's future make it easier or harder to write from his voice?

A. When I was writing Finn's perspective, since he didn't know what was about to happen, it was like I didn't know either. It was easy to compartmentalize. Up to his last second, Finn thought there was a future. He didn't even have a chance to know otherwise.

Like I said, living in that space of early grief was harder than I expected. I thought Jack would have a simple, straightforward grief that would be easy to depict. Except no one's grief is simple or straightforward.

Coming back to Autumn's voice felt like coming home after a long journey, but the longer I was there, the more that I discovered little things had changed. Autumn has been through a lot since the ending of *If He Had Been with Me*, and depicting how she has changed yet retained her essential self was a challenge.

Q. What do you hope readers take away from this novel?

A. I hope someday, when a terrible thing they could never have imagined happens, instead of hiding from their pain, they'll remember that the only way out is through. Grieve your grief, and memento mori.

Q. Friendship is as much a part of *If Only I Had Told Her* as the romantic relationships. Did you expect this? Do you have a preference for which you write?

A. Friendship was such an important theme of *If He Had Been With Me* that there was no way it wouldn't be a large part of *If Only I Had Told Her*. To me, there is no romance without friendship; otherwise, it's just sex. Therefore, to me at least, a deep platonic friendship and a romantic relationship aren't really all that different. I think writing a romantic relationship is a lot easier than depicting the incredible depths a platonic relationship can reach, which is why I've never written something without a romantic element. It's easier!

Q. Love and grief are powerful emotions. Did you have any takeaways from writing these experiences into your novels?

A. It's impossible to have love and joy without having grief. If we love someone, then we run the risk of losing them. When we're grieving, it's because we have lost someone precious to us. The only way to avoid grief is to never love anyone or anything, and that is no way to live.

Q. Do you listen to music while you write? What kind of music would your characters like?

A. Music is a massive part of my writing process. I create dedicated playlists that I listen to while writing, while thinking about a story as I drive or weed or pace around my home. Music is how I sustain the emotion I need to depict. Sometimes I'll have one song on repeat for hours or days if need be.

There are five songs that were intrinsically part of the drafting process of both *If He Had Been with Me* and *If Only I Had Told Her*:

"Funeral for My Future Children" by Anna von Hausswolff
"Half Acre" by Hem
"Emotional Champ" by New Buffalo
"How It Ends" by DeVotchka
"Hoppípolla" by Sigur Rós

If you look up that last one, make sure you read the English translation of the lyrics.

For Finn's point of view in *If Only I Had Told Her*, the songs I listened to on repeat were

"Like a Friend" by Pulp
"Waiting Room" by Phoebe Bridgers
"I'll Believe in Anything" by Wolf Parade
"Existentialism on Prom Night" by Straylight Run

Given that characters in *If He Had Been with Me* were using CDs, I've sustained that in *If Only I Had Told Her*. The CD that Finny is playing for Autumn on their last drive is Dashboard Confessional's 2003 album, and the song that makes him think of their summer nights together is "Hands Down."

For Jack's chapters, I listened to music that spoke to his grief more than his personal taste:

"Epilogue" by the Antlers
"Fourth of July" by Sufjan Stevens
"Wolves" by Phosphorescent
"Love Love Love" by the Mountain Goats

To help me find Autumn's headspace in the final section of *If Only I Had Told Her*, I listened to these:

"I Have Never Loved Someone" by My Brightest Diamond
"Dead Hearts" by Stars
"Adventures in Solitude" by the New Pornographers
"The Trapeze Swinger" by Iron & Wine
"Keep Breathing" by Ingrid Michaelson

Q. Your novels feature deep, meaningful emotions. How do you navigate that intensity while writing, and does it seep into other parts of your life?

A. It's the reverse of that, actually. My writing is how I process things from my past that are haunting me. If I can make myself cry while writing, then I'm going to be a happier person when I come out of my office afterward.

Q. Top five favorite books? (And would Autumn approve of this list or have her own suggestions?)

A. Autumn's top five:

Pride and Prejudice by Jane Austen
The Catcher in the Rye by J. D. Salinger
A Prayer for Owen Meany by John Irving
The Princess Bride by William Goldman
Rebecca by Daphne du Maurier

Mine:

Franny and Zooey by J. D. Salinger
The Heart Is a Lonely Hunter by Carson McCullers
Doomsday Book by Connie Willis
The Remains of the Day by Kazuo Ishiguro
The Blind Assassin by Margaret Atwood

Q. Sylvie has a connection with Sara Teasdale's poetry. Who is your favorite poet? Have you ever visited the grave of an author (or creator) you've admired?

A. My all-time favorite poet is e. e. cummings, who Sylvie would find enraging. Some other poets who haunt my brain are Mary Oliver, Elizabeth Bishop, T. S. Eliot, Emily Dickinson, and Elizabeth Barrett Browning.

Coach is also a poetry fan. In addition to reading "Ode to an Athlete Dying Young" at Finny's funeral, his advice to Jack, "the only way out is through," is from a Robert Frost poem.

I adore graveyards and visit several a year just to take walks. I like to visit the graves that no one visits, remove the moss or trace the letters to figure out names that are faded. I think as a writer, I would prefer someone to read my work rather than visit my grave, so perhaps that's why I've never visited any other writers' graves. However, I once had a drink in the building where Hemingway's favorite bar used to be, and I've been to Graceland three times to visit the grave of my fifth cousin twice removed, Elvis Presley.

Q. What advice would you give someone who wants to write?

A. Rule 1. If you think what you just wrote is terrible, it doesn't mean you are a terrible writer. It means you know what good writing looks like and maybe you'll be able to fix it. If you can't fix it yet, try pushing forward knowing you'll come back to it later.

Rule 2. Don't save good lines or ideas for later. Use them now, and let your brain come up with something even better as you go forward.

Rule 3. Don't talk about your book with other people. You need it to be fresh when it goes on the page. It's amazing how much inspiration can be lost by speaking about it.

Rule 4. Be suspicious of writing groups. Some people get community and encouragement out of them, but some people want to talk about being writers more than they actually want to write.

Rule 5. Start now. There's lots of competition and no time to waste.

lightning round!

Q. Who would you ask to borrow notes from if you missed class?

A. Finny would be the nicest about it, and while Sylvie's notes would be slightly better, she would be less easygoing about getting the notes back to her. Autumn did not take notes. Jack took notes, but they're a mess and only he can read them.

Q. If you could go on a road trip with three characters from *If Only I Had Told Her*, who would you pick? And who would drive?

A. I would love to go on a trip with The Mothers riding in the front so I could hang out with Finny in the back, like Autumn gets to do.

Q. Which character would you trust to house-sit?

A. Finny would be the house sitter. Sylvie is very responsible, but the temptation to throw a party would be too much for her. Jack and Autumn would forget to take in the mail or something like that.

Q. You are playing paintball with your characters. Who is on your team?

A. Sylvie has a strategy to win any and every game she encounters, and Jack won't have a problem shooting his friends with paint.

Q. Who bakes the best brownies?

A. Finny does because he follows the recipe but also adds

extra chocolate chips. Sylvie would try and fail to make brownie macaroons, and both Jack and Autumn would burn their pans.

Q. Which adult in *If Only I Had Told Her* would you chose for a parent?

A. I would like to live in Autumn's mom's perfect house, but Angelina's relaxed parenting style would probably suit me better. On the other hand, as someone with a loving and present father all my life, I don't know how I would have turned out if I'd had an absent parent like Finny and Autumn both had. Perhaps it would be the best then for me to go with Jack's parents, who are there when he needs him but also give him lots of space.

Q. You are attending Autumn and Jack's twentieth high school reunion with them. Who are they still in touch with? Who are they most excited to see? Who would they avoid?

A. Jack and Autumn are still in touch regularly, and I have high hopes that things may have worked out in the long term for Jack and Sylvie. Autumn would be excited to see friends like Brooke and Noah who she hadn't talked to in years. She would be cordial to Jamie and Sasha, who are no longer together, but I don't think she'd be as excited to see them as they would be to see her.

Q. You're joining movie night with Finn, Autumn, and Jack, and you get to pick. What are you watching?

A. I would give them a choice between two of my favorite movies:

Black Swan, a disconcerting psychological drama, or *Welcome to Me*, a raunchy comedy. Both films, in their own way, ask the same question: "What is the difference between artistic passion and mental illness?" If there was any disagreement about which to watch, I would suggest that we watch both. You should too.

acknowledgments

All hail Gina Rogers, narrator extraordinaire and the muse who brought Finny back to life.

Thank you to my agent, Ali McDonald, and everyone at 5 Otter Literary. You ladies are amazing.

Annette Pollert-Morgan, I could not have pulled this off without you. Well, maybe I could have, but I wouldn't be as proud of this book as I am without your tough love.

My family has been so supportive of me through all the ups and downs of my career. Rob, Austin, Mom and Dad, Elizabeth, thank you for everything. There just aren't words.

My son, Percy, was very patient as I took time away to write this book. He recently asked me if, after the book was done, I'd ever have to do this again. I'm sorry, sweetheart, but I am planning on doing this again.

Read how it all started for
Autumn and Finn...

Don't miss the #1 New York Times *bestseller taking TikTok by storm!*

one

I WASN'T WITH FINNY ON that August night, but my imagination has burned the scene in my mind so that it feels like a memory.

It was raining, of course, and with his girlfriend, Sylvie Whitehouse, he glided through the rain in the red car his father had given him on his sixteenth birthday. In a few weeks, Finny would be turning nineteen.

They were arguing. No one ever says what they were arguing about. It is, in other people's opinions, not important to the story. What they do not know is that there is another story. The story lurking underneath and in between the facts of the one they can see. What they do not know, the cause of the argument, is crucial to the story of me.

I can see it—the rain-slicked road and the flashing lights of ambulances and police cars cutting through the darkness of night, warning those passing by: catastrophe has struck here, please drive slowly. I see Sylvie sitting sideways out of the back of the policeman's car, her feet drumming on the wet pavement as she talks. I cannot hear her, but I see Sylvie tell them the cause of the argument, and I know, I know, I know, I know. If he had been with me, everything would have been different.

I can see them in the car before the accident—the heavy rain, the world and the pavement as wet and slick as if it had been oiled down for their arrival. They glide through the night, regrettably together, and they argue. Finny is frowning. He is distracted. He is not thinking of the rain or the car or the wet road beneath it. He is thinking of this argument with Sylvie. He is thinking of the cause of the argument, and the car swerves suddenly to the right, startling him out of his thoughts. I imagine that Sylvie screams, and then he overcompensates by turning the wheel too far.

Finny is wearing his seat belt. He is blameless. It is Sylvie who is not. When the impact occurs, she sails through the windshield and out into the night, improbably, miraculously, only suffering minor cuts on her arms and face. Though true, it is hard to imagine, so hard that even I cannot achieve the image. All I can see is the moment afterward, the moment of her weightless suspension in the air, her arms flailing in slow motion, her hair, a bit bloody and now wet with rain, streaming behind her like a mermaid's, her mouth a round *O* in a scream of panic, the dark wet night surrounding her in perfect silhouette.

Sylvie is suddenly on Earth again. She hits the pavement with a loud smack and is knocked unconscious.

She lies on the pavement, crumpled. Finny is untouched. He

breathes heavily, and in shock and wonder, he stares out into the night. This is his moment of weightless suspension. His mind is blank. He feels nothing, he thinks nothing; he exists, perfect and unscathed. He does not even hear the rain.

Stay. I whisper to him. *Stay in the car. Stay in this moment.*

But, of course, he never does.

Looking for more from
#1 *New York Times* bestselling author
Laura Nowlin?

Don't miss...

this
song
is (not)
for
you

#1 *new york times* bestselling author
of *if he had been with me*
laura nowlin